THE CARPET KING

The Carpet King

by Gregory Ward

LITTLE, BROWN & COMPANY (CANADA) LIMITED

Canadian Cataloguing in Publication Data

Ward, Gregory
The carpet king

ISBN 0-316-92232-3

I. Title.

PS8595.A73C37 1991   C813'.54   C91-09354-4
PR9919.3.W373C37 1991

Every reasonable effort has been made to trace ownership of copyright materials. Information enabling the Publisher to rectify any reference or credit in future printings will be welcomed.

Cover Design: Tania Craan
Editing: The Editorial Centre
Interior Design and Typesetting: Pixel Graphics
Printed and bound in Canada by Gagné Printing Ltd.

Little, Brown & Company (Canada) Limited
148 Yorkville Avenue, Toronto, Ontario, Canada

ACKNOWLEDGEMENTS

Many thanks to Bill Dendy and Jonathan Kearns for architectural insights, and to Robert Derot for his carpet wisdom. Thanks David Hindley and Gary Gray...the warmest, and to Colin Smith for saying the same thing over and over. Thanks to the girls with wax in their hair, and above all, thank you Alan Shirlaw for getting me out of that and into this.

For Pip

PROLOGUE

In November 1986, Kate and Hal Sebastian got sucked into a black hole in Delray Beach, Florida.

The condominium development was called Breakers II and would be ready in less than a year, the Toronto agent guaranteed them. With a down payment now, they would be renting their unit as soon as the building was finished, covering the mortgage and making some money. If they wanted to sell a year or two down the line, they would double their investment, the way things were going in Florida right now.

Their bank manager tended to agree. A free flight out of cold and grey Toronto to inspect the sun-drenched, oceanfront site convinced them.

Breakers II was completed on schedule, but by mid 1988, only half the units were occupied. Kate and Hal's was not amongst them. Kate flew back down to Delray at her own expense. The building looked all right; it wasn't in a swamp, she didn't see hospital waste on the beach, there had been no alligator sightings in the parking lot. Give it a little time, said the developer's representative. Was their rental price too high? By the way, had they ever thought at all about a Florida lifestyle?

Kate and Hal passed an uncomfortable summer. What they had bought themselves, it seemed on hot, sleepless nights, was not so much an unrentable and unsaleable three-bedroom condominium as a giant vacuum cleaner with a fifteen-hundred-mile-long hose, capable of sucking up cash at a rate of almost two thousand dollars a month.

On top of their financial anxiety came record-breaking temperatures and humidity in Toronto. The seasonal homicide rate doubled, even in that civilized city, providing further evidence that violent crime rides with the mercury.

And it was more than the numbers. In late June, a cleaner found the mutilated body of a nineteen-year-old exotic dancer in a motel room near the lake shore. "TA TA TA TA TA TA TA TA..." stuttered across the walls in pink spray paint. It seemed an eloquent enough comment on what was left of the body, until one of the detectives suggested it referred to what the knife had taken: the womanly parts that had been Lena DiMaio's stock in trade.

Toronto was still sweltering in September when a second "Graffiti Murder" exploded into a national sensation. The spray paint and the mutilation were the same, although the killer had doubled his efforts: the dead strippers were Mary Jo Korenycky and Sandra Dell.

The fear and excitement peaked in the fall, but were gradually buried under the layers of daily news. Over the long winter months, Torontonians would pause occasionally to wonder where the monster was hibernating, and whether the coming summer would be as hot and humid as the last. But most of the time, people forgot.

They had other things to worry about.

PART 1

CHAPTER
1

The trouble with Kate's husband was, he couldn't believe they were poor. Eating white bread and white sugar was poor. Reading tabloid newspapers, watching daytime TV. In Hal's mind it was impossible for two smart people with college degrees and current library cards to be poor. Poor was a state of mind. According to Hal, they "didn't have a whole lot of money right now," which was a different thing, no big deal, and why he was still happy to take piddling commissions like the Ancaster house.

One step took Kate across her husband's tiny office, crammed with the basic furniture of his trade: a drafting table, a Stone Age Pitney Bowes copier, a cabinet for drawings. The drawing spread out on the table this morning was typical of his restoration work: a gazebo, an elaborate confection of whorls and curlicues he was recreating for a Century House in Ancaster, Ontario. Typical, also, would be Hal's fee from the Ancaster Heritage Society, who used the house as their headquarters — he would be paid on an appropriately Victorian scale.

Not that Hal wasn't worth a great deal more. Scrupulous and intuitive, his work had garnered plenty of awards, but they were all more or less nominal, meaningless to anyone outside the narrow field of restoration architecture. It was high time he won a real prize.

Kate reached under the drafting table for her scuffed leather art case and drew out its contents with extra care because her hands were suddenly damp. Her nervousness was premature; the competition deadline was still six weeks away, although Kate had been on edge ever since Midland had announced it. Going over this material was supposed to give her confidence, to remind her how impressive Hal looked on paper: his Cambridge Ph.D., his teaching experience, nine years as a practising restoration architect, his awards...his inarguable *readiness* for a landmark commission.

The presentation kit was impressive, too, even in mock-up. It had been Kate's idea and her execution — a glossy, twice-legal-size folder adorned with her own sepia sketches of Hal's past projects, with inside pockets for typed material and the drawings. It didn't worry her at all that Hal hadn't started them yet; he was quick as well as clever when he wanted to be.

The trick was getting him to want.

Kate slipped the material back into the art case, lifted her head and sniffed.

"Bloody hell!" Her Englishness unfailingly came out in moments of stress.

The kitchen was full of smoke pouring out of the toaster like emissions from a toy factory. Kate yanked on the cord and gave the ejector an uppercut that knocked the ancient appliance off its feet.

Next time, she vowed, scraping black into the sink; one more time and it would end up springs and black crumbs in the road. Hal, of course, considered the toaster a modern classic, like the threadbare Harris Tweed she could never get him out of, like the rustbucket Chrysler Valiant parked in the alley behind the house.

Kate set out the scraped toast on plates and put a bowl of Cheerios in front of Rain's highchair. She had laughed when Hal proposed such a name for their daughter — Rain sounded like one of those daft hippie names from the sixties, Windstar or Leafsong. She had given in mostly out of surprise at his stubbornness; it was so unlike her husband to push that hard for anything.

She listened for a moment to the laughter from the bedroom and called, "Get a move on — it's ten to eight!" through the thin wall.

Thin walls, small rooms — the original spaces plundered to make additional rooms when the house was converted to a duplex. Confined to the ground floor, Kate and Hal made do by sharing a bedroom with their eighteen-month-old daughter because Hal needed the spare for his office. Renting the ground floor of the Grace Street house was never meant to be anything but an interim solution, until they had the down payment on a home of their own. Breakers II was supposed to speed that day, and now it was eating up the dream, every month another bite.

Hearing no progress from the bedroom, she went in. Hal was lying on the bed holding their struggling, half-dressed daughter in the air, shaking out laughter like silver coins. Kate almost forgot to be angry.

"Wonderful! *You* take her to Mrs. Gee's because *I'm* leaving at eight-fifteen with or without her." Mrs. Gee — Mrs. Giaraldi, the inexpensive, reliable Sicilian lady who babysat Rain — lived on Kate's bus route to work; for Hal it would mean a special trip in the car, twenty minutes there and back.

He plonked Rain down and sat up, blinking through shoulder-length, dark blond hair. He swept it back and reached over to the night table for his glasses — the same little round, gold-rimmed pair he proudly claimed to have worn, with updated prescriptions, since the Summer of Love. "Is something burning?"

With a growl of frustration, Kate crossed to the bedroom closet. She found a wide plastic belt to cinch her sweater-dress (and restore her pre-Rain waist), then rummaged for shoes to go with the belt. She found one.

"I saw Rain with it," Hal said. "Where's Mummy's shoe, Monkey?"

Kate rifled the crib at the end of the bed where Rain had lately taken to hoarding things, found the shoe wedged behind a bumper-pad.

"This can't go on, Hal. Rain is one-and-a-half years old. She needs a room of her own...we need one!"

Hal tugged Rain's polo sweater over her head, kissed the face that popped out. "We don't *have* a spare room."

"We have your office."

"So where's my office supposed to go?"

"Downtown, where offices *should* be. Not taking up desperately needed space in cramped, horrible ground-floor apartments!"

Hal raised his eyebrows. "Fine, I'll phone the movers. How does thirteen hundred a month sound? We can call it Breakers III."

"It'll sound just fine when you've won this competition. So will a new apartment...maybe even our own house one day before we kick the bucket."

"Such a quaint English expression!"

"So will a proper car instead of that sieve on wheels. Right now I'd settle for a decent fucking *toaster*!"

"Fucking!" echoed Rain.

Hal beamed. "Doesn't Mummy say awful things?"

"So you'd just better win, mister." She opened a dresser drawer and threw balled-up baby socks and woollen leggings at him. She picked up her brush and swiped at her hair, thick and dark around her pale winter face, hennaed these days to hide a touch of grey. Kate was thirty-six, one year younger than her husband.

Hal asked: "You're getting a printing estimate on your folder?"

"It's only an estimate. You don't have to worry." She glanced at his reflection in the dresser mirror and saw his cautious, concerned expression. She wanted to slap him when he looked like that. She threw down her brush and crossed to the bedroom door. She stood for a moment, drumming her fingers irritably against the wood, watching him shake Rain down into her red leggings.

"Wake up, Hal! You think the Vanguard is going to fall into your lap? You think the Midland Development Corporation is just going to hand it over? So what if it costs a couple of thousand to give us a competitive edge? Jesus Christ, Hal, what do you want?" She laughed mirthlessly. "As if I didn't know. You don't want a damn thing, do you? You'd be happy to spend the rest of your life in this pig hole, writing cheques to Florida and...and drawing *gazebos*!"

Grace Street was a mess in April, a long range of grimy, curbside ice-hills rich with winter deposits — old newspapers and candy wrappers and cigarette packs — blowing loose as the ice melted into roaring drains.

Kate saw the bus coming as soon as they rounded the corner onto Harbord. Rain saw it too and struggled to get out of her stroller.

"Gee Gee! Gee Gee!"

Kate wedged the art case between her knees and lifted Rain out, holding her over one arm while she collapsed the stroller with a practised jerk. As usual, there was no empty seat and nobody gave her one, so she rode standing with Rain in her arms, packed ever tighter, assaulted by the glum faces, the garlic and cigarette breath and body odour.

"Gee Gee," Rain persisted.

Every day she got excited on this bus and the same emotions deadlocked in Kate: gratitude for finding a good, affectionate person to take Rain, bitter resentment of the nine hours, five days a week, somebody else was spending with her daughter. Picking her up after work last night, Kate had been horrified when Rain actually clung to Mrs. Gee.

"Thatsa your Mummy!" The woman had a way of talking to Rain, at once pacifying and scolding, that seemed to bring instant compliance. She had presented Kate with a drawing Rain had made during the day — purple wax crayon on orange construction paper, a wobbly circle.

"Circle! Firsta time!" Mrs. Gee crowed proudly. Kate had given her daughter a felt-tip and paper when they got home, but she couldn't, or wouldn't, do anything but scribble. Of course not — eighteen months was much too early for circles. All the same, with Rain asleep in her crib and Hal out at a Preservation Committee meeting, Kate had sat in the bathroom and cried through half a toilet-roll about it.

What else was she missing? What real developmental landmarks had been passed in the consecrated gloom of Mrs. Gee's house, amidst the Jesus pictures and the variety store Dresden and the plastic-covered furniture?

Kate's arms tightened around her child as the driver announced her stop next. Her lips found the tip of Rain's ear, cool and tender as a new leaf.

Something else when Hal got the Vanguard — she was going to quit work.

Kate Sebastian laboured as a paste-up artist for *T.O. Time*, a bi-weekly news and entertainment magazine. At age thirty-six, she should have been art director, or at least assistant, but had blown her chance of normal promotion by taking two leaves of absence in the last five years. The first, to prove she could make a living painting portraits, had failed; during the second, pregnancy leave to have Rain, she had missed the office shakeup, her best opportunity to lobby for the position she deserved. When she got back ("lucky to have a job to get back to"), they had already hired Kelly Obe from outside.

"See you in fifteen?" Kelly breezed as they passed in the corridor just after nine. "I think we'd better have one last look at that pen piece."

Kelly was referring to a vapid article on the fountain pen fad. She was dithering over the headline style, whether to go with spidery handwriting and ink splotches or Times Roman. Kate had spent half of yesterday afternoon recutting and repasting *The Write Stuff* for Kelly Obe.

Fifteen minutes was adequate for the production manager, Mike Herlihy, to estimate four thousand dollars on a limited run of twenty of Kate's folders. The make-up cost was the killer, he said, starting up the printing press; it wouldn't cost a whole lot more to run off a thousand.

"Sorry, Katy." He looked regretfully at the glossy folder on his desk. "You did a nice job." She had always been on friendly terms with Mike; he knew all about the Vanguard competition that was the reason for these folders and about Kate's hopes for Hal. "If it makes you feel any better," he said, "it doesn't sound like *anyone's* going to be restoring the Vanguard unless Midland gets rid of that guy in the Doyle Hotel. It was in the paper again this morning; he still won't budge."

"Carny Danial? They'll buy him out. Everyone's got a price."

"Don't be too sure. They've been trying for months."

Kate had seen the article too, had been trying not to think about it. The Midland Development Corporation, which owned the Vanguard, had bought out all its tenants or allowed their leases to expire, emptying the historic downtown building for restoration and remodelling. In the case of Carny Danial, who leased the Doyle Hotel on the Van's south-east corner, there had been a computer error; his lease had been renewed. Now Danial wouldn't budge for love nor money. *The Globe and Mail* said Midland was taking him to court for the second time.

Mike was looking at his watch as if their business were concluded.

"I still want those folders, Michael. If it's the same price for two hundred, I'll take two hundred. Hal can always use them."

Mike shrugged. "That's up to you. I'm glad it's not my money."

"It is."

"Say what?"

Kate smiled. "Sort of. It won't be production money — it'll come out of the promotions budget, but you control it."

Mike reclined in his chair, watching her with guarded amusement. Kate leaned across the desk and made neat brackets of her hands. "We say it was a sample run for a dead promotional offer. From the food section. Readers' all-time favourite recipes, loose for convenience inside a glossy menu. Except it never went ahead, right? The food editor got the chop last month, as you know. We simply backdate the invoice and they'll chalk it up as another of Jay Temple's follies. Jay's gone to Halifax. Who's going to check?"

For a moment Mike looked impressed. Then he chuckled. "Jesus...for a moment there I thought you were serious."

She stiffened. "Why shouldn't I be? Have you any idea how much overtime I've put in at this magazine? If they'd been paying me by the hour instead of a pittance of a salary, they'd owe me *fifty* times what it'll cost them to absorb one lousy print run!"

Mike smiled from his big chair. "Life's a bitch, Katy."

She swept her material back into the art case and zippered it with an indignant flourish. At the door she stopped and turned.

"Michael..."

"What?"

She smiled sweetly, batting her eyelashes. "Of course I'd pay it all back."

Kelly Obe opted for the handwritten headline, which would mean reassembly, not that Kate was going to touch it today. "Once bitten..." she told George Reathkin as she put the work aside. "I'm not going to look at it until the silly cow's changed her mind a couple more times!"

She busied herself assembling the galleys and white prints for a sports car ad for the early June issue. Since the shakeup, the magazine was aiming younger — fewer articles with half the copy, more big fun pictures and advertisements, lots of trendy black and white. The girl in the car ad, shampooing her Toyota MR2, looked about seventeen, Kate thought morosely; gorgeous, too, with her brush-cut and her cheekbones and her baby tits digging through her wet T-shirt.

"Mmmnn," murmured George, ogling across Kate's table until she whacked him away. "I'm looking at the car!" he protested.

"Sure." Kate liked George. He was cute, still puppy-plump, a condition he tried to hide with unstructured suits, a designer beard and a rakish gold earring.

"I've got an MR2 on order," George said. "I didn't tell you, did I? A red one."

Kate looked at him in surprise. "Well, well. How much are they paying *you*?" He looked away, embarrassed. "I'm sorry, George, it's none of my business." And why shouldn't Boy George have a sports car? Twenty years old, single, probably still living at home.

They worked for a while in silence, cutting and waxing and rolling copy and pictures between the keylines, assembling Kelly Obe's vision of her vain magazine, doing Kelly's dirty work. Kate thought bitterly about her exchange with Mike Herlihy; she should have known it would come to nothing. She would have to borrow the money, that was all.

It doesn't sound like anyone's going to be restoring the Vanguard.

Kate felt a worm of fear twist inside her. What made Mike such a goddamn expert? Of course someone was going to restore the Vanguard. Hal was. Her husband was.

"Kate? What are you doing?"

She looked down where George was looking, at the artboard where her X-acto knife was buried. A six-inch incision ran diagonally through the newly pasted MR2 advertisement, cutting the car and the pretty girl in half.

CHAPTER
2

Compared to most other strip clubs, like Fantasies in the east end or the French Quarter down on the lakeshore, the Doyle Hotel was respectable. Located in the heart of the financial district, the Doyle did most of its business at lunchtime, catering to a regular pinstripe clientele that came in from the office towers surrounding it. You could take your client to the Doyle, confident not only of lovely ladies, but of a clean and comfortable place to sit, of fast, smiling service and of the conspicuous absence of pimps, thieves and dope dealers.

The Doyle Hotel was exceptional because of a hale seventy-one-year-old gentleman called Denys Danial, though everyone called him "Carny" because of the pink carnation that was never absent from his buttonhole.

Carny had been the Doyle's leaseholder and manager since 1966, by which time he had already been there twenty years, coming straight out of the army to work for his father and his brother, Lawrence. It had been a regular restaurant and bar in those days, right up until '64 when his father died and Lonnie took to wearing a black toupee and had his thick glasses tinted, like Roy Orbison. Right after that he got the girls in.

Nobody could believe they were brothers. Lonnie was in pig heaven as a club owner, the life and soul of the party, kidding the customers, screwing the dancers, drinking the bar stock — a life-style that required only two years to kill him. Carny was an anchorite by comparison: moderate, reclusive, whippet-thin. Ironically, he had a natural disregard for sex that was one reason, along with his abundant kindness, why the girls always brought him their secrets and their troubles.

But the biggest difference between the brothers was one of vision. This went beyond the fact that Lonnie was almost blind without his glasses (which had kept him out of the war), while Carny had normal eyesight.

"Gotta move with the times," Lonnie had told him when Carny protested the introduction of the striptease. "Times change, man." But Carny feared and hated change, had always struggled against it, was still struggling almost a quarter of a century later.

The rousing jangle of his Westclox Big Ben came as a blessed relief this April morning. Carny silenced the alarm and lay for a moment in his English striped pyjamas; as all too often these mornings, they clung to him, damp with perspiration. Carny's fear of change, more specifically his fear of losing his business to the Midland Development Corporation, ran so deep it had by now permeated his dreams. In them, Midland hovered beyond reason, a blind, invisible fury, poised to tear his life out by the roots and suck it into the air.

Carny came fully awake and swung his legs over the bedside. He peeled off his pyjamas, then catapulted himself into a cold shower to blast away all residue of his dreams. The morning shower was always cold — an army habit, a long-established routine and in Carny's mind one reason why, at seventy-one, he was still sound in his mind and in his trim body, why his business was still in the black.

Routine was Carny's ticket. Not that all his routine activities were "good" for him: two eggs sizzled in butter would follow his shower; he would smoke an unfiltered Player's after the dishes. But he never overdid these small vices, always had two eggs but never three, smoked exactly twenty Player's every day at rigorously observed intervals, never twenty-one.

Regularity had checked his weight at five pounds either side of 130 all his adult life, kept his blood pressure low, ordained that his bowels move every morning at exactly seven-fifteen, after his coffee and before his first cigarette of the day.

On fine mornings he smoked it in the War Room, which looked east and caught the morning sun, firing up with a monogrammed Ronson lighter that regular habits had prevented him from losing over the years. While he smoked, he feather-dusted the trophies and photographs weighting the walls, taking solitary pleasure in the *puff puff* of the duster, the strong blue cigarette smoke twisting through the sunbeams.

Carny enjoyed housework, chipped away at it every morning so that he might never come home to an untidy house. He had tried a cleaning woman a couple of years ago, very briefly, a widow who had talked too much and moved things around, introduced unfamiliar odours, then frightened him to death with arrangements of fresh flowers and finally a heart-shaped box of chocolates. With more than enough company at work — especially female company — Carny had come to depend on his off-hours of solitude.

Most of the framed photos in the War Room were of Canadian soldiers wearing Service Corps insignia. Featuring prominently was a small, wiry captain with terrier-bright eyes and a clipped moustache. Carny caught his reflection in the glass as he flicked and fluttered: the moustache was snow white after forty-five years, but tummy was still flat, back straight, chin up!

Preserved, he thought with a chalky smile, as he dusted off the canned K Ration (K for Keepsake) of forty-five-year-old meat and vegetables on the shelf beside his medal. One of these days, he had long promised himself, he was going to make a night of it — open and eat the damn thing with the Band of the Royal Scots Dragoon Guards thumping on the record player. But he always lost his appetite for the idea when he tried to picture the War Room shelf without the dull, blemished ration tin next to his Military Medal, D-Day, second wave. Together they perfectly symbolized the logical idea of service and reward as it had existed in Carny's army, the sensibleness, even, of Carny's war. He had no real memory of its unpleasant side, the German shells falling behind the lines where his field kitchen was located; at the time, he had been too busy getting soup on and latrines built to see them as anything more than an inconvenience.

Carny squashed out his cigarette and carried the ashtray out to the kitchen garbage. He gave the feather duster a flourish inside the garbage bag, replaced it on the designated cup hook in the housework closet, then made a final survey of the kitchen to make sure it would be nice to come home to.

He opened the back door to test the weather, found it unusually warm for April, and went to get his car keys and his mackintosh from the hall closet; no sense in getting fooled by a promising morning. He backed the Buick out of the detached, single garage, shut and locked the garage door, then left the car to warm up while he stood on the sidewalk in front of his house, looking up at the roof.

He remembered now. Last night, while he had lain awake listening to the wind, the Midland worrying had become general worrying. In a bleak no man's land between wakefulness and sleep, he had imagined something rapping at his house, testing its fabric, seeking entrance.

This morning, of course, after a cold shower and a good breakfast, he was looking for some loose flashing or a flapping shingle. Seeing nothing amiss at the front, he went around to the back yard. There wasn't a lot of house to inspect. It was the same two-bedroom bungalow Carny had occupied since he was demobilized in '46, one of the veterans for whom such houses had been provided on a government subsidy. A serviceman needed to be married to qualify, as indeed Carny had been for ten not very happy months, before Dilys electrocuted herself in the bath with a Bakelite hairdryer.

The roof at the back was fine too, and while that pleased him, of course, it was disturbing to think that he had imagined the noises. Dreams were dreams, but hearing things...

Unsettled, Carny drove to work with extra caution, although he was never anything but a textbook driver. He observed speed limits and came to a full stop at stop signs; his hands remained firmly at three and nine o'clock, never crossing when he turned the Buick's ivory-coloured steering wheel, slightly yellowed now like his cigarette fingers.

People used to honk at him, honk and tailgate and glare, but not any more. Oh, maybe they tailgated a bit, but it was out of curiosity and pleasure now at the sight of a nice-condition '65 Buick Wildcat, original paint, one owner. Carny was in no way passionate about the Buick. He wasn't that kind of man. He had driven lots of other cars over the years, courtesy cars and rental cars, and had never noticed much difference. He had owned the Buick this long for the simple reason that nothing had ever gone seriously wrong. There were simple reasons for that too: clean oil and plugs, regular lubing and tuning, rustproofing and shampooing and plenty of wax. Simple maintenance.

Carny sat tight near the intersection of Jarvis and King, dapper in his light wool jacket and bow tie. Isolated from the fuming swell of rush hour traffic in his enormous car, he waited patiently for the city to move its own sluggish morning bowels.

When the intersection cleared, he turned west on King and then north onto Court, then west again along the narrow alley behind his hotel to the spot bespoken for his car, between the Doyle's service entrance and the fire-escape exit.

He did not take the service entrance. Instead, he walked back around to King Street where the hotel fronted, gratefully aware of the massive building that housed his premises. He could feel the Vanguard's dark, protective mass looming above him, solid as a mountain, though had he looked up this morning, he would have seen it shimmer slightly as the fumes rose off four lanes of traffic on King.

Carny loved King Street. It was broad and dignified, truly the king of streets, although in forty-five years he had seen it change; skyscrapers had stolen the sky, fifty cars a minute spoiled the air. So many cars that Carny began to feel their effect as he walked along the street — a shortness of breath, a whiff of nausea. He could have spared himself the fumes by entering his hotel from the alley rather than the Doyle's front entrance, but Carny would no more have considered that than omitting the daily buttonhole that earned him his nickname.

"You're in the paper again, Carny." A pink carnation nodded in the flower-seller's unsteady hand. Always pink, which had been Carny's mother's favourite colour. "Midland's takin' you to court again," the man went on. "Says you're costing them close to half a million a month holed up in the Van. That right?"

"They're exaggerating, Horace." Carny took the flower, inserted it in his lapel, gave it a little tug to secure it.

"Think they can win?"

Carny smiled at the flower-seller. "Of course not, Horace. I've got a lease."

"Paper was callin' you 'The Doyle Diehard.' I mean…half a million a month! Shit *me!*"

Carny shut his eyes for a long moment, inhaling the carnation's candy sweetness. He abhorred coarse language, had heard too much of it in his life. He reached into his pants pocket for the two-dollar bill folded and waiting there for this express purpose.

"Nah. Forget it. S'on me today."

Carny straightened, his cheeks flushed as though catching some of the carnation's pinkness. "I've been overpaying you for one carnation six days a week for twenty years. Would you mind telling me why today should be any different?" He held out the money but Horace pushed it away.

"For luck." Horace said. "What's wrong with that? One for luck."

Carny rolled up the bill and wedged it, like a wafer in vanilla ice cream, into a bunch of long-stemmed white roses. He snatched his hand away as a needle pain seared his finger.

Horace crinkled up his watery eyes and chuckled, rolling out the fumes of his habitual liquid breakfast. "See that? You've offended Lady Luck!"

Carny inspected his finger, squeezed out one fat red drop, licked it away, then turned to the door of his hotel.

"I don't need luck," he said with quiet dignity. "I've got a five-year lease."

CHAPTER
3

The Vanguard Building admitted Carny Danial and stood, black and impassive, over the shining river of cars. It saw the river slow midmorning, swell again at lunchtime, obeying the city's tidal impulses. A number of people stopped to look up at the building that had made the news again, others to buy flowers from Horace. Still others, all men except for the dancers coming on shift, followed Carny into the Doyle Hotel.

The idea of a bite and a floor show had occurred to Hal Sebastian, too, on his way there, but the thought was swept away the moment he emerged from the King Street subway and looked up.

Built as the flagship of the Vanguard Insurance Company in 1889, the Van was simply overwhelming — a block-long, seven-story sandstone dreadnought. It had stood on King Street for a hundred years, deep-rooted, solemn, self-righteous as the bewhiskered moguls who had commissioned it from the great Henry Hobson Richardson.

Conceived in the architect's celebrated Romanesque style, the Vanguard's King Street elevation was composed of a gabled, châteauesque roofline linking four great towers inset with massive rounded arches. At each corner of each tower, a round decorative chimney (sixteen altogether) soared up to the green copper roofs, all aimed at the sky like a battery of mortars.

Soot-blackened and bellicose, the Vanguard would never concede pride of place to the stalagmite glass towers, many times its height, that crowded in on it. If anything, the Van *gained* status from their flimsy impossibleness.

And the glass towers kept no secrets.

Hal raised his camera, a vintage Leica, and took three exposures of the main entrance archway. A month ago, standing here on the south side of King, he had first suspected that the Vanguard was keeping secrets from him. It was whispering, something old buildings often did to Hal: a wear pattern on a floor leading to a blank wall, a sudden resonance in an otherwise solid surface, an unexplained step in a floor or ceiling. With the Van, it was Richardson's main archway, simply too grand, too far upstage from the flanking arches to account for what lay beyond — a mean vestibule crammed with stairs and elevators, whittling down to a narrow passage that cut through to the back alley.

Hal was far from a specialist on Richardson Romanesque, but he knew the man better than this; for all his machismo, Richardson never lost his integrity, would never have created a Disneyland entrance for a down-market lobby.

Yesterday, finally able to free up some time from the Ancaster house, Hal had come back with his suspicions, a hand drill, a hobby knife and a finishing hammer. Thus armed, he had made his first real sortie into the warren of silent, empty offices that was Richardson's dreadnought. By four o'clock, after a day of discreet boring and cutting and sounding, he had been thrilled.

"Doctor Sebastian, I presume?"

Hal lowered his camera and looked round. "Hi Jules."

"All I can say is this had better be good. I had a Nautilus machine booked for noon."

Hal chuckled. "I'm sure it's breathing a sigh of relief."

The fact that Julie was five foot two in no way lessened the impression of strength; it was in her clear, direct gaze and confident smile as much as in her body, hidden now by comfortably loose jeans and jean jacket over a thick turtleneck sweater. Her gymnast's poise, even her black hair bunched into a muscular pony-tail, denoted power. Hal had taken to her the moment she appeared on his site last summer in Port Hope, to gain field experience after her fourth year at the School of Architecture. Her childlike sense of fun was charming in someone of high intelligence, but Julie was also diligent; she had more than worked her passage in Port Hope. After that, they had kept in touch.

"So what are we waiting for?" she demanded. "Show me the big secret."

Hal smiled. "Patience...if you're going to get anything from this exercise, we have to take the clues one by one. I want you to have an AHA experience!" He pointed across the street. "That's where we're going in, the main entrance, which is also your main clue." She frowned across King Street. "You won't see anything from outside, Jules. We have to go in."

She bowed her head, a contrite Chinese maiden with praying hands. "Yes, Sebastian-san."

"Wait a minute, that's *Japanese*."

Hal was still rummaging for his lens cap as Julie left the curb and stormed King Street's four perilous lanes of traffic, stopping two of them. Second-generation Canadian, Julie was bound by none of the traditional constraints on Chinese women. If she graduated highest in her class this summer at the University of Toronto, it would be because she had the intellect and the discipline to do the work, but above all, because she loved old buildings.

Hal waited until after the traffic had backed up from a red light before crossing. For the first time he regretted not wearing a sweater under his Harris Tweed — the day was betraying its sunny beginning, grey and gusting now. He was glad to be under the too-grand Romanesque arch, unlocking the modern glass door with the key he had procured from Midland's maintenance office. He locked it again behind them.

Julie walked ahead of him into the vestibule, staring up at the arch, the squeaking of her Nikes on the terrazzo echoing in the emptiness. She rotated slowly, taking in a small, undramatic vestibule

28

with a bank of three elevators and a side door to a stairwell, the whole thing clad in dingy travertine.

"It ain't Richardson," she said. "It's been refinished. Horribly."

"Only refinished?"

"No. They downsized it. It's much too small for the entrance arch."

"Good. So the vestibule would have to be much grander to keep scale with the arch. Or..." Hal's grey eyes sparkled. "Or it could *lead* somewhere grand. Your next clue, by the way, is donuts."

"Hello?"

"The kind with holes in the middle. A stack of them." Hal grinned at Julie's consternation. He was having the time of his life. "Let's go," he said. "The third floor is where the real detective work starts."

The elevators were disconnected so they used the stairwell. On the first and second floors they passed identical deserts of beige carpet that seemed to stretch forever under low, acoustic-tile skies. The monotony was relieved only where the workers had left their marks on the carpet — worn patches and coffee stains and cigarette burns.

"The open-plan office," Hal eulogized. "Modern working conditions for modern people!"

Julie shook her head in disgust. "I'll bet there are twelve-foot ceilings under that hideous tile. Give me ductwork!"

They continued up the narrow, echoing stairwell to the third floor, Hal panting slightly from the effort of keeping up with her. The third floor, like those above it, was largely original: a maze of narrow, gloomy corridors featuring lumpy plaster and dark panelling. Except for the corner offices with their fine arched windows, most of the workrooms were small and dingy. Those sentenced to work their lives here must have found the atmosphere every bit as dispiriting as the open plans below. Passing these deserted and condemned offices, Hal could imagine the whole Dickensian cast — the grim martinet and the sour spinster, the Young Turk and the breathless secretary and the drab clerk with inky fingers. They all whispered too.

As they neared the centre of the maze, the atmosphere lightened as the materials changed. Drywall instead of plaster, hollow-core doors in place of heavy oak. Gone was the panelling and the dark wood trim.

Julie said: "It's like we passed some sort of invisible border."

"Not so invisible. Look here." He led her back to the point in the corridor where the change seemed to begin, squatted at her feet and carefully peeled back the square section of brown carpet he had cut away yesterday. "Took a bit of archaeology, but there's your border." He ran his finger along a seam between two different subflooring materials, old spruce planking and newer plywood.

Julie shrugged. "So? They patched the subfloor. They probably damaged it when they renovated."

"Ah, but there's a patch of plywood in the middle of every floor. From here on up it's supporting the same renovated island — new walls, doors, everything. The whole core of the building is modern."

Hal remained squatting, watching her think. He was pleased he'd invited her; it was fun leading her down the trail he'd broken yesterday.

"New floors to support...I dunno...heavy modern equipment? Mainframe computers?"

"Try again."

"Okay, they took out supports underneath. Yeah! They took out the supporting walls when they knocked out the open-plan offices downstairs. Bigger spans, so they needed..." She frowned. "But it's the same on every floor, right?"

"That's right. From this floor on up there's all kinds of support."

"Fire damage? No, fire isn't selective. Water? Something that would damage just the core of the building..."

"Damage?"

She began to look cross. "Sure. They replaced..."

"Replaced?"

Julie got mad. "Okay, smartass, tell me!"

Hal waited, knowing she wouldn't give up. "Something up here that has to do with the arch down there," she mumbled. "Something..." A slow smile began to transform Julie's face. "Hey...I know." Her voice rose with excitement. "*Nothing* got damaged, right? Nothing got replaced. Because that's exactly what was down the middle of the original building. Nothing!"

"Go on."

"Donuts!" she cried. "A stack of them! The entire building was a stack of donuts with a seven story hole in the middle!"

"A *hole*? My dear young lady…"

"An atrium!"

"Thank you." Hal beamed. "An atrium, from a glass roof down to a wide, sunlit courtyard. Which is why…?"

"Which is why the main archway is so grand!"

"AHA!" cried Hal. "Sometime in the thirties they slung all this plywood across the atrium to create extra office space. They did it on every floor, even used up the open courtyard on the main floor. Then they added insult to injury by downsizing the vestibule. Doing that, and eliminating the atrium and its inner courtyard, threw the scale of the entrance completely out of whack."

Hal's voice dropped to a stage whisper. "But do you want to know the *good* news? Midland doesn't know it's here! They included structural plans in the competition package and the plans make not one single reference to a lost atrium." He jabbed a finger at the ceiling. "They don't even show the glass roof!"

"The atrium roof is still up there? The original?"

Hal got up from his squatting position, grimacing at his cracking knees. "I'd put money on it."

Julie trooped along beside him, back towards the stairwell. "You mean you haven't been up there yet?"

"I was saving that for you."

"Aren't *you* sweet."

"Besides…" He dangled a second key. "I didn't have the key to the roof stairs yesterday."

"Jerk!"

Seven stories above King Street the wind was vicious. It shoved the door back in Hal's face, then reached into the stairwell housing, biting through his Harris Tweed.

It was an acceptable price of admission. The glass roof of the atrium was there, a vast square pyramid of glass, hundreds of panes, boarded over on the inside and painted a smeary black. Hal guessed it would be almost invisible from the skyscrapers around it, blending in with the surrounding tar roof.

He turned up his collar and huddled inside his jacket as they made a fast lap of discovery and inspection, shouting against the wind as it cuffed away their speech.

"It's wonderful!" Julie yelled. "But how will it help you win the competition?"

"Midland wants a showplace," Hal shouted back. "So I'll design the atrium right back in. The basic structure is still here. Rip out the plywood, scrape off this black paint and there it is. Big arch from King Street into a sunny courtyard, shops and restaurants on the first two floors, offices above that with gallery frontage and natural light."

"What's to stop others submitting the same design? Sounds pretty standard urban chi chi to me."

The wind snatched away Hal's laughter. "Nothing. But all the other competitors are big firms with restoration departments — not specialists. Unless they do their archaeology, they'll propose their atriums from scratch — new side walls, new roof, the whole schmiel. An extra two million to build something that's already here. See it from Midland's point of view: Sebastian sleuthed it, Sebastian's two million low...who would *you* give the job to?"

They completed their circuit, Hal pleased to note that the glass roof was virtually intact, then headed back through the sculpture-garden of ventilation and air-conditioning forms, towards the stairwell housing.

The truth, Hal admitted to himself on the way down, was that he only half-believed his own argument. Maybe one side believed it, the idealistic side; but the grown-up Hal knew that the best proposal was no guarantee of getting a job. There could be an inside track, a chance the work would go to an insider once Midland had picked the other competitors' brains. But he couldn't tell that to a beginner. Julie had plenty of time to get cynical without a head start.

Hal also knew that he didn't care which way it went. Not really. Not the way, for instance, that Kate cared. He had long ago found a comfortable niche in small, hands-on restorations, free of pressure and politics and self-styled experts and generous budgets that suddenly dried up, just when you'd fooled yourself into thinking you could do a half-decent job. Not that it wouldn't be fine to get a landmark commission like the Vanguard and have it the way he wanted, but that was asking for the moon. It would be fun working on the competition, but if he didn't win...

I'm a small-timer, Hal realized with a slight, not unpleasant, shock, because he had never thought of himself in exactly those terms before. Another truth he wouldn't reveal to Julie.

Kate, of course, already knew.

When they reached the second floor landing, Hal pushed open the door to the lower open-plan office. "Let's cut through here. There are fire stairs at the east end that go down to the back alley. I'd like another quick look at the north elevation."

Julie followed him across the beige desert, towards a grey steel door in the east wall of the office, bisected at waist height by the regulation panic bar. Hal knew the layout from the competition drawings. Beyond the door, the fire stairs were shared by the adjoining Doyle Hotel, which had an identical fire door. On both doors, the opening mechanism was located on the inside to prevent entrance from the opposite premises.

Halfway across the open office, they heard the whine of a power tool coming from the fire stairs. One of the maintenance people, Hal thought; their work went on even in an empty building. As they neared the door, the electric whine came again with another sound over it, a jagged rasp — some kind of cutting attachment on a power drill.

"How hungry are you?" Hal said.

"Starving."

"Good. I know a great little..." He stopped, surprised by a sudden flurry of activity beyond the door, the clatter of tools being hastily collected and stowed, a metal tool box snapping shut, hurried footsteps disappearing down the stairs.

Hal pushed on the panic bar and entered the stairwell, just in time to hear the door to the alley crash open and shut at the bottom of the stairs. Hal could hear the distant throb of music from the Doyle Hotel; he could feel it, a pulse of bass and drums in his shoes.

He stood for a moment, knitting his brows, staring at the Doyle's fire door across the landing, at an EMERGENCY EXIT sign, wondering why the sign should be on a door that didn't open from this side, and at least a foot below regulation height.

He went back into the office. Julie was over by the north wall, at one of the windows overlooking the alley. "What was he doing?" she asked. "Why did he take off like that?"

Hal shrugged. "Beats me."

"It was kind of spooky." Julie bit her lip. "He looked up at me. He looked right up at the window as if he sensed me watching."

"You saw him? What did he look like?"

"Green coveralls, tool box. Early twenties. Ordinary. Well..." She smiled. "Ordinary to me. You'd probably have at least one more thing to add."

"I would?"

"He was Chinese." Julie laughed at him, her black almond eyes sparkling with mischief. She bowed prettily. "Thank you, Sebastian-san, for most AHA morning! Now I buy lunch for illustrious master as small token of esteem."

Hal smiled and returned the bow. "Thank you, Julie Lee." He liked saying her name; it sounded like sleigh bells. "There's a good place on Wellington if you..." He felt the fleeting caress of her pony-tail, soft and herbal-scented as she swept past him towards the fire door. "Where are you going?" he called after her.

"We are going next door."

"Are you crazy?"

"Curious! I've never been in one of those places before."

"Julie...wait up!"

But she was already on the stairs.

CHAPTER
4

The first song was always fast. Strut your stuff, show off your costume. The shape of things to come.

Second song, part of the gift wrap came off. Tits, but unless they were perfect or made of silicon, which Tyah's weren't (maybe six out of ten but not high 'n mighty, not nineteen years old anymore), unless they were like Felice's tits, you concentrated elsewhere.

Legs, in Tyah's case. Slender and sinuous from eight years of dancing, six hours a day, six days a week. Legs a mile long in five-inch heels and a high-cut G-string. Legs with a velvet, black-light tan. Take them on a leg trip, all the way to the little vee of daylight where good thighs part at the top.

You're once...twice...three times a lady...

The third song was always slow and they got everything, which disappointed them if only they could admit it, because the most perfect body in the world looked sexier with *something* covered up. But they were paying four bucks a beer to see pink, so...

Tyah slipped the side bows of her satin G-string and rolled over on the fake fur rug, facing the audience on all fours. Pussy cat. Slowly she collapsed her arms, leaving her bare bottom in the air, proffered to the back of the stage where a plate-glass mirror reflected her to the sea of male faces. She drew her knees together as she snaked off the G-string, compressing her twat into a neat bun.

Pussy.

A somersault, and now she was turned around on her back on the rug, looking at them through wide-apart thighs, catching eyes full of stubborn expectation as though the big thing was still supposed to happen — a cuckoo was going to pop out, an oracle was going to tell them something they needed to hear: *Go home, pick up some flowers for the wife, pick up a treat for the kiddies, make yourself feel better!*

The slow song finished. Tyah put on her robe to enthusiastic applause, gathered up her costume and dragged the rug off the stage. Clyde, Carny's deejay, was already pitching the next dancer in his slick jive: "Gentlemen! The show that never ends. Keepin' you on the boil, *at* the Doyle. Put your hands together please, for some serious striptease...the very very lovely...Felice!"

Tyah crossed the club, greeting her regulars, logging table dances for when she got back from the dressing room. She noticed the little Oriental girl check her watch and go, leaving her male companion to finish his beer.

Tyah had noticed her immediately. A fully clothed female in the audience was a rarity and meant one of three things: she was here for a job, she was into women (extremely rare) or she was slumming, with a guy, somewhere she normally wouldn't be caught dead in. Like this girl. Tyah had passed their table on her way to the stage, had seen Shane checking the guy's camera. No cameras was a house rule in every strip club in the world, but the girl had made a big fuss, almost getting them thrown out before her friend smoothed it over.

He looked equally out of place amongst the business crowd, with his long hair and his old tweed jacket. But he was paying for his beer like everyone else, so Tyah gave him a professional smile as she went by this time, and he smiled back, a nice easy smile that made her think of Fletcher — as if she thought about a whole lot else but Fletch these days!

She moved through the hustling waitresses and the cruising table dancers to a doorway in the back corner of the club marked STRICTLY NO ADMITTANCE — EMPLOYEES ONLY. Tyah pushed the door open and saw Felice at the top of the stairs in her new outfit, already half a song late.

"C'mon Felice, you're on!"

"Shit!"

Felice was struggling to button wide white suspenders to the waistband of her black satin pants. Tyah ran up. "Let me do it!" She dropped her own costume on the top step and unzipped the pants to expose the waistband, making it easier to get the buttons through the stiff leather grommets. "I'll change the buttons tonight, put on smaller ones. Hold still!"

The costume was brand new, Tyah had put the last stitch in this morning. Fletcher, who had seen the outfit on Tyah's cutting table, called it her "tuxedo for the libido." The tux itself was bolero style with exaggerated shoulder-pads — not that Felice needed them. Underneath the black satin pants was a "formal" white G-string to match the white bow tie and the white suspenders that were just wide enough to cover Felice's nipples.

Felice was squirming with impatience. "Jesus, Ty! I got to go on!"

"There…" Tyah was zipping her up when the door burst open at the bottom of the stairs.

"How about some pussy out here, Felice? Soon as Tyah gets the fuck out of your pants!"

"Fuck you, Shane."

"No thanks, Tyah, you're not my type. Felice's my type, aren't you sweetheart?" But he said it to Tyah, smirking and squeezing his racquetball, tossing it hand to hand. Shane had tried professional boxing before he was a bouncer, but his hands had failed him as much as his attitude. Despite an otherwise stocky, powerful build, Shane's hands were abnormally small, hardly bigger than a child's. He had a deep complex about them, worked constantly on his rubber ball to try and build them up.

"NOW, Felice!"

Felice ran down. Shane barged into the club ahead of her, letting the door swing back in her face.

"Your shoes!" Felice had left her black pumps at the top of the stairs. The younger girl turned, reached up to catch, but for a moment Tyah withheld them. "What's he mean, you're his type?"

"Just gimme the fuckin' shoes, Ty!"

Tyah folded her costume with expert care before hanging it on the rack at the back of the dressing room. It was another of her originals, a cowgirl outfit in soft white leather, embroidered and glittering. Miniskirt, vest, gauntlets. She handled each piece with the same loving care, knowing down to the last rhinestone and sequin how many painstaking hours had gone into it.

By now Tyah was designing and making costumes and clothing for a number of friends. Her next job was for Felice's brother, Marc, who had ordered stage outfits for his whole band. It was her most ambitious project to date and would mean welcome exposure now that the band had a regular TV spot in Montreal. Tyah's old Singer was on its last gasp — she would need some professional equipment pretty soon, which didn't come cheap.

Which meant it was time to get down to the combat zone: for every song that played itself out downstairs, Tyah was losing five dollars' table-dancing money.

But she needed to be alone a few minutes more, away from the music and the people. It was a luxury to have the dressing room to herself; an hour ago, at opening time, there had been fifteen girls at the mirror all bitching at once. There were still fifteen lipsticks and mascara brushes littering the counter, enough pairs of jeans and street shoes on the floor to open a thrift store.

Tyah waded over to her tote bag and slipped into her table-dancing gear — a store-bought polyester camisole combination, easy to get in and out of. Then she lit an Export Light, pulled a chair out from the makeup counter and put her long legs up.

As she smoked, she could hear Felice's second song pulsing up through the floor, an old Elvis rocker called *Little Sister*, which was pretty much how Tyah viewed their relationship. Felice worked out of Montreal where she had a place with Marc, but she always stayed with Tyah when she was in town. A good arrangement: they liked each other's company, Tyah could do her big sister act and it saved them both on food and rent.

She could hear the wolf-whistles drowning Elvis as the tux came off, could picture Felice with the white suspenders stretched taut over those glorious tits. She had the shoulders to carry them — and the cheekbones and the eyebrows and a mane of black hair. She had everything, certainly everything she needed to become a legit model. She was wasting herself stripping, as Tyah had been telling her since Christmas. She would broach the subject again tonight, along with the less pleasant one of Shane Pilch, Scum of the Earth.

But Tyah didn't want ugly thoughts right now. She pulled on the Export and blew a slow, satisfied stream at the mirror.

She was doing pretty good, finally. It would be three years in June since she had checked into a detox centre on her twenty-fifth birthday with a two-hundred-dollar-a-day heroin addiction. Three years and she was still clean as a pin, nothing more than the odd joint for partying.

She had been on probation all this time (it was up in June) but they had been the best three years of her life. They had produced Fletch, the first good man after a string of losers, her first car, a pretty, two-bedroom apartment in the Beaches and the discipline to work her hobby into something that might be profitable enough, in another year or so, to let her quit dancing.

Three good years that had instilled a simple and unshakeable belief: your money could go into your bloodstream or your bank account, but not both. Which was why, to minimize temptation, Tyah worked exclusively for Carny Danial.

Tyah listened for a moment to the whirr of Carny's adding machine behind the wall of mirror tiles separating the dressing room from the office. One of those tiles, as everyone knew, was a two-way mirror that Carny's brother had installed years ago. Lonnie had died before Tyah's fifth birthday, but the story lived on: how Lonnie got so spoiled for kicks he had to peep into the dressing room to watch the girls putting *on* their clothes!

But the mirror posed no threat to privacy these days. Carny had long ago boarded up the window, because he was a gentleman, an otherwise extinct breed in this business. Sure, he was strict; he came down hard on intoxication, tardiness and "improper conduct," a relative term that could mean soliciting, fighting or a table dancer allowing a customer to touch her in a dark corner for an extra ten. First timers got a warning, second offenders had their pay docked, third time out, blacklisted — girl never worked the Doyle again.

But if you were straight with him, Carny stood solidly behind you. If a dancer was in trouble, he was there: advice, a useful name, a place to stay — even cash in a pinch. And there was a payback: his girls put on the best show in town and they looked happy, which was always good for business.

Tyah stood up, took a last pull on her cigarette and squashed it out. On her way to the door she blew a smoky kiss at the mirror-tile wall where Carny's adding machine whirred on.

She did another show at five o'clock but up till then, and for an hour afterwards, she worked the tables.

Tyah never had to cruise very long to scare up dances — there was always someone catching her eye, or else one of her regulars showed up and kept her occupied for an hour or more. It wasn't really dancing; for five dollars a song she was an animated statue beside the guy's chair, so close he could smell her spice, feel her heat, the caress of her hair, the occasional press of bare flesh against his clothing. But no touching. The slightest touch from a customer and a discreet hand signal produced Shane. Infractions were rare, but still Tyah preferred the centre tables where the level of intimacy was lower.

She discouraged the talkers, the guys who asked "Why do you do this, Tyah?" or "You just don't seem like a stripper," even as their eyes drifted back to her body. She never asked a man's name until he was a regular. She never accepted presents or invitations to dinner from regulars or let them talk dirty to her. She just stripped and smiled, thinking about the thousand dollars she could pull down in a fair week.

At six o'clock, her shift was finished and Tyah got dressed, longing to take her scrutinized, aching anatomy home, away from the smoke and the din. Felice would be a while — she was up in Carny's office getting a lecture for being late on at lunchtime — so Tyah shouldered her tote and wandered down to the bar and ordered a Diet Pepsi from John.

"That guy ever come back for his camera?" Tyah asked. She had noticed it behind the bar earlier in the afternoon, had looked around for the hippy-professor with the nice smile but found him gone. Now his camera was gone too.

John cast his melancholy eyes at the empty shelf and shrugged. "No one come to me. Maybe the guy talk to Shane about it. Seen the paper today?"

"I heard."

There was a *Toronto Sun* lying on the counter. John unfolded the fat tabloid, flipped past the Sunshine Girl (on the meaty side today) to page three. "Read that." He went away to take orders from three waitresses who had materialized at the bar, leaving Tyah to read:

VANGUARD STILL MONEY PIT FOR MIDLAND.

When you gotta go, you gotta go — so they keep telling Carny Danial, also known as "The Doyle Diehard." Mr. Danial is leaseholder and manager of the Doyle Hotel, a bar featuring exotic dancers in the monolithic Vanguard Building on King Street East. He is also an expensive thorn in the side of the Midland Development Corporation, which owns the Vanguard, but they can't seem to pull him out.

It is two years since Midland got the go-ahead to develop the historic Vanguard into an office and retail complex. To that end they have bought out the leases of all tenants in the grand old building, or allowed them to expire. All except Mr. Danial's lease which, according to Midland, was renewed accidentally a year ago.

"It was a computer error," Midland spokesman Graham Sawtrell claimed in an interview yesterday. "Mr. Danial's lease extension agreement was the result of a clerical oversight on the part of one of our junior employees. No one should be made to pay this dearly for an honest mistake."

By "dearly," Mr. Sawtrell is referring to the estimated half a million dollars a month it is costing Midland to carry a big, empty building in a prime downtown location. Six months ago, Midland failed in their bid to oust Mr. Danial in the Ontario Supreme Court. Mr. Sawtrell announced yesterday that they have appealed the ruling. A date for the hearing will be set next week.

Mr. Danial, whose father and brother were in business at the Doyle before him, has been operating the tavern on the corner of King and Court Streets since 1969.

"Carny took over from Lonnie in '66, didn't he?" John would know, he had been working at the Doyle since Carny's father's time.

"Caught it, did ya?" John yanked open the refrigerator, pulled four beers in his fist. "It's plenty long enough if you ask me, stubborn son of a bitch. Midland offered him a king's ransom to vacate, now them high rollers gonna soak 'im." Tyah watched him top the four bottles in a single fluid motion and swing them onto a waiting tray. "I know what I'd do, I'd take the money and run."

"Me too."

"But you can't talk to him. 'I've got a lease…I've got a lease.'" John sniffed disapprovingly and produced a cocktail glass out of thin air. "Ought to be in Arizona or some place, boring the other old farts with his war stories."

There was no parking spot on Tyah's street, even for her little Chevette. But the fresh air was welcome after the Doyle fug, and they enjoyed the block-long walk home.

It was a picturesque neighbourhood, sloping gently south from the bustle of Queen Street to a band of parkland and the April-sharp horizon of Lake Ontario. The grass was already reasserting itself in bright green patches; here and there snowdrops pushed through, squeaky fresh.

"I've got a confession," Tyah said as they walked. "I forged your signature on an application form." Felice said nothing but she knew what Tyah was talking about.

"You're wasting yourself, you know that? All's you have to do is audition for their modelling course, what the fuck's so hard about that? They've even got a branch in Montreal. If they like you — and they're gonna *love* you — you'll be working right away."

Felice looked bored. "Yolanda what?"

"*Bates*! Yolanda Bates Agency. Jesus, forget it, sorry I fucking mentioned it!"

Tyah lived in a well-maintained, three-story, white stucco building where she had a lakeview, ground floor apartment. Tyah unlocked the front door and took a deep breath of heavy, tropical air. "What do you think? Guy moves in, brings all his friends with him."

By Fletcher's "friends" she meant the fifty-odd house plants of every shape and size, from a family of common and garden monkey plants clambering around the window to some rare and valuable orchids. Fletcher was a partner in a year-old enterprise at Bay and Davenport called the Plant Kingdom, a growing business, as he could now joke.

"My God!" Felice dropped her tote bag on the pastel dhurrie and turned around, taking it all in. She had come in from Montreal this morning and it had been a month since she was last here. "You and Fletch...you're *living* together?"

Tyah grinned and made a pistol at the coffee table, at a framed photo of Fletcher that used to reside by her bed. "Pow! Another good man down!"

Felice hugged her, genuinely pleased at the news. Then she picked up her bag. "I'm real glad for you. But two's company, eh? I'll leave the pants."

"What are you talking about?"

"Look, I can stay at the Doyle, the rooms are fine." She meant one of the three bedrooms on the third floor, for out-of-town dancers, the only hotel rooms Carny maintained.

Tyah marched towards her, grabbed Felice's tote and forcibly peeled off her denim jacket. "You're not going to the Carny Hilton or any place else. Now give me the pants and go make coffee. You're pissing me off."

"You sure?"

Tyah laughed. "Think I'm worried about the competition? Think my old man's going to look twice at a dog like you?"

Felice gave her the finger and went off to the kitchen. Tyah carried the black pants into her workroom. It was a tiny room, cluttered with dressmaking equipment, racks of clothing and paper patterns, bolts of material and endless boxes and tins of thread and toggles and zippers and pins and a thousand other things, some of them a mystery even to Tyah.

She opened her button tin, stirred around until she had six the same, then laid the pants out on her cutting table. There was a button attachment on the Singer but Tyah preferred to sew by hand when she wanted to wind down after the club.

She was on the fifth button when the coffee arrived. Felice watched over her shoulder as Tyah's expert fingers jabbed and plucked at the needle. Felice sniffed, sipped her coffee and sniffed again.

"Caught a cold in there, did you?" Tyah asked.

No reply.

Tyah looked around. "Snowing was it, in the kitchen?"

Felice shrugged nervously. "I'm sorry. You want to do a line? I figured you don't..."

"Figured right." She turned back to the work, wound off the button, brought the waistband to her mouth and snipped the thread with her teeth. "Is that what Shane meant? You're his type?" She swivelled around to face her friend. "How long has this been going on?"

"Come on, Ty, it's just a little blow. There's no problem."

"Oh, you don't think so. Let me tell you, Shane Pilch isn't nice company, Felice. You remember Starlene? No, I guess she was before your time. Well, Starlene was a character, right? Always cracking jokes. Till one day she cracks one about Shane, about Shane's weird hands, something like: 'Shane got off to a bad start in the fight game 'cause they don't do boxing gloves in infant sizes.'" Felice shrugged. "Okay, Starlene told shitty jokes, except this one got around to Shane and the next day she didn't show for her set.

44

Or the next day. We figured she'd left town. Then six weeks later someone sees her dancing in Gary's."

"Where?"

"Scarborough. A biker joint. So I cruise out and there's Starlene wearing body paint, right? Big horrible fucking flowers and butterflies and shit like that. Know why? Bruises like you wouldn't believe. And she's limping...*six weeks later*." She gave Felice a level stare. "That's your friend Shane."

Felice shifted her weight uncomfortably. "Why didn't Carny fire the guy?"

"What for? You need proof, and Carny couldn't prove nothing. Starlene wasn't going to say shit. One: she's scared, with good reason. Two: Shane's the snowman, right Felice? Nobody says dick about Shane because you're all getting high as kites off of the guy. And Carny can't prove nothing 'cause he never deals on the premises. Am I right?"

Silence.

"How much you pay for that gram? Eighty? Ninety?"

Felice mumbled reluctantly: "Eighty."

"That's a nice price these days. But it'll start going up now, you'll see. Pretty soon you'll be paying a premium, just like at the 7 Eleven, right there when you need it. And you *will* need it, little sister."

Tyah looked at the younger girl for a long moment, then reached up and lightly touched Felice's face before swivelling back to her table.

"Okay. End of lecture. Fuck...I do sound awful straight these days!"

As Tyah reached for the last button, a dark curtain of hair fell across her vision. She felt a baby-soft cheek against her own as Felice whispered: "I think you sound nice."

Tyah finished the sewing, then took Felice through the sketches for Marc's costumes, and at seven-thirty Fletcher came home with another friend.

"Fletch! You're crazy!"

Preceding him through the door, to a fanfare of rude remarks from the women, was the biggest cactus Tyah had ever seen outside of a cowboy movie. Fletcher heaved the giant clay pot onto the dhurrie and dodged out the door. "You three have fun now, y'hear?"

"Fletch!" bawled Tyah. "Get back in here, you fool!"

Fletcher reappeared with two paper sacks, which he set down beside the coffee table. "Had ourselves a little celebration at the store," he drawled proudly. "Record sales so far this month. Gave m'self a little bonus." He went to pat the cactus, then remembered the spines.

"You're drunk," laughed Tyah.

"Bullsheet, senorita!" Like a conjurer, Fletcher pulled grocery items from the first sack and arranged them on the coffee table: two pounds of ground beef, a family-size packet of chili powder, a giant tin of kidney beans, a bag of onions. From the second, a forty-ouncer of Cuervo Gold, half gone.

"Margareeetas!" he cried. "We got triple sec?"

"Nope."

He gave his best Jack Nicholson grin. "Clear fluid it is, then! Hey…" He went after Tyah, on her way to the kitchen with the groceries. "Don't you touch them makin's! Chili is man's work, always was, always will be." Laughing and sparring, Tyah let him bump her out of the kitchen, neatly catching the rolled-up Baggie he tossed into the living room.

In a minute he was back with three straight shots of Gold, which they drank with salt licks and lime kisses. Then they smoked the munchies joint Tyah had rolled from the good stuff that Fletcher's partner, Willi Gillens, grew under optimum lighting conditions in the basement of the Plant Kingdom. Fletcher put ZZ Top on the stereo and cooked chili while the women found a home for the cactus, which they christened Bonus and then changed, giggling like schoolgirls, to Boner.

Tyah stole glowing looks at Fletcher in his apron. He was a pretty man, though of a securely masculine type that could afford the long, dark lashes around his violet eyes, the movie star teeth and the deep cleft in his chin that Tyah so loved to explore with her tongue. Even at the stove, in an apron, he moved slow and easy, at peace with himself.

Fletcher's cooking was terrible. His chili was more like hamburger soup, but the joint had done its work. With muffled grunts of pleasure, elbowing each other for place on the sofa, they devoured two bowls each and mopped up with hunks of soft white bread. They washed the chili down with ice-cold beers, then Fletcher cracked a fresh pack of Camels and they sat back, cradling full tummies, and smoked the best cigarette of the year.

Tyah and Felice did the dishes while Fletcher played deejay, and when The Eagles' *Peaceful Easy Feeling* came on, he sauntered into the kitchen and led Tyah out by the hand to dance, slow and peaceful and easy.

It was a perfect way to end the day, to close her eyes and feel her man's arms around her, to lay her head against the firm pillow of his chest and feel his square hand in her hair. She must have dozed off for a moment, because when the album side ended and she opened her eyes, Felice was standing in the open doorway with her quilted denim jacket on, tote bag in her hand, smiling at them.

"I've got the pants," she whispered. "Thanks a lot. And thanks for a great dinner, Fletch."

Tyah gently released Fletcher and followed her friend into the vestibule. "Where the hell are you going?"

"I called Carny. He's expecting me."

"Don't be crazy."

Felice had made up her mind. "I'll see you tomorrow in the combat zone." She opened the front door and the cool night air slipped in. She hesitated a moment, then pushed it almost closed. "Know something, Ty? This modelling thing...maybe I'll give them a call. Yolanda what was it?"

"Bates!"

"Yeah. Bates." Still Felice lingered, nibbling the inside of her cheek as though there was something else, difficult to say.

"What is it, Felice?"

"I dunno. Shit. Today in the club, for the first time, something made me feel...I dunno...ashamed. You ever feel that way?"

"What was the thing?"

"When I was table dancing, I seen this little Chinois...this Oriental..."

Tyah remembered: the Chinese girl with her smart, educated face, slumming it for an "interesting" half hour in the dark place Tyah spent half her life. "Yeah," she said. "I remember the girl. She was with a guy, he brought in a camera."

"What?" Felice looked puzzled.

"Sure. The guy she was with had a camera. Shane checked it, she gave him a hard time."

Felice was shaking her head. "No. I'm talking about a man. A Chinese *man*. I was dancing for Wally, right? Big fat guy, regular guy."

"I know Wally."

"I'm dancing for Wally, maybe twenty minutes, I see this little Chinese guy sitting off in the corner, watching me. Staring at me. He was..."

"What?" said Tyah. "Jerking off?"

"No. Just looking at me. I dunno." Felice shrugged and opened the door again. "I'm sorry. I didn't mean to spoil a nice evening with this shit."

"Felice?" Tyah looked into the young girl's eyes, measuring, encouraging the fear there. The mostly unadmitted fear that every stripper had felt since the horror last summer. It may have lost its edge over seven months, but it was always there.

Side two of the Eagles went on in the living room. "Watcha doin' Ty?"

"Okay, Fletch, just a second." She turned back, reached past Felice and shut the door. "You're gonna stay here."

Felice's dark eyes flashed. "Open the door, Ty."

Tyah considered. "Okay, but I'm going to drive you."

"Ty..."

"Can it!" Her scowl became a smile. "You know me — I drive great when I'm stoned!"

It was a quarter past eleven when she got back. Fletcher was watching the television. "Look at you," she said. "Figured you'd be in your bed by now."

Fletcher thumbed the remote, killing Arsenio Hall. He got up and took her hand. "*Our* bed, darlin'. I can't be there without you."

Moonlight streamed through the bedroom window. Tyah held him away from her. "I want to look at you," she said, and began to undress him with trembling slowness, in loose time with *Peaceful Easy Feeling*, which she could still hear in her mind, or maybe it was in her heart. When he was naked she said: "Lay down, Fletcher."

She stood by the bed for a full minute, awed by the beauty of his body bathed in moonlight, aching to touch it, and to be touched. "My man," she whispered, scarcely able to believe it. When she could wait no longer, she undressed herself and lay down beside him. They kissed and caressed gently, tentatively, filled with wonder, their breath quickening as their hands journeyed languidly, teasingly, inevitably, between each other's legs.

Tyah moaned with pleasure as he played her. She kissed him harder, open-mouthed, hungry now. She held his head in both hands, her smile becoming one of mischief as her tongue flicked into the deep, deliciously stubbled cleft of his chin.

"See what I'm doing? Now you do that to me." Before he could misunderstand, she guided him down, between her breasts, over her belly, down...

CHAPTER
5

April warmed to May on Grace Street, and mid-month came a week of impatient summer weather. It drew out the Mediterranean families who filled the air with the oily smoke of barbecuing fish and the incessant, squabbling din that would continue all summer. From behind the fence, Kate could hear the inevitable *swish swish swish* of Bruno Valente, a retired hospital cleaner, sweeping his concrete garden.

Bruno sweeping. The sound of summer. Hearing it on the Friday morning at the end of that hot week, Kate realized with a deep, sinking feeling that she had lived here seven years.

She crouched, dispirited, at the base of the fence. Planting perennials had seemed like a good idea this morning when she had called in sick to the magazine, but now she had lost heart for such a commitment to the shabby, rented garden.

"See, Monkey? You've made a face. There are the eyes, there's the nose. Shall we make a mouth?" Kate added a bit of stick to the stones Rain had arranged on the flower-bed. "How about a head?" Kate began to draw a circle around the stones, but Rain snatched up the stick-mouth and scrabbled in the dirt to spoil the face. She threw the stick down and toddled towards the house. Kate went after her. "Stay out here, Rain. Daddy's working." The child ignored her, climbed on all fours up the steps and toddled through the open back door. What the hell, it was lunchtime anyway.

Spending a stolen weekday with her daughter had been a sublime thought this morning, but Rain had been sullen since breakfast — paying me back for all the days she doesn't have me, Kate thought. She couldn't win!

She stood on the bald patch of lawn behind the house, kneading crusted soil from her fingers. The Grace Street house was a skinny, two-story Victorian with a frowning gable and small, dark windows. Cold in winter, an oven in summer, the duplex was in dismal shape. In wet weather, a leaking eavestrough drooled through the north wall where the brick needed repointing, which accounted for spreading yellow blotches on the ceiling, like urine stains on a mattress. Hal corrected most problems, but the masonry needed major work — eventually they would have to call the landlord, who would doubtless respond by putting up the rent.

Seven years, etched into her soul like a tally on a prison wall.

It was the waiting that was unbearable. Easier for Hal, a week away from the competition deadline, working all hours to finish the drawings. But there was nothing for Kate to do now except wait. Her mock-up had become camera-ready art that had gone to the printer with an order for two hundred folders (they could be used whenever Hal bid on a job), for which Kate owed the bank $4318. Hal's displeasure had soon passed; he was preoccupied with the drawings, and really he was as little interested in disbursements as he was in *making* money. Mike Herlihy, on the other hand, reminded Kate almost daily that she had gone out of her mind. Maybe he was right. But owing the bank a bit more didn't seem half as crazy as missing a chance to change her life.

Swish swish swish...

To change this.

Hal came through the back door, blinking in the bright sunlight with Rain in his arms. "There's Mummy!"

"You look like a ghost," Kate said, going to them. He set Rain down, removed his glasses and rubbed his eyes. He was pallid and unshaven, his hair licking out like a bedraggled feather where he rested his head in his hand to draw.

"Mummy lookit!" Rain waved a postcard at her.

"It's from the Boys," Hal said, sitting down wearily on the sun-warmed steps.

The Boys were Murray and Tom, the couple who rented the upstairs apartment, away on a long-saved-for holiday in the south of France. They were well, the postcard said, Antibes was heaven, they were eating much too much. They signed themselves "the Michelin Men." Kate turned the card over and gazed at a Côte d'Azure seascape.

Suddenly Hal reached forward and caught her hands. "Why don't we go somewhere? Right now."

Kate shrugged. "Why not? I'll go call Air France."

"I mean a drive. Let's just get out of here for an hour or two."

She frowned. "I thought you had all kinds of work to do."

"I have been working, round the clock," he said indignantly. "I need a break." His grip tightened. "Come on. The three of us. We haven't done that in ages. Just for a couple of hours. Let's just point the car and go."

"You promised Julie you'd have the elevations ready for colouring on Monday. Are you going to make it?"

"Hey!" Hal's grey eyes flashed angrily.

"I'm only thinking..."

"Don't push it, Katy. Okay?"

Kate drove. They went east on Highway 401 with no real plan other than getting out into the country. The Chrysler's droning soon had the desired effect on Rain; at the Metro border she stopped wriggling in her car-seat and crying for dropped toys and took her afternoon nap.

At Ajax, Kate lost Hal as well. At first she was annoyed to find herself alone on a journey she hadn't wanted to make in the first place, listening to him snore. But after a while the highway started working a kind of hypnotism on her, and she began to enjoy the act of driving without traffic lights and stop signs — the sensation, though mild in the Chrysler, of speed. The idea had been to leave the highway for a country drive, but now she felt as though she could keep going on this straight, soothing grey road, on and on without stopping, all the way to the sea.

Near Oshawa she got held up behind an old, right-hand-drive Rolls Royce with Quebec plates, which seemed an odd combination. *Je me souviens* said the motto on the fleur-de-lis plates.

Kate did remember, although the car in her memory was a Bentley, not a Rolls, of the same vintage and with a similar body style. It had been black with demure navy leather; Grandy would have had no time for a white car — *nouveau riche,* he would have said, unless you lived in a hot climate, in which case there was some excuse. Grandy was fastidious about "good form," perhaps because he had attended only a minor public school, or perhaps because he was, essentially, a self-made man.

Kate's grandfather had been a widower in his mid-sixties when her parents died in a sailing accident in the English Channel, and Kate moved into the big country house in Worcestershire. She had uncles and aunts, all claiming her; it would be only natural, they protested, for a six-year-old girl to want to be raised with her young cousins. But after a number of stormy, tearful sojourns with her various relatives, Kate rejected them all and returned to Grandy and Nan, his housekeeper.

Grandy's business was biscuits, which had made him a modest fortune. A rangy, shrewd-eyed man in chalkstripes, it was hard for people, even his own family, to imagine him playing enchanter to a young girl. Yet Grandy was the star around which Kate's life orbited. She did go away to school, of course, but at the end of each term she would sit in the window seat overlooking the long drive, breathless with excitement as she waited to glimpse the black Bentley. Grandy always came in person to fetch her from school; no matter what his business agenda, he never missed, never once sent Pearce the chauffeur.

Then it was home to the enchanted house and garden, sometimes with a school friend or two. To the summerhouse and the swimming pool and the trout pond, to a fourteen-foot Christmas tree and outings to the ballet and the pantomime, to *Alice* and *The Arabian*

Nights, beside a roaring fire in Grandy's Havana-scented study. Later on there were tennis and pool parties for her young teenage friends and Continental holidays, ski trips to Chamonix and Kitzbuhel; although Grandy organized chaperones for these, he didn't come himself. Right up to the end he was actively running his business.

Grandy died when Kate was sixteen, having made what should have been ample provision for his family. But he had also made a disastrous error.

He had long been advised that the family holdings should be more diversified. Kate's trust, for instance, consisted almost entirely of shares in the family business. But Grandy was fiercely proud. Every year showed robust gains, he argued; such a sturdy, secure basket was designed to hold a great many eggs. But when he died, when the business went to his son Terry, the basket began to unravel.

Uncle Terry had been a dogged and dutiful lieutenant, but left on his own, he had no feel for business, no ability to grasp the big picture, none of his father's decisiveness. He wavered on almost every issue, and when he finally made one of his invariably bad decisions, he blamed his managers for the results. If there was one thing Uncle Terry *had* inherited, it was his father's pride, and it was pride that led him to resist the merger that might have saved his company from ruin.

Kate was twenty, beginning her final year of art college, when Uncle Terry called the hospital to say he had drunk a bottle of oil of wintergreen. Indecisive to the end, he had left the call too late; by the time they pumped his stomach, the poison had done irreparable organ damage.

Long faces at the funeral grew longer at the family meeting afterwards. The biscuit business was in receivership with nothing on the books but red ink. Their stock, including Kate's entire portfolio, was practically worthless. There would be enough to see her through her last year of college, but after that she was on her own.

Kate was at an age (and a time and a place) when such news was less than earth-shattering. None of her art college friends had any money, and she was enjoying her independence and life in London. After college she got a prestigious, if ill-paying, job with Sotheby's, lived with her two best friends in a flat furnished in budget Scandinavian and seemed perfectly happy for five years. Kate surprised even herself when she applied for a transfer to Sotheby's Canadian office.

She had met Hal when he was a graduate student at Cambridge. They had been lovers, briefly, and had parted friends when he returned to Canada. That had been easier, somehow, in the early seventies. Certainly Hal was at the back of her mind when she took the transfer — she knew he lived in Toronto — and it seemed only natural for them to get together when she arrived and learned that he was available. Natural to be in his bed again on those cold Canadian winter nights. Natural, eventually, to stop paying rent on two separate apartments when they seemed to spend all their time at one or the other of them.

Perhaps it was the physical distance from England, from the spurned relatives, that allowed Kate to start missing Grandy and the life she had lost for the first time in years. Since her marriage, having realized that, in Hal's case at least, "architect" was *not* synonymous with security, her nostalgia had become chronic, a constant ache that could flare up from a number of irritants: a photograph of an English country house, a whiff of cigar smoke, the aroma of leather upholstery in a car. *This* car, this Rolls Royce ahead of her on the 401, even in *nouveau riche* white, tugged at her, set her yearning for the style and security of her childhood, the lifestyle that had slipped away.

Kate signalled right, into the feeder lane for Exit 440, Bond Head. She had no knowledge of the place, but Bond Head sounded like it would be on the lake. Hal was still snoring lightly beside her. They had been out exactly one hour. Taking the lakeshore route home would use up more than that, but after seeing the Rolls, the highway had somehow lost its magic. So instead of using the Bond Head exit to loop onto the westbound lanes, Kate motored south towards Lake Ontario.

She found it at the end of a long avenue of stately maples. White picket fencing on both sides protected prosperous-looking Cape Cod cottages, grey clapboard with clean white trim. The end cottage was the largest and finest, facing south over the water. Kate slowed to see the family, just arrived in a Jeep wagon, getting the jump on their fine weekend. The woman, young and pretty — younger than Kate — watched the Chrysler with vague animosity as she herded two infants and a dancing Irish setter away from the road. Kate flushed and accelerated away; it stung her to see herself through that young woman's eyes, another day tripper in a beat-up car, ogling the "quality."

She slowed again at the water's edge, then stopped, her westerly return blocked by the wide creek she had been following down from the highway. Here the creek formed the access channel for the Bond Head marina, a growing forest of masts as the Travelift launched craft for the season.

She dragged a tattered map from the glove box, confirmed that she would have to retrace her steps to the 401 and drive home on it after all. There was no continuous lakeshore route west; all along the coast it was interrupted by creeks and marinas and industrial parks. But the road did go east, to Port Hope where Kate's map ended; a narrow country road winding through farmland and small lakeside communities.

She glanced at the dash clock, then at her sleeping husband. Rain began to stir in her car-seat, alerted by the lack of motion. Just a short way, Kate decided, throwing the car into gear. Just until they reached the next access road up to the highway.

They climbed steadily, levelling out along hundred-foot bluffs above sparkling water. On the inland side of the road, apple orchards in full, fragrant blossom stretched as far as the eye could see. After half a mile, the road wound north away from the lake around the perimeter of a dairy farm, where another fragrance wafted into the car.

"Poo!" said Rain, coming awake.

"Cow poo," Kate informed her. "That's a real country smell. Look!" A herd of black and white Holsteins watched the Chrysler's progress, hardly more animated than the plastic cows on Rain's toy farm.

Kate smiled at her daughter's wide-eyed reflection in the mirror, a touch sadly to think that these were the first real cows Rain had ever seen. Grandy's house had been surrounded by farms. The animals, the good smells, the distant chugging of a tractor borne on the breeze on a summer afternoon — these were among the treasured memories of her childhood. And as she drove, she thought again, enviously, of the pretty, affluent young woman she had seen just now at the gate of her country retreat.

Gradually the road descended, winding and dipping through stands of dense white cedar, playing peek-a-boo with the lake. Had her map been larger, Kate would have seen this same road continuing all the way to Kingston, as it had done for 150 years. But long before that, it passed through a dwindling hamlet called Wesleyville, population: thirty-five. Kate saw a ruined one-room school house, abandoned so long that willow saplings had grown to young trees inside, forming a living roof. But the sparse cottages were well maintained, and so was a tiny variety-store-cum-post-office outside which five old boys turned slow heads to watch them pass. Their interest peaked when Kate stopped in front of the building at the end of the village, a Victorian country church standing behind respectfully manicured lawns.

It was here, on the gravel shoulder in front of the church, that Hal woke up.

Kate woke him up.

"Babe, you've got to see this." It took him some grunting and blinking before he was fully conscious and sitting up. "Look there!" she told him.

Hal smiled. It was lovely, he agreed. Mid-nineteenth century. A hall church. Tall, Gothic-arched windows on each side, a neo-classical facade with pilasters and a triangular pediment on which the datestone read: "Wesley United Church 1860." Other than that, the construction was simple, sturdy red brick and white-painted wood.

Its symmetrical prettiness alone would have caught Kate's attention. But what had made her stop the car, her heart suddenly, foolishly beating, was a bright red and yellow realtor's sign on the lawn.

"Who can it belong to?" she asked. "Who can sell a church?"

"The church can. United Church in this case." He looked back at the village. "What's this place called?"

"Wesleyville. It seems almost deserted."

"There's your answer: congregation's gone. Meanwhile the United Church has to pay rates and upkeep. Flogging a dead horse. Little gem though, isn't it? Someone from the city will snap it up and do a number on it. Make someone a nice hideaway."

Kate twisted around in her seat. "Look! There's a clear view of the lake! And all these trees!" The church was surrounded by smooth, long-limbed sugar maples. Freshening green now, in summer they would form a cool, bountiful canopy. Behind the church, beyond a tidy cemetery, a knoll rose gently to a stand of mature white pine.

"It's an absolute dream." Kate scrabbled in the glove box for a pen and an unpaid parking ticket to write on.

Hal frowned. "What are you doing?"

"I'm getting the name of the agent."

"What for?"

"Fun." She finished writing, opened the car door and swung her legs out. "You coming?"

He looked at the clock. "We're going to be into the rush hour if we don't head back right now."

But Kate didn't hear him. She was standing up outside the car, taking deep, greedy breaths of Wesleyville air.

CHAPTER
6

Graham Sawtrell was in his early fifties, a big, jovial Englishman with a weekend sailor's ruddy complexion.

"They're tarting up the boardroom so we'll have to make do in here," he told Hal and Julie as he welcomed them into his office. "Hope we don't cramp your style."

The executive vice president's corner office was anything but cramped. A handsome room, wood panelled and leather upholstered. The window-wall provided a spectacular twenty-third-story view of the city. Hal looked for the Vanguard, three blocks east, but found it hidden by a tower.

Two other Midland people rose from an oak table to greet them. Sawtrell introduced Jack Haines, VP finance, and Larry McIsaac, engineering, both middle-aged and suet-plain in sincere business blue. Sawtrell then turned to a third man who had not risen, on his immediate right. Ron Allis was around Hal's age, lean and elegant in a silky olive suit. He looked up from his papers, unsmiling, and offered a cool, effortless handshake.

"Ron's our real-estate consultant," Sawtrell told them. He gestured for Hal to go on his left with Julie beside Hal. "Ron likes us to build buildings that people want to rent, buy things in, park their bloody cars in. And we try to please him the best we can." He sat down, a signal for everyone else to follow suit. "In other words, when we build — in this case, restore — it's Ron's job to see we don't have our heads up our backsides."

Haines and McIsaac glanced at Julie, found her smiling. Hal smiled too; with his polished bluster and that accent, anything Sawtrell said would sound like the right thing.

"So tell us, Mr. Sebastian: where, as they say, is *your* head at?"

Hal got off to a good start. The Vanguard's hidden atrium came as a complete surprise. None of the Midland people made any attempt to hide the fact, and they were quick to appreciate the value of Hal's discovery. Apart from the first and second floors, Hal explained in his preamble, apart from the open-plan floors where the original structure had been replaced with columns, the whole atrium was intact, including the roof. It would be a relatively easy matter to rip out the core of the building, enlarge the lost windows in the atrium walls, then add the office and retail galleries.

There was no way of knowing how many proposals were already in, but from the slight, unconscious smile on Jack Haines's face, Hal suspected he was low so far, even by the two million he had estimated.

"What do you think, Larry?" Sawtrell said pointedly. "See anything you want to talk about so far?" McIsaac had been looking sheepish from the start, understandably. Hal expected him to wriggle on the pin now, to nitpick, to look for a way to gloss over the fact that his department had missed the building's biggest single design feature.

To McIsaac's credit, he came clean: "What can I say? We started out with the previous owner's drawings and I guess we inherited their limitations. Congratulations, Hal. You did your homework better than we did."

Jack Haines beamed. "Costwise, it's got to be better than starting from scratch."

"That's all good to hear," Hal said, trying not to sound as encouraged as he felt. "But so far the credit has to go to Henry

Richardson — it's his design." He paused, smiling now. "This is *our* scheme."

Hal felt a surge of pride as Julie handed round the kits and he saw their reaction to the glossy, illustrated folders adorned with Kate's sepia sketches of his past projects, titled and dated. Hal still thought some of the credits were misleading —a complete town hall where he had rebuilt only the front steps, a cathedral church where he had merely advised on dry-rot in the vestry — but Kate had rationalized by pointing out how much good work had been omitted.

Inside each kit was the meat of the proposal: Hal's resumé, the design drawings for the Van, detail drawings and typed material. When this was removed, the inside of the folder showed Kate's full-colour rendition of the atrium, looking skyward from the courtyard, revived Romanesque glory with all the conveniences — elevators, escalators, code-conforming yet unobtrusive safety features. The new galleries, blending perfectly with the original Victorian shell, teemed with Kate's thrusting figures.

"Very nice," said McIsaac.

"Super job!" concurred Haines.

Sawtrell said: "What do you think so far, Ron?"

Hal looked anxiously at Allis, who had not yet shown a flicker of emotion, making copious notes with a slim fountain pen. "Let's keep going," he murmured without looking up.

For the first time, Hal sensed trouble. Allis carried weight here, that much was clear. Whatever he said was going to be definitive. He exchanged a sideways glance with Julie: what was with all the note-taking?

Hal addressed specifics — underground parking, energy systems, the Van's exterior treatment, including the giant task of scrubbing away 150 years of grime, which, in the interest of preserving the fine stonework details, was *not* to be sandblasted.

The Midland people listened attentively, asking questions only to clarify Hal's intent, appreciating that objections should be raised later, *in camera*, as the basis for picking a winner.

Then, out of the blue, Ron Allis spoke. "These railings around the galleries..." He said it quietly in a dead voice, yet there was immediate silence around the table. Allis trailed his manicured forefinger across the detail drawing. "These railings are highly visible from the courtyard, yes?"

"Absolutely, at every level," Hal replied evenly.

"What do you propose they be made of?" Allis sounded almost bored, like someone who must constantly deal with predictable inferiors.

"Originally, this sort of detail would have been wood or cast iron," Hal explained. "Since there were no galleries as such, we're inventing here, but cast iron feels about right. Cast iron rails with tempered glass shields below; plexi's cheaper but it scratches."

Allis's pink and pearl finger descended to the retail galleries on the first two floors, accessible from the courtyard by steps and escalators. "Here as well? Cast iron hardware?"

Hal nodded, frowning slightly; the man was sniffing at a bone, getting ready to pick it.

"Brass," Allis said. He spoke to Sawtrell exclusively, an open affront to Hal and Julie.

"Sorry, I didn't catch that," Julie said. She had heard him perfectly, cast her words with ill-concealed annoyance. Hal gave her a warning nudge under the table.

Allis looked pityingly at her. "Brass around all the galleries and for the stair-rails up to the shopping levels. Brass on all the doors, awnings, all the visible hardware."

"Awnings?"

Hal nudged her again. Allis glanced disdainfully at the shopfront detail on page five, and then addressed Hal as if Julie no longer existed. "I was wondering why you omitted awnings from the drawings."

Julie was unnudgeable. "They weren't *omitted*, Mr. Allis. There aren't any awnings because the sunlight enters vertically from the atrium roof; there's no need for them. Awnings would also obscure the Romanesque arches that form the shop windows; these round arches are a vital theme throughout the building."

Allis spoke as if to a precocious child. "If you are conversant with available statistics, you will know that awnings on shopfronts create a marked increase in retail sales. So do greenery, plants and trees, of which I see altogether too little, especially in the courtyard. Brass has comparable drawing power. It symbolizes warmth, integrity, old world charm, particularly appropriate, I would think, in a restoration like this."

"I see." Julie nodded in mock enlightenment. "*Ye olde worlde charm*. How silly of me." She looked sideways at Hal, stupefied.

With a decisive snap of paper, Sawtrell flipped to the next item, the cost breakdown, attempting to melt this sudden ice with more of his British bluster. "Here we go, the moment of truth. Of course, Jack over there's already had a boo at this." He gave Julie a confidential, mollifying wink and stage-whispered: "For Jack it's like peeking at the dirty bits!"

"Fine," she replied. "Let's see if we can give Jack a hard-on."

She allowed only the briefest pause, in which even Sawtrell was caught off-guard, before moving on to the figures she had crunched and double-crunched on her computer. As Hal well knew, developers normally viewed elemental cost breakdowns with more than a grain of salt. But from the start, Julie had Jack Haines on the edge of his seat.

As soon as Hal saw that she was in complete command of her material, he let his mind wander, first to the little Sony under the table, positioned in the open mouth of his satchel. The tape was running fine. Hal preferred it to writing notes, a discreet and efficient way of chronicling meetings. From near the floor, the excellent broad spectrum microphone could pick up someone stirring coffee at the opposite end of the table.

Reassured that the Sony was recording, he considered Ron Allis, so far the only fly in the ointment. Nevertheless, he was probably — depressingly — right about the Vanguard. That popular taste would forever be imitative and mediocre was one of the realities that had long ago nudged Hal into the slow lane where he could motor happily, at his own modest speed, enjoying the scenery.

Julie was just wrapping up when Sawtrell slipped away from the table to take a call at his desk. Hal heard the terse rhythm of his conversation, felt a ripple of subdued anger. Why shouldn't the man get angry? One didn't get to be executive vice president with nothing but a talent for making off-colour remarks in a posh English accent. Sawtrell put the phone down and came back, smiling, his genial self again. He did not resume his seat, but stood in polite silence beside his chair until he had everyone's attention.

"Don't mean to rush you good people, especially after a first-rate presentation." He looked around the table. "Absolutely first rate, wouldn't you say?"

Haines and McIsaac took Sawtrell's lead, assenting enthusiastically. Allis gathered his papers with a vague, ambiguous smile.

The convivial host, Sawtrell moved casually around the table until he was behind Hal and Julie with his hands resting intimately on the backs of their chairs. One couldn't help but admire his diplomacy, the painless way he was killing the meeting. Hal felt clumsy before him, actually kicked over his satchel as he rose to accept Sawtrell's warm, powerful hand. "Thank you again, both of you," Sawtrell enthused. "You'll be hearing from us in short order." He hovered, saying more of the right things as papers were shuffled and briefcases snapped.

Allis left first. Julie went to the washroom, suggesting that Hal meet her by the elevators. Haines and McIsaac left together after handshaking and compliments. Perhaps now was the right moment to ask the obvious question.

"What about the 'Doyle Diehard'?" Hal said it casually, shouldering his satchel. "Is he going to be a problem much longer?"

Sawtrell smiled. "How are you at praying?"

"Rusty."

"Then practise." He laughed. "Pray for Mr. Carny Danial's speedy demise. A falling brick, a runaway streetcar…anything like that!" Sawtrell lounged in the doorway after Hal went out, called past him to Jack Haines who was picking up an inter-office call at the secretary's desk. "How about it, Jack? Our Mr. Danial…are we going to hit the magic number soon?"

Haines smiled painfully. "Couple more zeros on the end ought to do it."

"See what I mean, Hal? Pray!"

As promised, Hal called Kate immediately from a phone in reception. In a subdued voice he told her the meeting had gone well.

"Oh, babe!"

"Don't count your chickens, Katy."

"But they liked it?"

"I guess so."

"What d'you mean you *guess* so?"

Hal looked cautiously around. "I can't talk here. I'll tell you everything tonight. See you in about an hour."

"Oh, babe!"

He waited for Julie by the elevator, in the no man's land between Midland and Kreeg Advertising, which occupied the other half of the floor. It was five o'clock on a Friday and the corridor was packed with workers boarding downbound elevators, the advertising people generally more flamboyant, more fashionable than the Midlanders. A few people had ridden up, including a slight Asian man who sauntered off the elevator in jeans and a tight polo shirt. He caught Hal's eye, jerked his thumb towards the door marked KREEG ADVERTISING ASSOCIATES.

"Midlan?"

A heavy accent, but Hal understood. He pointed out the opposite door and the young man swaggered through it. He looked like a courier, Hal speculated idly, though presumably couriers had to be able to read English. This guy couldn't: the company name was written large as life on Midland's door.

Hal forgot about him as Julie arrived and they rode down in a packed elevator. This wasn't the place to talk either, so he waited until the ground floor lobby to begin the post-mortem.

"So what do you think?"

Julie threw herself at the revolving door and spun out into the clamorous, downtown afternoon. The fresh summer weather of the previous week had become unseasonably humid — more like August than May. Hal felt the polluted air settle against his skin like a damp poultice as he left the air-conditioned building, quickening his pace across a wide forecourt crowded with workers streaming home for the weekend. He caught up with Julie at the top of six shallow steps descending to the sidewalk, now crammed with pedestrians waiting to cross Bay Street, huddled against the traffic fumes and din.

"I thought it went okay," he said encouragingly. "I liked Sawtrell."

"He was buying Allis's shit, you could see he was. Jesus, Hal...brass and awnings! And plants, don't forget the plants, lots of greenery! He doesn't want a building, he wants a fern bar! I'd rather have my head up my backside!"

Hal smiled. "It's always a two-way street — they'll make concessions too. We could still end up with something good." Julie shrugged, staring out across the traffic. "Okay," Hal conceded, "so they need to learn about quality. So we learn 'em — *work* with them, open their eyes. It's either that or walk away and let them *really* screw up a nice old building."

Julie turned on him. "Rah rah rah!" Then all of a sudden she was smiling her sweet, shy, Chinese maiden's smile. "Sound like movie, Sebastian-san. *Old* movie!"

"Thanks a lot."

With unexpected force she reached up and grasped his shoulders, pulled him down and lightly kissed his cheek.

"What's that for?"

"You did pretty good."

Hal grinned. "You too. I assume you have a licence for that mouth?" 'Let's see if we can give Jack a hard-on'?" They laughed together and people passing them couldn't help but smile to see their glow. At last Hal unbuckled his satchel to get his wallet. "You want to brave the subway? I doubt we'll pull a cab in rush..." He frowned into the open satchel. "Shit!"

"What is it?"

"My tape recorder. I must have left it under the damn table."

Julie chuckled. "Getting good at this, aren't you? Wasn't it your camera last time?"

66

He darkened. "Yeah...I suppose I could have another try at the Doyle."

"You didn't get it back yet?"

"I spoke to the bartender, the bartender said I had to see the bouncer, the bouncer wasn't there...nice little runaround." He backed away. "I'll see you later, partner. You were totally awesome. I'll call you first thing tomorrow."

Hal rode back up to the twenty-third floor. As he stepped out, he noticed the adjacent elevator closing, caught a two-second glimpse of blue jeans and a polo shirt and the flat, pale face of the Asian courier-that-wasn't on his way back down.

Sawtrell's secretary was on the phone; she smiled in recognition as Hal passed on his way to the office. The Sony was still recording on the last few inches of tape. He switched it off and packed it into his satchel, nodded at the secretary and returned to the elevator for the tedious, floor-by-floor descent.

There but for the grace of God, Hal said to himself, as body after hot, tired body piled in around him. He thought of Kate who became one of these drones five days a week. And she did it for him, too, didn't she? And for Rain. He thought of all her hard work for this meeting — the folders that had so impressed them — and felt a sudden pang of love and gratitude.

Okay, he would pray. To Whoever. For Kate's sake at least, he would pray for a brick or a runaway streetcar.

The humidity shocked him a second time as he revolved out of the building. He was surprised to see Julie out on the forecourt, pushing towards him against the crowd.

"Guess who I just saw?"

"Ummm...Ron Allis and you tripped him down the steps."

"That guy from the Vanguard, the guy who ran out into the alley."

It took him a moment to remember. "You waited here to tell me that?"

"I was just standing checking out the building when I saw him come out."

Hal grinned. "Sure it was him? I thought all Chinese people look alike!" Julie didn't crack a smile. "Okay, it was the same guy. So what? Like we figured, he's probably a Midland employee. Their maintenance office is here, this is where I got my Vanguard keys."

She shook her head. "I don't know, Hal. This sounds crazy but it was like...even with all these people out here, he *knew* someone was watching him. He wasn't even heading in this direction but he stopped and looked around at me."

"I wouldn't worry about it. I'm sure you have a million guys look at you."

"No. It was just like at the Vanguard. Creepy."

Hal waved baby-style with his fingers. "Goodbye. Go home. Get some rest. You've had exams, you've been working your buns off, you're going gaga."

Julie shrugged and turned away. Then she looked back again and smiled lasciviously and threw him a cute, mid-stride wiggle — "Have fun at the Doyle!" — and then she was lost in the crowd. It was only then that Hal remembered the man on the elevator — blue jeans and a polo shirt and a flat, pale face. But there was probably no connection. There were thousands of Chinese people in Toronto.

CHAPTER
7

When Kate received Hal's call from Midland, she was barely able to contain her excitement. She immediately called her sister-in-law.

"The presentation was fantastic, Biz! They loved it!"

"He hasn't won yet," Elizabeth cautioned her. "Don't count your chickens."

"Phooey! Listen, could you do us a huge favour? I hate to ask, but could Rain sleep over with your guys tonight? Hal's been working so hard on this thing, I was hoping we could get into a little candlelight and wine. Would you mind?"

Elizabeth laughed in her knowing way. "It's fine, Katy. You may have the bedroom to yourselves!"

It would work out well, Elizabeth assured her; Rain's two-year-old cousin Frazer would be thrilled to see her. Elizabeth was taking Jonathan, her eldest, to his clarinet lesson at six, so she could pick Rain up from Mrs. Gee's on the way.

Before she left work, Kate called Mrs. Gee to beg an hour's extension and introduce her sister-in-law. With no need to pick up Rain, Kate took the subway home for a change, hoping that it would be cooler underground than on a crowded bus, and that the walk from the station might help to calm her down.

It was too warm in the Grace Street apartment to even think about cooking. Nevertheless, she wanted to be home with Hal tonight, so she called Gourmet Express (to hell with the expense) and ordered blanquette de veau and chocolate mousse for seven-thirty.

Relax, she told herself, unconvinced that she really wanted to — it was exciting just to be so excited! On the other hand, she didn't need to be a nervous wreck when Hal got home. She poured a glass of cold white wine and put on the most relaxing record she could think of — Antonio Carlos Jobim — and bossa nova'd circuitously to the bathroom, leaving behind a trail of discarded clothing.

She took a cool shower, humming *The Girl from Ipanema*. After it, talcum-smooth and scented, she delved into her underwear drawer for a shallow, glossy box that had not been opened for a very long time. She put the box on top of the dresser, raised the lid and, with her fingertips, lifted out two morsels of white, lace-trimmed silk.

Kate slipped them on and padded back to the bathroom, taking sinful pleasure in the chafing of French lace between her legs. She faced the long bathroom mirror, then turned sideways, looking at herself more critically than she had dared to do since her pregnancy. After Rain, Kate had given up on ever feeling sexy again, but at last, for the first time in almost two years, she decided she could once again do justice to costly silk and lace nothings.

She went back to the bedroom for a dress and lace-bordered G-string chafed her again. This time Kate encouraged the blush of desire between her thighs, a delicious glow radiating into her belly and down into her legs. Weak-kneed, breathless, she turned and pressed her back against the cool closet door, her fingers straying to the dampening silk triangle, slipping under the lace border into the tiny pocket. Her knees gave way, her back skidding down as she found the slick, aching part.

No...not yet!

With an effort of will, Kate removed her hand, turned and opened the closet. While her breathing slowed, she chose a virginal white cotton dress to keep the lingerie secret until Hal took the dress off. By which time she would be chafed to delirium!

She found a bedsheet for the table cloth. She gathered a sheaf of cutlery, the candles, the wine glasses and the little spray of freesias she had bought at the subway station, and set up their romantic dining room in Hal's office.

He had finished the competition drawings with two days to spare, and the Ancaster house had resurfaced. The skinflints wanted the porch restored next, and Hal was naturally thrilled to comply. Never mind, Kate thought as she snatched the drawings off the table; that porch would mark the end of an era. They were onward and upward now!

When the table was clear, Kate lowered it and tilted it level. She laid the cloth and two places, then added the flowers and lit the candles. She was standing back with the smoking match in her hand, admiring the way the glasses caught the dancing candlelight, when the phone rang.

It was Elizabeth to say that everything was fine, Rain was happy as a clam and wasn't the humidity incredible for May? "Probably another of those lovely greenhouse effects!"

"Should I say goodnight to Rain?"

"Listen, if it ain't bust...we'll call you if there are tears at bedtime."

"I appreciate this, Biz."

"By the way," said Elizabeth, "did you hear back about the church?"

Kate hesitated a moment. "Yes. The agent called last Monday."

"And?"

"Well..." Kate paused again, smiling, winding the telephone cord around her finger.

"Well what?" Elizabeth sounded suspicious. "Don't you play coy with me, Kate Sebastian. What have you done?"

Kate giggled. "I put in an offer."

"You did *what*?"

"Hal doesn't know yet. I'm going to tell him tonight. That's part of the reason for the candlelight and wine."

Elizabeth sounded stunned. "It's a good thing Rain's over here — she won't see Daddy having a coronary!"

"He'll come around. I'm packing hundred-dollar French lingerie!"

"I don't know what to say. What if Hal *doesn't* get the Vanguard? You can't afford..."

"He *will* get it! Anyway, I made the offer conditional on my husband inspecting the property and liking it. I said he was out of the country on business for the next three weeks. By then we should know definitely that we've won."

"You little schemer! And the vendor went for it...three weeks on a conditional offer?"

"They're glad to get any kind of offer. It's been on the market over a year. No one ever goes to Wesleyville."

"Maybe there's something wrong with it," warned Elizabeth.

"Are you kidding? I played hookey from work and went over it with the agent. It's fabulous. They want a hundred and fifty but it's a full acre and the building's in perfect shape. The outside woodwork needs a little scraping and painting, but that could be fun this summer."

"Oh sure!" Elizabeth laughed. "Rain can help too, right? Finger painting with exterior enamel — whoopie! I'm assuming, of course, that you've rented the condo."

"Any day now. Just this week we had a couple of serious inquiries. We're advertising in..."

"I don't believe I'm hearing this! You've lost your cotton-picking mind."

"Why? I just told you — it's a conditional offer." Hal's older sister was practical to a fault, probably something to do with having three little boys.

"All right." Elizabeth sighed indulgently. "What's it like inside?" She chuckled. "Do you get to keep, like, the choirboys and stuff?"

The ecclesiastical trappings had long ago been removed, Kate told her. But there was pine panelling and sixteen-inch-wide floorboards and the ceiling went up forever, which meant they could put in a loft with bedrooms. A wood stove could go where the altar used to be, with a Navajo rug against the wide boards, sunlight pouring through tall Gothic windows. Maybe they could track down a carved lectern or an old harmonium at some county auction, a link with the past. She saw the walls pure white, cool and inviting after the heat of the city, a background for the canvases all that sunlight and tranquility would inspire her to paint.

"It sounds wonderful, Katy. Just don't get too high on it in case you have to jump off. You're not rich and famous yet."

Kate laughed. "Hal's going to be famous — I'll settle for rich!"

CHAPTER
8

"What camera?" the bouncer wanted to know.

But then a kid came in and the bouncer had to see his ID, which the kid didn't have. The bouncer sent him packing, along with his underage buddies ogling the promotional glossies outside the club.

It was the same bouncer who had checked the Leica, no doubt about it. Hal remembered the rubber ball; the guy was still squeezing it, slinging it hand to hand. Abnormally small hands, Hal noticed this time; almost deformed. Sharp little fists to dent people with.

Hal waited nervously by the club's inner door. It opened every few seconds as dancers and customers passed in and out, releasing a tide of rock music, a sweet and sour reek of cigarette smoke and beer and perfume. When the kids had gone, the bouncer came back.

"You still here?"

Patiently, Hal went over it again: "Last month, I came in with a camera, an old Leica IIID. You told me I had to check it. You said you'd keep it behind the bar until I left."

"I said that?"

"Yes. I remember you clearly." The insolent expression hardened. We've crossed the line, Hal thought. But then the bouncer sauntered away again to clown with a stripper coming on shift, a hatchet-faced girl with a bad smoker's cough. Hal heard her call the bouncer "Shane."

This wasn't going to be as simple as Hal had thought.

He moved aside to let a trio of businessmen pass into the club, razzing each other to hide their guilty excitement. When Shane realized that Hal wasn't going away, he came back, coiled and dangerous, crushing the rubber ball.

"You're beginning to get on my fuckin' nerves, you know that? In or out, okay? In or fuckin' out!"

Hal went in. He would find the manager. With luck that would be something other than the creature of Hal's imagination — an obese satyr wired on coke, getting a blowjob under his desk while he made phone calls to mobsters, only too happy to unleash Shane's pointy little fists.

Hal navigated as far as an illuminated cigarette machine and waited there for his eyes and ears to adjust to the gloom and the punishing music. On stage a naked girl with tan-lines was spread-eagled on a fake-fur rug. Table dancers prospected through the audience or posed on their boxes, the nearest one tilting her body six inches from the customer's face, prying herself open like a gynecologist's patient. Strange to think that normal life continued only a few yards away beyond the doors, on a regular street full of regular, fully clothed people.

He could see the whole room now, from the stage to the bar at the back, buzzing with activity as waitresses in French maid costumes hustled to keep the Happy Hour happy. He spoke to a waitress going by with a tray of beers but the music buried his words. He shouted to the next one who shouted back that if he wanted a drink he had to find a table. Finally he asked a cruising dancer who didn't know whether the manager was in or not, but told him to check the office and pointed out a door on the far side of the room next to the deejay's booth.

He skirted the tables, side-stepping busy waitresses and slinking dancers, moving towards this quieter place beyond the epicentre of the music. As he passed the sound booth, he could see the deejay behind his window, a skinny black man in an oversize suit who was watching him with interest. Hal paused by the manager's door to read: "STAFF ONLY — STRICTLY NO ADMITTANCE." He glanced around for Shane, then pushed it open to reveal stairs up.

"Bro!" Hal spun round. The deejay came out of his booth, his body jiving loose inside the big suit. "What you want, man? You can't go up there."

Hal let the door swing shut behind him, crossed to the booth. "I need to see the manager."

"What for? Lookin' for a job? Job involving pussy, right?" The ultraviolet light caught a blaze of teeth. At least he was friendlier than Shane. "You outta luck — Carny ain't here."

Carny? Of course...the Doyle Diehard! In the tenseness of the last few minutes Hal had forgotten to make the connection. "I'm not looking for any kind of job," he told the deejay. "I'm..."

"Take some advice, man: pussy job okay for 'bout ten minutes, after that it aaaall look alike. Black pussy, white pussy, cowgirl pussy..." He grinned past Hal and ducked back into his booth.

Hal turned. A long-legged dancer was closing the stairway door behind her. She was dressed in elaborate Western rig, everything in white — hat, boots, gauntlets, waistcoat, leather microskirt — all embroidered and fringed and rhinestoned. She smiled at Hal as she sashayed past, glittering. Suddenly she turned and made a pistol with her fingers.

"Heeey...I remember you! You were in here with an Oriental girl." She saw his surprise and laughed. "Listen, pal, girl comes in here wearing all her clothes, I usually remember. Shane checked your camera, right?"

Hal nodded, impressed. "Quite a memory. Unfortunately, Shane's isn't as good as yours."

She narrowed her eyes. "You didn't get it back?"

"No, I didn't. I was just talking to him, or trying to. I'm afraid Shane's playing hard to get."

"Figures. You'd better talk to Carny."

Hal looked at her apprehensively. "Is that going to help?"

"Can't hurt. Carny's pretty straight. If Shane's still got your camera, Carny's about your only hope. He's out doing the banking right now. Give me your name and number, I'll tell him."

Hal carried his satchel to the nearest table. He printed his name and office number, feeling guilty as he did so — seeking help from Carny Danial when he had spent the last half-hour praying for bricks and runaway streetcars.

He handed the slip of paper to the cowgirl. "I really appreciate this...?"

"Tyah."

"Thanks, Tyah. I hope it isn't going to be a problem for you."

"No problem for me." She smiled. "Maybe for Shane."

"I take it he's not..."

"On my 'A' list?" She gave a dry laugh. "Try 'Z' list!" She glanced at the slip of paper and inserted it in her vest pocket, then she tipped her white Stetson. "Stick around awhile, Hal Sebastian. Have a beer, catch the show."

Hal watched Tyah's long, pretty legs carrying her to the stage as the deejay pitched her. He couldn't very well ignore the invitation after she had been so helpful. He would have to have one beer.

Tyah was sensational and the audience let her know it, whooping and hollering and clapping in time with the shit-kicking country music. She did much more than take off her clothes. She had a goofy, hayseed routine that was funny *and* sexy. She performed cartwheels that ended in the splits with the heels of her Western boots inches from the happy stageside faces — *Oklahoma* with an X-rating. She walked on her hands and did the Texas two-step on her hands to a song called *Bareback Rider*, proving she really was riding bareback under that tiny skirt.

But eventually — inevitably — the slow song came around and she was no longer a cowgirl, just a girl without clothes on a fake-fur rug. A pretty girl, sure, but lying back with her legs wide apart, Tyah proved the deejay right: black or white or cowgirl, all looked the same.

Hal drained his beer and stood up. He had got as far as the cigarette machine by the exit when he almost collided with Jack Haines.

"Small world!" Haines shouted in his ear. "I won't tell if you don't! You coming or going?" Hal said he was on his way home. "I was just thinking about you," Haines confided. "Hell of a presentation you gave us today. Come on, let me buy you a beer."

Hal smiled regretfully. "I probably shouldn't. My wife's expecting me home for dinner."

Haines hesitated, blocking Hal's exit. He looked suddenly uneasy. "Listen, could I have a word with you?"

Puzzled, Hal let himself be steered towards the bar and took a stool next to Haines, who was already ordering. Hal reassessed him: not quite the mild accountant of the meeting. But the man was uncomfortable about something, a feeling that was already transferring itself to Hal. Haines finished ordering and cut him a quick nervous smile, then immediately looked away at the stage where Tyah was finishing her set.

Hal was in too much of a hurry for business etiquette.

"What did you want to tell me, Jack?"

Haines looked back and he was no longer smiling. "I didn't keep you here to make small talk, Hal. I meant it when I said I was impressed with your presentation. I like you and I like your associate and I like your work. I shouldn't tell you this, but yours was the last entry and if it was up to me there wouldn't *be* any competition."

But...

Unspoken, yet Hal could hear it louder than the blaring music.

The beers came. Hal sat very still, gnawed by apprehension, watching Haines pour to the top of his glass...a slow, scrupulous inch of head.

Haines looked up from his perfect beer, saw the suspicion building on Hal's face and nodded, gravely, to confirm it. Hal seemed to hear the words before Haines spoke them.

"Having said what I think of your work, Hal, it's extremely distasteful to me to have to tell you this."

CHAPTER
9

At seven-thirty, Gourmet Express arrived and Kate paid a tired young man in a tuxedo sixty-five dollars with tip. The styrofoam containers were faux-granite.

At eight o'clock, Kate transferred the tepid food to plates and put them in the oven. Then she tore off the lace underwear, which was rubbing her raw, and put on comfortable cotton. She poured herself a second, large, consolatory glass of wine and drank half of it in two gulps.

Where *was* he?

At eight-fifteen, on the verge of angry tears, she called Midland and was told that there were no late meetings in progress; Graham Sawtrell's group had broken up at five.

Kate began to feel anxious. Hal was forgetful, but not about things like this. He was considerate: if he said he would be home in an hour, he usually meant in an hour. It had now been over three.

She missed Rain now, wished her back in the empty crib in the bedroom. She even missed the usual Friday night racket from up-stairs — the Boys playing Liza Minelli at concert volume — for-getting all the times she had been driven to pound on the ceiling with a broom.

It was so quiet that she jumped, spilling wine down her white dress, when she heard Hal's front door key.

Kate marched down the narrow hallway, anger displacing concern. "Great! Thanks a lot! You said an hour. Why the hell didn't you call me?" He stood in the open doorway, swaying slightly. "Have you been drinking?" That much was obvious. "Have you been somewhere with Julie?"

"I have to tell you something, Katy." He backed up against the front door until it was shut.

"You can try 'sorry' for a start! You said an hour. I hope you like sixty-five-dollar shoe leather because that's what you've got for dinner!"

He stared at her, grey eyes swimming behind his glasses. He said levelly: "We're not going to get the Vanguard."

Kate had obviously misheard him. "What did you say?"

"A guy called Karel Lorenz is."

She stared at him. "What are you talking about? You just called me to say they loved the presentation. You said that. You said..."

He reached towards her. "Come on. Come and sit down."

Kate recoiled from his touch. "Start making sense, Hal. This is a competition. You've only just submitted and they liked it. They *loved* it! So what the Christ are you talking about?"

Dejectedly, Hal told her about meeting Jack Haines at the Doyle Hotel. How Haines had overheard Ron Allis on the phone in an empty office after the meeting saying that he could not work comfortably with Hal Sebastian. Allis sensed potential conflict, "an attitude problem," an unwillingness to follow through. He did say, however, that he thought the Sebastian proposal was the right approach — or would be after Karel Lorenz had made the necessary changes and taken charge of the project. Allis didn't think there would be any problem with Sawtrell.

"I know Lorenz, Katy. He's a fat cat, a yes man, a good brass-and-awnings man. And he's on the inside track. Haines told me he works with Allis all the time. There's not even anything illegal about what they're doing because we got nominal payment for our submission. It belongs to Midland."

Kate stood in place, her only movement a slight shaking of her head, an unconscious expression of disbelief and denial. Like someone in a dream she followed her husband into the office, listened to his subdued compliments on her table, felt him take her glass, let him replenish it, heard him ask what happened to her dress. He kept on talking, apologizing, but his words fell behind the other sound in her head: a vibration that had begun, low and mournful, in the hall, rising in frequency and volume until now it was an unbearable pandemonium.

It stopped.

For a brief moment Kate was conscious of her husband standing across the table, raising his glass to his sorry mouth. She heard him say: "Maybe it's all for the best, babe."

And then she exploded.

"NO!"

Her hand scythed over the table sending plates, flowers and candles crashing across the floor. One of the candles, a stub by this time, was still guttering as it rolled into the corner, licking at the stack of Ancaster drawings.

With a shout Hal was over to it and on his knees, pounding at the flame. When he looked up, Kate was thundering over him.

"It is *not* for the best! If you think I'm going to take this lying down like a piece of dogshit you're wrong. My God, how could you even *contemplate* letting them get away with it?"

"Kate, listen..."

"No!" Her hand scythed again, terminally, drops of blood flying from her cut fingers. "*You* listen to *me*! This is not over yet, do you understand? This is very, very far from over!"

CHAPTER
10

John was the last employee to leave. Carny stood watching the barman put on his raincoat, jingling the keys to hurry him along.

"What you need a coat for? Must be eighty degrees outside."

"Rain can't hold off much longer," John replied. "Radio said it's gonna pour." He did up the big buttons one by one, with agonizing slowness.

Carny shook his head. "You do that about the same speed you polish glasses."

"Maybe. But you ever see me break one? In forty years you ever?" John stooped to put on low rubber overshoes.

"Good grief, man, it's May!"

"Snowmelt or downpour, feets get wet just the same." John walked an hour to his house on Niagara Street every night, whatever the weather. Like Carny, he was a creature of neatness and habit. They bickered because they were alike. After forty-five years together, there was a working lifetime of respect and affection between the two men.

At last John was ready. "Okay?" Carny said. "Can we go home now and get some sleep?"

"I can. You'll go up to that office and worry. You better stop it, too. Worryin's bad for the ticker."

"Not this again."

"Sure this again. Why don't you take the money, fly south like an old bird's s'posed to do?"

"You of all people asking me that?"

"You ain't no spring chicken, Carn."

Carny chuckled as he walked through the lobby to the main door. "And where are you going to get another soft touch like this one, working for an old duffer like me, too senile to notice all the liquor you've been watering over the years, all the short shots!" Carny unlocked the big door with a grunt of effort, reached down for the handle and missed and suddenly he wasn't sure of anything except that he was being supported under his arms.

"Whoa, big fella!"

Gradually his head cleared. "I'm alright." He put weight on his legs. "Lemme go, I'm fine."

John held onto him. "See what I told ya?"

Carny shook him off, made a show of steadiness as he walked back to the bar, then rested up against it. John went behind, to the bar phone. "I'm going to call you a cab."

"No, you're not. I'm not leaving my car in the lot."

John was so surprised he put the phone down. "In the lot?"

"You heard me!" Carny snapped. "Some so and so's been parked in my spot all day so I'm in the lot. Dollar seventy-five the half hour, can you believe it? You could *buy* a car for a dollar seventy-five a half hour!" He made a disgusted sound. "Money! They're either grabbing it off you or trying to ram it down your throat. You want to know why I'm not in Florida? Because it makes me happy as a clam to make a nuisance of myself here!" He swivelled on the bar stool, away from John. "There. I feel better!"

Carny surveyed his premises with fierce pride. The cleaners would come in the early morning but he always had the waitresses straighten the chairs and empty the ashtrays and wipe down the tables before they quit. Just like his other home, he couldn't stand to leave the club just any old how. "Forty-five years I've been running this business," he said fervently. "They might just as well try and get rid of the cigarette smoke!"

Finding himself behind the bar, John's hands automatically strayed here and there, wiping, straightening, buffing, which in turn made him argumentative. "Forty-five years? C'mon Carny, you didn't take over till Lon died."

Carny didn't turn round. "Oh no? I was running things the second I was out of uniform, John Gidney, and well you know it. What did Lonnie know about running a business?"

The bartender chuckled. "He knew one thing, and it's kept *you* in the black ever since."

"I don't know what you're talking about." Carny kept his back to John, craning his neck as though the club were full of people.

"I'm talking about the girlies, aren't I?" Carny heard the wheezing that passed for laughter with John. "Well, ya didn't run it then, did ya? When Lonnie got the rude girlies in!"

Carny ignored the bait. "I was the eldest. Only reason Dad handed over to Lonnie was because he missed the war. If it hadn't been for Lonnie's eyesight, Dad would've made me manager from the word go and he told me as much!"

"Lonnie may have been shortsighted but he sure as shit saw the future when he got the girls in!" John wheezed a bit. "'Over my dead body,' you said. Hah! Laced up straighter'n a Sunday-school teacher, told him you'd quit on the spot!" John took a fit of wheezing.

"I stayed because the business would have folded if I hadn't." Carny swivelled round, shot his friend an acid look. "There was such a thing as loyalty then."

"Hogwash! Business was booming. You knew it was the smart move. All the old places gone now but you're still here and you know damn well why. Tits and ass, buddy, tits and..." John stopped, embarassed. The expression was taboo at the Doyle, had been since the murders last summer.

Carny climbed off the stool, walked back to the front door with John on his heels. "Where you going, Carny?"

"Get you out of here. I've got some things to look at in the office."

"See? Going up there to worry." John watched his boss unlock the door. "Why don't ya let me drive yous? I can handle that big boat."

"Scram."

John looked at him hard for a moment, deciding whether or not Carny's stubbornness was life-threatening. Finally he shrugged. "You're the man." He stepped out into the soupy night air. "Holy…Feel that, will ya? It's gonna be another one just like last…" The barman stopped himself a second time.

"See you tomorrow, John." Carny withdrew his head and pushed at the door.

"Boss?"

"What now?"

"We was all behind you over Shane. Just wanted you to know that."

"Goodnight, Johnny."

Carny locked the door and returned to the bar, where he turned off the house lights at the master panel until the only light was a thin yellow frame around the stairway door. He walked towards it, the camera strapped to his shoulder bumping softly and rhythmically against his ribs.

"A customer has come to me personally about some lost property" was how he had put it to Shane.

"What are you talking about?"

"Did you take the camera, son?"

Shane had turned nasty right off the bat. "What is this? Guy brings in a camera, I check it. What the fuck do you pay me for?"

"So you *do* remember." Carny had felt Shane's compact bulk tightening, dangerous energy charging the air around him.

"That's full of shit."

Carny smiled then. He had waited a long time to say this. "Let me tell you what I *don't* pay you for, Shane. I don't pay you to steal my customers' property. I don't pay you to harass my dancers. I don't pay you to sell cocaine, on or off my premises. In fact, Shane, I don't pay you, period. Not any more."

Shane relaxed then, quick eyes steadying, fixing Carny insolently.

Everything relaxed except the little hands, busy with the rubber ball. "Go fuck yourself!"

"Fine. Shall I do that before or after I sign your paycheque? It's Friday night, son."

Shane looked worried for the first time. "You can't do that."

"I can and I will unless I have that camera behind the bar at closing time, in which case your cheque will be in the mail. If you need to go home to get the camera, you're welcome to do that. If you want to lodge an official complaint with the Ministry of Labour, you're welcome to do that too."

Poor Evelyn. Whenever Carny found himself regretting never having had children, he thought of Evelyn Pilch producing Shane. It was only because of her that Carny had hired the boy, the fact that Evelyn had danced at the Doyle for fifteen years before she went off the rails and drank herself to death. He had disliked Shane from day one.

He felt it again as he climbed to the office: the dizziness, the insubstantial, papery feeling in his chest. He stopped, unable to take the next stair, leaning against the wall. I look like a drunk, he thought — like Lonnie. He immediately straightened.

Tired, that was all. Bone tired.

At last he reached the top of the stairs and paused again for breath. Carny was looking down a corridor, towards the door to the fire stairs, at the opposite end. Beside it on the left was his office, just beyond the dressing room. On the right side, narrow stairs led up to the third-floor rooms where his out-of-town girls boarded. He could hear a radio playing softly up there.

The door to the club was always locked after hours, but his boarders had keys to the door at the bottom of the fire stairs, the same one Carny used himself to leave the building at night, right by his parking spot in the alley. The boarders could come and go as they pleased, as long as they didn't bring men into the building. Carny had his operating licence to think about and besides, while those girls were under his roof they were also under his protection.

Carny unlocked his small, windowless office and switched on the desk lamp. He unshouldered the camera and put it down, a big paperweight, in the tray of bills and bar receipts and junk mail — the nightly paper harvest. Usually he made a short hour's work of it before he went home; right now he could not have been more daunted by the prospect of auditing General Motors.

Later, he promised himself, after a little nap. A cat nap. Recharge the batteries for an hour's work, then home.

He shut the door and sank into his old leather swivel chair, snug as a ball in a catcher's mitt. He rolled forward and picked up the camera again, fitting his fingers to its familiar shape. A Leica IIID! It was like some kind of compact time machine, whirling him back forty-five years and five thousand miles, to an allied forces base in Germany a month or so before he was demobilized.

To the victor belong the spoils, which had meant a Luger side-arm or a ceremonial SS dagger to one man, a terrified fourteen-year-old daughter of the Reich to another. Carny's plunder had been a Leica IIID camera identical to this one — Wehrmacht issue, with a shutter-delay, so you could push the button and run and be in the picture with your goofy buddies. Carny had sold it on the transport home, but not before it had snapped most of the pictures in the War Room.

A Leica IIID! Shane couldn't have known what it was or he'd never have exchanged it for a week's pay. A collector's item worth a pile today. The owner, Hal something — Tyah knew who he was — the guy would have every right to be pleased when he turned up to claim it.

He put the camera down, leaned back and shut his eyes. He could still hear the radio upstairs in Suzanne's room, too faint to bother him. One more week for Suzanne, shape up or ship out. She was consistently late, drank too much. Sloppy. He would be sorry to lose Felice, though. He wondered vaguely if she had left yet. Tyah was taking her out somewhere, to celebrate Felice's last day. The stamina of these kids…work all day, then off to parties at two o'clock in the morning! Good kids though, especially Tyah. As good as he'd ever had.

With the last of his energy, Carny reached out to switch off the desk light.

There.

For a few moments he watched the after-image of the bulb burning against the black, fading as wakefulness faded. He barely registered a faint sound from the fire stairs, a door opening then quietly closing again. Felice, he thought dreamily.

Had he been awake, Carny would have countered that assumption with the fact that no one had come down from the third floor, no one had passed his office to enter the stairwell. Someone returning, he would have decided, faulting that induction when no other sound followed, nobody coming up the stairs, none of his boarders. He would have gone to investigate, annoyed to find the stairs in darkness and the light switch ineffective, although the stairwell had been brightly lit just before. A fastidious housekeeper, Carny would have gone to fetch a new bulb.

But as it was, on this strangely humid late Friday night, Carny Danial slept.

CHAPTER
11

Suzanne Pelletier was in bed but not asleep. She was humming to the radio, a tuneless, distracted sound. Her left hand gripped a plastic glass one-quarter full of Southern Comfort. Her right hand was under the covers, her fingers tracing the line of her caesarian scar while she thought about her three-year-old, a little boy with black hair and blackberry eyes living at her mother's place in Dorval. Suzanne's mother had a drinking problem. Sometimes, Suzanne suspected, her mother went out and left the little boy alone. She probably left matches all over the apartment. If Jean-Claude woke up...Suzanne's free hand went from her belly to her mouth. Her humming stopped as she began to chew what was left of her thumbnail.

Joan, who called herself Nicole because *anything* sounded sexier than Joan, was sitting on the edge of a faded, overstuffed armchair. She was wearing a long T-shirt, which rode up around her waist as she trimmed her pubic hair with nail scissors. She had done the bikini line earlier with Neet.

Nicole had a husband, at least the Parry Sound Jail had him right now after he'd violated his probation with three more break-ins. Nicole was going to visit him on Sunday. The bus fare alone represented a day's table dancing, so Nicole snipped and neatened, catching the trimmings in her left hand, hoping like hell she wouldn't get her period before Sunday.

Felice was the only one dressed, waiting by the window that overlooked the corner of Court and King Streets, watching for Fletcher's pickup.

A lot had happened to Felice since the night she'd eaten chili with Tyah and Fletch. Not only had the Yolanda Bates Modelling School accepted her, they had offered to pay her full tuition if she agreed to contract with the Yolanda Bates Modelling Agency upon graduation. Less than one in a hundred girls had their tuition paid, Mrs. Bates had told Felice. "You're an investment, dear." She was to start Monday. Carny had taken her off tomorrow's roster so that she could catch the early train and have Saturday afternoon in Montreal to buy the things she needed for school on Monday.

She turned away from the window. "What's the time?"

"Two-oh-five," Nicole informed her.

Suzanne, from her bed, said: "Carny fine me twenty fuckin' dollar today. What's the matter wid him? Run dis place like it was army or something. Fine for dis, fine for dat." Suzanne's first week at the Doyle had been a disaster for everyone.

"Carny's an all right guy," Nicole corrected her. "Give me half a week's pay for nothing when they took Justin down. Put me on the bus his own self. You tell me another owner'd do that."

Felice turned back to the window. "How long I got to wait for these people?"

Nicole stood up, dropped her trimmings in the waste basket and stretched, her pubis visible as a diminutive, perfect triangle. "I'm going to bed." She padded over to Felice, kissed her. "I'll see ya in *Vogue*, eh?"

"*Hustler!*" Suzanne tittered.

They ignored her. Nicole padded to the door. "Where you going with Ty?"

"Some booze can Fletcher knows about."

"Can I come?" said Suzanne.

"You *are* a fuckin' booze can," Nicole said on her way out.

Felice eyed the phone booth glowing emptily three stories below, at the corner of Court and King. There used to be a pay phone on the landing but it rang at all hours with friends and boyfriends, and had been removed at the boarders' request. "I'm going to go call." She went out, a shimmer of tight red satin and raven hair. Through her alcohol haze, Suzanne listened to the diminishing clatter of stiletto heels, falling silent as Felice reached the carpeted second floor. Suzanne sighed, thought about trying to lose a little weight, toasted the thought with a slug of Comfort.

Entering her room across the landing, Nicole had found a little gift-wrapped box on her bed. There was a card, pink hippos doing the cancan. "Au revoir. Love from Felice." The farewell gift was a Cyndi Lauper cassette, just because Nicole had mentioned she liked one of the songs. She ran back into Suzanne's room, where Suzanne was refilling her plastic glass.

"Where'd she go?"

"Went to phone."

Nicole unlatched the window and pushed it up. The third floor was air-conditioned like the rest of the club; she felt the night, sticky and bad smelling, press in around her.

Carny had a rule about calling from the windows but this was important. Felice had an early train, Nicole might not get another chance to thank her. Maybe she could sing something. She worked it over in her head a little bit, looking to Cyndi Lauper's biggest hit for inspiration: *Girls Just Want to Have Fun.*

Behind her Suzanne said: "Tell 'er to get me some smokes, eh?"

"Maybe she's not coming back."

"If she is, okay? Large Rothmans." She pronounced it "Rotman's."

Slob, thought Nicole. All she needed was Suzanne drunk, smoking in bed across the landing.

A full minute passed and she was still waiting for Felice to appear from the alley at the back of the building.

"Where the hell is she?"

Suzanne sat up in bed.

Nicole said anxiously: "Maybe I'd better go see. She could've fell on the stairs, hurt herself." She moved closer to the window. "Wait, here she comes!"

But it wasn't Felice. The girl had brown hair, not black, and she was sauntering, going nowhere in particular. A car turned up Court off King, slowed as it passed the girl who bent down to talk to the driver.

" 'Ooker," observed Suzanne, who had joined Nicole at the window.

The prostitute got in the car, which pulled a U-turn back to King and drove east. They watched until it was two disappearing points of red light at the end of the block.

Suzanne started to bite her nails.

Nicole was saying "I'm going to…" when they both spun round at the sound of feet on the stairs and there was Felice in the open doorway looking pale and frightened in her stocking feet. She quickly shut the door behind her and leaned back against it, panting.

"What is it?"

"You okay?"

"I…I don't know. I think there's somebody in the stairwell."

CHAPTER
12

Tyah was wearing new black leather pants. She had finished them exactly ten minutes ago, which was the main reason they were late. Fletcher wore the ones she had made him for Christmas. The Leather Twins. Fletcher thought that was seriously overdoing it, but Tyah had told him extreme party measures were called for tonight. He mellowed after a joint of Willi Gillens's latest monster hybrid that contained, according to Willi, "an indecent amount of THC." Tyah rolled a second one for the road.

They were finally in the vestibule with the door shut behind them when the phone rang.

"Maybe it's Felice wondering where we are." Tyah dithered. "Shall I go back?" Fletcher threw up his hands. Tyah cursed, unlocked the door and ran in to the phone.

It was Willi, sounding upset.

Fletcher took it. He listened, appalled. "What? Give me a break!" He looked at Tyah in dismay. "Okay, Willi…okay, I'll be right down."

"What is it, Fletch?" Tyah followed him to the bedroom where he began stripping off his party clothes. Apparently Willi had just received a call from the station that monitored their alarm system.

A half hour ago, the ceiling sprinklers had let go. No fire, but the cash, the computer and some valuable, hydrophobic desert plants had all taken a bath. He had to go down right away.

Fletcher threw on jeans and a sweatshirt. "Tell Felice good luck — if she *wants* my luck tonight!"

"You need me at the store? We could both come."

"S'okay." Fletcher rummaged in the dresser, then tossed something, a slender metal shape, across the bedroom to her. It was the canister of Mace he had picked up on a buying trip to the States after the murders last summer. "Man-in-a-can, okay? You two shouldn't be tripping around at night without some protection. You got gas in the Chevette? We can pick up Felice if you want — I'll drop you at the booze can."

Tyah went to him, hugged him tight. "You care about me." She said it somewhere between wonder and contentment. "Yeah, I got gas. Think you can meet us later?"

"If we get swabbed down in time."

She kissed him. "Call us at the can if you need a couple more deck hands."

"Love you." Smiling, because they said it together.

Tyah found the Chevette keys, then spent a fruitless minute looking for her umbrella. She ran to her car through thick, warm rain.

CHAPTER
13

Nicole said: "But you didn't see nobody?"

"Just the sound." Felice shrugged. "I dunno. Maybe I'm crazy or something." All three of them were sitting on Suzanne's bed. In the light, in the company of her friends, Felice's terror was fading.

"I couldn't make the light work," she explained. "So I start going down in the dark. But then I get this crazy feeling like...like I'm not alone."

"Did you hear a voice?" demanded Nicole.

"Non. I hear something scratch on the stair and I get the *chair de poule*...the goose's flesh, you know?" She looked appealingly at Nicole. "I couldn't go down."

Nicole realized they had unconsciously joined hands, like three scared little girls at a pyjama party. She tore hers away and stood up. "This is stupid. Somebody better to go see if Carny's still here. I'm sure I heard him in his office a while ago."

Felice shook her head. "There was no light under his door. I think he's gone."

"Somebody should go make sure," Nicole said.

Suzanne drew the bedclothes up to her chin. "Don't look at me. I'm not going."

Nicole gave her a look of disgust. "I'll bet it's nothing. Only Carny and us got keys, right?" She glared at Suzanne. "Did yous give any keys out?"

"'Course not. Hey, maybe it's Carny. Some of dese old guys..."

"Don't be a fuckin' re-tard!" snapped Nicole. "Carny's super-straight." She grabbed the matchbook from Suzanne's night table, started for the door. "Enough of this baby shit. I'm gonna to light a match at the top of the stairs. We'll soon see..."

Nicole froze, staring at the door knob inches from her hand.

It was moving.

"Nicole?" Felice whispered. "*Qu'est ce que...?*"

And in the blink of an eye there was a fourth in the room, a terrible, cat-quick figure with glittering hands that touched Felice then Suzanne then twirled back for Nicole who had time to see her friends on the bed as surprised, seated figures in a strange tableau, with scarlet ropes springing from their necks. She didn't have time to scream.

CHAPTER
14

In Carny's dream he had somehow smashed up the Buick and the body shop had done a horrible job of repairing it. The fenders bulged unevenly and the trunk was swollen almost as big as the passenger compartment. It was covered with lumps as if the filler had been slapped on by chimpanzees.

"Got a problem?" inquired the body shop man as he made out the bill for thousands of dollars. Unable to find words of protest, Carny wrote out a cheque. The man took it and then, with the illogicality of dreams, handed fistfuls of money to Carny.

He was just thinking how unbearably the shop smelled of spray paint, wondering how could they stand it all day even with masks on, when he began to wake up.

For a few moments he was astonished at how the dream — at least the spray-paint smell from the dream — lingered. Then, very gradually, it occurred to him that the smell might be real.

Carny came fully awake and sat up with a start. He was thinking about getting up to investigate the smell when he heard the *sound* of spray painting in the dressing room, at least the rhythmic clatter of a ball bearing, someone shaking a spray can to mix the paint.

Shane! was Carny's instant thought. He had seen the Buick gone, had assumed the office was empty. He might have known Shane would be a sore loser.

There was only one way to be sure.

Carny now did something he would not have dreamed of doing under any other circumstances. He turned on the desk lamp and reached for his paper knife (a freebie from some long-ago Molson rep) and used it to remove the two Phillips screws holding the cardboard-mounted poster of Niagara Falls in winter over Lonnie's two-way mirror. The peep-hole. Carny turned the desk lamp off again before lifting away the light cardboard square.

He saw, standing in the dressing room, a small, slight figure holding a flashlight. A shadow-figure, but he knew right away it wasn't Shane.

Suzanne? Stupid-mad because he had fined her?

The dim figure stood at the far end of the dressing room, lazily shaking the spray can while the curious flashlight played over the rack of dancers' costumes.

Not Suzanne. It was a man. Carny became more certain of it as the figure crossed the room towards him, until he was standing less than two feet away, gazing at himself in the mirror tiles.

There was light on him now, reflected off the mirror from his flashlight. Carny was looking straight into a pale, flat Oriental face, smiling with arrogant satisfaction.

And so near! Carny got a cold shiver at the thrill of his concealment.

But what should he do? The intruder would hear every word if he tried to call the police. Alerted, he would run. It was a crazy situation. But then Carny had the crazy thought to match it.

He glanced down at the Leica on his desk. Why not? Even if the film wasn't fast enough for hardly any light, wasn't it worth a try? He picked the camera up and tossed the strap over his head.

Carny's fingers danced over the familiar settings. He wound on, felt the resistance that meant it was loaded, set the aperture wide open and the shutter speed for a fifteenth of a second. Then he stood up and leaned over his desk and very quietly placed the lens against the window — he'd need it rock-steady at a fifteenth.

The man began spraying, but Carny was too busy to look, in too much of a hurry to focus the moon-face before his subject moved away from the window.

It was now or never.

Smile for the cops, kid...

The shutter was louder than Carny remembered or expected. The intruder froze, listening, and the face grew in the window, inches away now, pale cheese in the flashlight. Then, with a suddenness that made Carny gasp, the window went black.

In pitch darkness, straining to hear, Carny felt the first chill of real fear. He groped through the dark to confirm that his door was locked, although the single Yale lock offered little comfort. If the intruder tried...

His boarders...his girls!

A sudden fog of terror closed around him. In his curiosity and excitement, he had forgotten all about the dancers upstairs. Carny quickly pulled himself together. All right! Enough fun and games. It was time to act his age and call the cops.

He had the receiver in his hand, his finger poised to dial, when one of the dressing room stools exploded through the mirror-window in a rage of glass.

Carny reacted just quickly enough to protect his eyes. He saw the flashlight wagging crazily as the man smashed at the jagged glass remaining in the window-frame. Now there was a skinny leg on the sill as the Chinese braced himself to swing up and through.

Heedless of the stinging glass on his desk, Carny fumbled desperately for the paper knife, his only possible weapon. He could already see a much more wicked glitter in his assailant's hand, but for one moment the man's balance was precarious on the sill and that moment was Carny's.

Without thought, fuelled by instinct and adrenalin, he lunged towards the silhouette behind the light. There was a high-pitched cry and the shape fell back into the dressing room, carrying the paper knife with it.

I've killed him! thought Carny. *I have killed a man*!

He fumbled crazily, whimpering, cursing the desk lamp that was nowhere to be found. Then he heard a movement from somewhere in the dressing room.

"Who are you?" he cried out to the darkness. "What do you want?" But his tremulous old man's voice shamed him. Barely able to control his trembling, Carny floundered in a crunching, stinging sea of glass until he had located the telephone, which had been swept onto the floor.

He squatted over it in the dark, wincing as the receiver touched his face where it had been gashed by flying glass — he could feel the blood running down his neck, soaking into his collar. He stabbed the phone cradle and got a tone, found the nine-hole on the dialling ring, which now came off on the end of his finger.

"You bastard!" he bellowed in fear and rage.

Silence.

Very well. He would go out. He wasn't going to stay here like a cornered animal. He was going down to use the bar phone.

Again he thought of his boarders, and that lent him a sort of courage. Unlocking his door with blood-slick fingers, Carny stepped out into the dim light of the corridor. He would walk past the dressing room door and down the stairs, unlock the club and call the police from the bar phone. But first he would go up and

TA TA TA...

check on the

TA TA TA TA TA TA TA TA...

It was sprayed in pink, all the way along the corridor, which was why the dream of paint had been so strong. Could he still be dreaming? God of Mercy could this be a nightmare?

Somewhere in Carny's brain an electric alarm began a guttural jangling, a slaughterhouse sound signalling the nightmare realization of what the pink letters meant. It was also the cue for a slender figure to step silently out of the dressing room and face him down the corridor. One hand was glittering, the other was outstretched towards Carny.

"Camera," urged a soft voice. "Camera."

Carny had forgotten the Leica strapped around his neck. He lifted it over his head, looped the strap around his hand and tested its dangling weight. The Chinese advanced slowly, keeping himself under rigid control. I've hurt him, Carny thought.

"Stay back!" He commanded, once again dismayed by the warbling impotence of his voice. That, and the certain smile on the man's face, caused Carny's illusion of his capability, if not his courage, to slip away suddenly. There was only one possible option for him, he realized, and it was not hand-to-hand combat.

Carny turned and fled towards the fire exit, threw open the door and staggered down into the darkness. The Buick...if he could just get out to his car...

He was halfway down to the alley door when his pursuer burst into the stairwell.

Please God...

He could hear the young man on the stairs behind him, closer, his breath a furious hissing. But now Carny was two steps from the door with his car keys in his hand. A few more seconds and he would be out, into his car with the doors locked, honking bloody murder as he ran the bastard down!

Carny hurled himself against the crash bar and collapsed out into an empty alley.

For a moment he stood, swooning, staring at the empty space where his Buick should have been, instead of in the parking lot at a dollar seventy-five a half hour. Then he remembered his peril and began to run as he had not run in many years, towards the lighted street at the alley's mouth. He heard the fire door crash open behind him, heard splashing steps no more than twenty feet away and closing.

Now the nightmare fell into a classic paradigm as the slice of sane, lighted world at the mouth of the alley receded even as Carny fled towards it. He could see a streetlight with the rain slanting across it. A taxi passed; he could hear the swish of its wet tires. Yet all of it seemed everlastingly unattainable. Somehow it reminded him of the wedge of magic, pantomime street beyond the courtyard that Jimmy Stewart could see but never reach in *Rear Window,* from the days when they made movies Carny could enjoy.

Now a late pedestrian hurried across the scene, angled pictur-esquely against the slanting rain.

"Help!" Carny tried to shout, but, true to the nightmare, his words came out as a weak croaking and the oblivious pedestrian passed out of the picture.

He staggered on, pain blooming in his face as the rain washed his gashes, the joints of his knees grating agonies. The light foot-steps were very close behind him now.

Carny was preparing to call again, drawing a breath like rustling paper that gave him no air, when he came level with the service entrance to his hotel. It was from this doorway that the hotel gar-bage had been collected earlier in the night, leaving a patch of ooze now blended to a slick scum by the rain.

It happened so quickly that Carny wasn't aware of losing his legs, of the camera flying out of his hand. Suddenly he was sprawled on his back on the wet pavement blinking up at a crouching silhou-ette.

"Back off, motherfucker!" cried a voice he knew. "Back...OFF!"

Carny could smell leather and perfume and then there was a hissing sound and he could smell something else and felt a sudden, screaming pain as though his eyes were filled with broken glass after all. Somebody cried out — maybe himself — and then he heard footsteps splashing away.

"It's okay, Carny...it's okay, man...he can't hurt you now. Let's get you up."

Tyah's voice carried to him through a dense jungle of pain. Carny felt himself being lifted, then carried. When he tried to open his eyes, they were smarting floodgates, blood or tears, he wasn't sure. "Where...where's the Leica?" he gasped. "Where's the camera?" Then his memory reached back through the jungle and he began to writhe in her arms.

"The girls...upstairs!"

"What?" Tyah's grip on him was suddenly desperate. "What did you say?"

Carny tried to speak but he was drowning. Struggling and drowning in air, like a fish. He had the papery feeling again in his chest, and then something was tearing the paper, trying to tear out his heart.

CHAPTER
15

Tyah dropped her quarter twice before she got it in the slot, before she remembered you could call emergency for free.

She told the operator who she was and where Carny was and that he had been assaulted. She requested an ambulance and police. "Tell them..."

The girls upstairs.

"...tell them the Doyle Hotel. Rear entrance. For Chrissake, hurry!"

Tyah ran through the rain, back to her car. Carny was unconscious. He had fallen sideways, his head resting on the driver's seat. His breathing was shallow and ragged. Tyah lifted him straight and reclined the seat. She saw a deep gash in his forehead on which the blood was beginning to congeal, smaller cuts on his cheeks and his hands. All through his clothing were specks of bright glass, glittering like rhinestones. She gently loosened Carny's fingers from his big key ring and ducked out of the car.

There was nothing more she could do for him right now. She closed the car door and turned to face the dark maw of the alley. No way she was going to wait here like a wet rag for the cops to arrive. She retrieved the Mace from her pocket and started forward.

Halfway down the alley, streetlight was defeated by shadow. The rain was easing off now, but from all around her came the sound of dripping water — a million drips in fantastic syncopation, like crickets in high summer. Tyah forced her steps forward, her right hand welded to the Mace can. Willi's shit was a little *too* good; she was going to have to fight it — hard — for control of her imagination, before it gave her the willies. Ha ha.

She tried two keys before she found the one that opened the fire door. The light switch didn't work, but a flick of her lighter assured her that she was alone in the stairwell. She removed her shoes and used one of them to wedge open the heavy steel door in case the cops arrived when she was inside.

At the top of the stairs she could smell spray paint. On the other side of the connecting door, along both sides of the corridor, Tyah could see why.

But only for an instant. Less than a split-second of gaping horror before her stoned soul shrieked denial and her brain, obedient to that, turned to

the sound

faint but wonderfully reassuring, of a radio playing up on the third floor, an old Aerosmith classic, Steve Tyler sounding raunchier than ever on *Walk This Way.*

Why not? She could do that.

No problem.

She went up the narrow stairs, calling: "Felice!" Maybe the radio up there was louder than it sounded. "Feliiiice!" Tyah was so late. Felice would be wondering where she had gotten to.

Walk This Way.

She knew which was Felice's room. She opened the door.

It was empty.

Nicole's room was empty too.

They were in the third room. The new girl's room. The sloppy one. What was her name? Suzanne?

Right.

Suzanne.

Right.

Tyah's mind had become like a gramophone with its needle stuck in a scarred record. Freshly, deeply, obscenely scarred.

Suzanne. Right. Suzanne. Right.

Stuck, so she didn't have to make anything of the scene before her, of the carcasses laid out, side by side, on a carpet soggy with blood. Of their throats that had been broadly cut. Of the radical mutilation that had removed the softest parts of their bodies, those that could be taken quickly, by scalpel, without cutting bone. Of the butcher's counter that had been Suzanne's bed.

The pink letters had been sprayed all over this room, too, but Tyah did not permit herself to see that either. Not yet.

The gramophone needle was still in its rut when strident voices sounded on the floor below. Tyah didn't hear steps thundering upstairs, or the young cop splashing his boots in the doorway, or his older partner's oath.

Still stuck when he told her to turn around slowly and drop the canister, to hold her hands away from her body. The needle didn't jump free until she felt a jolting grip on her arms.

Then she started to scream.

CHAPTER
16

Hal avoided King Street East until one fine late-morning, two weeks after the murders, driving by the Vanguard on his way out to Ancaster.

King was still crawling with thrill-seekers come to see the forbidding, gloomy place where triple-mutilation murder had been committed. After two weeks, the show no longer included detectives and forensic experts passing in and out of the Doyle in a steady stream, but the demonstrators were still out in force.

Mostly women, they had been called together from across the country by anti-pornography groups and social activists as soon as the headlines broke. As their placards and chanting and news interviews attested, they saw in the butchery the latest symptom of a rampant disease, one that could not be cured until all the pornographers and sleaze merchants in Canada had been run to ground, starting right here at the Doyle Hotel.

Graham Sawtrell, in the limelight as spokesperson for the Midland Development Corporation, registered his company's official outrage, side-stepping media questions about future plans for the Vanguard Building. Such questions, he made it clear, were premature and inappropriate while Carny Danial, still the leaseholder for the Doyle, remained in critical condition in his hospital bed.

The cynics had a field day with Midland: the company could afford to be sober and sensitive, they said, now that public opinion — public *pressure* — was growing daily in the company's favour. And this was true. Ninety percent of the angry, frightened people-on-the-street on the nightly news thought Midland had been losing its corporate shirt long enough; it was high time they were permitted to cleanse the Vanguard of the vicious smut that provoked acts of sexual violence, and put those nice shops and restaurants in its place.

Caught in the circus on King Street, Hal was half an hour late for the site meeting with his contractor — too bad, since Dale Coombs was unfailingly punctual. The Ancaster Heritage Society had claimed from the start that their budget couldn't handle a specialty contractor, which was fine with Hal; he would have chosen plain old Dale anyway.

"I can't save a stick of it, Hal; you know I would if I could. Timber's rotten right through to the brick. I'll have to scrape off the whole porch, start from scratch."

Hal leaned back against the Chrysler's warm, faded paintwork, nodding his agreement. Thanks to Dale, the restored interior of the house was a work of art; his gazebo, perfect down to the last intricate fret, had transformed the garden. If he said the whole porch had to go, so be it. "There's a bright side to it anyway," Hal said. "It'll be easier to clean the masonry with the porch off."

"For sure."

"While we're on the subject, have a look at this." Hal led Dale to the side of the house, showed him a round patch of cleaned brick below one of the graceful sash windows. "I did that yesterday. See that glow?"

Dale grunted appreciatively. "Like old gold." It did look like that, shaming the rest of the house with its mantle of grime.

"It took a 130 years to get that patina," Hal told him, "so we're going to look after it. You don't have to baby the place — it's good hard limestone — but no sandblasting!"

Dale chuckled. He had worked for Hal too often not to know the eleventh commandment by now. He rasped his calloused hands together. "Do we get to the good part now?"

His face lit up when Hal spread out the porch drawings on the Chrysler's warm roof. Hal's turn to listen now as Dale gave his expert opinion on the suitability of cedar over pressure-treated jack pine, where to use pegs and where nails for historical accuracy, how best to match the main roof shingles without incurring the expense of slate. Dale was excited; it would be infinitely more rewarding for him to build from scratch rather than work the drawing into the existing dilapidated structure.

By two o'clock they had covered enough ground for Dale to cost the porch. Hal waved the contractor's pickup out of the circular driveway, pulled his brown bag out of the Chrysler's glove compartment and took it to the green, sequestered lawn beside the house.

He picnicked under a spreading oak, munching contentedly on a ham and Swiss. From here, his round patch of cleaned brick looked like a gold coin, the first from a rich find. Not a bad metaphor; he *was* an archaeologist in a way, exposing history in vertical layers. That was especially true for the restoration of commercial buildings, those shopfronts in Port Hope, for instance, where he had first met Julie: Victorian under Art Deco under Vinyl Siding — each stratum telling tales on the next.

Hal took his last bite of sandwich and leaned back against the oak's massive trunk, savouring the drowsy hum of insects, the fragrance of new-mown grass. A warm summer day, a good plain lunch, work he loved…he was perfectly happy without the Van.

Going by the place this morning had only strengthened that conviction. To think that he had been at the Doyle the night of the murders, that maybe he had looked at those very same pristine young bodies just hours before…

How could he wish for any project facilitated by that? No doubt about it, the restoration would shoot ahead now. Sawtrell's falling brick, his runaway streetcar, had struck with unimagined swiftness.

Kate, on the other hand, was still obsessed — the Vanguard or bust. She couldn't accept that Midland had paid for the proposal; a token sum, admittedly (it hardly covered paper and Xeroxing) but they had *bought* the work, which meant it was theirs to do with as they pleased.

Stubbornly unconvinced, Kate had sought their friend Ross Ames's free legal opinion. Whereupon Ross, to Hal's surprise and annoyance, had turned Kate's obsession into a righteous crusade. In Ross's opinion, there had to exist for the competitors a *reasonable expectation* of adequate reward, just as someone buying a lottery ticket reasonably expects the grand prize to exist in a pot somewhere. A competition with a predetermined (or inside) winner was like a lottery with an empty pot, and that, according to Ross, constituted criminal deception.

It was exactly what Kate wanted to hear. Every night for the last two weeks, she had left him to put Rain to bed while she went to the library, feeding the flame with back-issues of newspapers and business magazines — anything she could find on Midland. She was cooking up a strategy, "groundwork" as she called it. But for what? How could they possibly afford a lawyer to take the matter any further?

Hal loved his wife. He tried to see that she needed a buffer from her disappointment, a parachute to slow her fall. He could understand her dissatisfaction with Grace Street, her frustration at working all day while someone else spent time with Rain. But to blame their situation on him...Oh yes she did. He knew, for instance, what she thought of this Ancaster project, how it symbolized for Kate his lack of drive and ambition.

But didn't he have a right to happiness too? Certainly there was financial pressure on them, but whose idea had it been to invest in Florida in the first place? Hal loathed Florida, even as a place to put money. Breakers II had been one hundred percent Kate's doing, and now that her get-rich-quick scheme was squeezing them dry, it was somehow *his* mess!

Hal clenched his fist, balling up his sandwich bag. He stood up and walked, head down, across the lawn to his car. He had a three o'clock appointment at a hardware store in Hamilton that specialized in antique and reproduction fittings. He still needed a lot of little things for this house — hinges, doorknobs, window fastenings. He was looking forward to choosing them. The finishing touches. He liked that part a lot.

CHAPTER
17

Tyah waited until Fletcher's pickup was out of sight and then, on tiptoes, she reached up into the topmost monkey plant growing in the window. She took down a cellophane bag containing a tenth of a gram of Iranian brown heroin and her syringe.

She stood very still, listening to the workday morning quiet in the building, savouring this moment. She was high now and she hadn't even started; high just knowing the next half hour was guaranteed good, right here in her hand.

Tyah had made a half gram from Hyacinth at the beginning of the week and had used it carefully, smoking dusters — heroin and tobacco. Yesterday she had skin-popped — nowhere near the vein — which was all that was going to happen this morning, just to get her through some mad, bad days.

She took the big scented candle from the living room table into the kitchen, got distilled water and a teaspoon and cooked her last tenth in the spoon over the candle flame.

Fix, whispered the quiet, inevitable voice. *Just once. How can it hurt? Just once doesn't count...*

The soft voice was scary but it was sexy too. It made her horny. Weak and curious and hot. Like being a virgin again.

Yeah yeah yeah...

Hypnotized, she went to the bedroom, got the thin leather belt she never wore but had never thrown out, with the extra hole near the buckle and faint teeth marks on the other end.

Dry hump. Just to see how it feels...

She tied her left arm off above the elbow, amazed how it all came back, the sweet taste of the leather as she drew the belt tight, the sticky sound when her teeth let go. After three years of sleep, the vein awakened. A little miracle, it stirred, swelled, showed her a tumid purple profile. She touched it with her finger, felt it fat and springy.

Come on, baby. Let me put it in. Just for a second, honest. Just for a second, I'll pull right out...

With all the old breathless fascination, she watched the bright needle questing in the cradle of her arm, how the baby-soft skin dimpled then surrendered.

For a few seconds Tyah thought she could still go back. She waited to hear the voice again so that she could defy it, but there was no sound in her head now. Just the dead silent glare of shocked white skin and the red-black meat and the blood, right on cue.

In the early afternoon, she went down to the French Quarter club to find Hyacinth.

"Look who it is. Looking for a job, Ty? Can't be, you're the one works exclusively for Carny right? So how is everything at Saint Mike's?"

"Fine, Shane."

"'Fine, Shane'? That's not what I hear. You know, I always wondered what hospitals do with them. You know, like...*after*. They send a hearse or just drop 'em into the incinerator or what? S'funny 'cause you always see those chimneys on the roof, right? Always smoke comin' out."

She waited, fighting the desire to claw his eyes. He was waiting too, for any excuse to throw her out, which Tyah couldn't let him do.

"What you want? Talk to Sam?" Shane meant Sam Wexel, his

new boss. "Be my guest." He moved aside, hands working on the ball, back and forth, the way other wired tough guys chew gum. He called after her into the din: "Sam knows all about you, Tyah. Your tits'll be around your fuckin' waist before you work a day here! Nobody likes a snitch, Tyah. Only place you're ever going to dance is Carny's fuckin' grave!"

The Quarter was a big club, as big as the places out by the airport, but older and seedier. At mid-afternoon it was half full. Vanessa was on stage, her slow song. Tyah caught her eye and motioned discreetly towards the back of the club. She drank a beer while she waited, acknowledging dancers she knew. Those who had worked the Doyle remembered that she had been Felice's friend and offered condolences. Thanks…yeah, a terrible thing…sure, everyone was scared…no, she hadn't heard anything new.

The French Quarter attracted a very different clientele from the Doyle. Stallions with jacked-up Firebirds outside, their hair worn long at the back in oily curls. Flash pimps, posses of Jamaicans, round-tables of South American guys talking hush hush, serious business. Dope city.

Vanessa's set finished. She was so black, all Tyah could see was a disembodied white teddy approaching her table, and the yellow-whites of her eyes. At six foot in her stocking feet, Vanessa had one of those bodies God must reserve for blacks as partial compensation for all the shit. The joke was on the men that pursued her long enough to find out that Vanessa's preference lay elsewhere. She reached the table, extended a long, exquisitely muscled arm to touch Tyah's cheek and slid into the opposite seat. Her touch didn't make Tyah feel uncomfortable — everyone knew Vanessa and Hyacinth were an exclusive item.

"How's Carny? Still unconscious?"

"He's holding his own. I'm going over to Saint Mike's after. Is Hyacinth around?"

Vanessa kissed her teeth in pure Jamaican scorn. "Where you been, girl?"

"Sitting home. Why?"

"She busted."

"Shit!"

"Tell me 'bout it! Me still hustlin' bail. Got a spare ten thousand?" She gave Tyah a wan smile. "Now you got a problem too, right? Big problem?"

"Nah, just chipping."

Vanessa looked concerned. "Wha' for? You was straight so long. Cops sweat you?"

Tyah stared into her beer. She could still hear the relentless, goading voices, just as loud and clear as if she were still downtown under the hot light: "Tell us again...tell us again in your own words, Tyah...tell us again exactly what you saw." Even dosed up to the eyeballs with Valium, it couldn't have been any rougher. Then Detective Hamray, deadly smooth:

"You've been a great help to the investigation, Tyah."

"I *saw* the killer. Why doesn't anyone believe me?"

"You thought you saw an Asian male assaulting Mr. Danial in an unlit alley, but he wasn't committing serial murder. There's a difference, wouldn't you say?"

"Felice told me, just a few weeks ago, she saw..."

"Come on now...how many Asian men go to strip clubs? Hundreds?"

"He ran out of the Doyle after Carny. I saw him."

"Is that right?" Hamray peered intently at the file. "You actually saw him leaving the building?"

"I saw an Asian guy attacking..."

"'An Asian guy' she says. You should check out an atlas sometime, Tyah. Big place, Asia. How many people, you think?"

"I don't know. Millions."

"Millions? How about half of the world's population, Tyah. I mean are we talking a Kampuchean or a Mongolian or a Chinese or a Bangladeshi? A Filipino, maybe. How about a Sumatran?"

She'd met know-it-all cops like Hamray a ton of times — so much to teach the world, so little time.

"Know something, Tyah? You know what's going to happen when this department announces Toronto's answer to Jack the Ripper is 'an Asian guy'? We're going to drown in crank calls, maybe even start a little race war. All because Tyah Whiteside, as usual, was too fucked up to be a reliable witness."

He watched her, mocking her surprise. "Oh. Didn't they tell you? They found a roach in your ashtray. Still got goober on it. Probably wouldn't have noticed except your car still smelled like a Woodstock reunion. Good stuff, though. Excellent stuff. Could've wrung the THC out of that little number."

Hamray let his hand stray to her file at the edge of the table. He flicked it open, turned it around so that Tyah could read again the terms of her probation and see that she still had two months to go. Hamray smiled. "Smoke that good ought to be illegal, if it isn't already."

Vanessa kissed her teeth disgustedly, grazed Tyah's hand with long, cool fingers. "What you g'wan do?"

"It's okay." Tyah took a swallow of beer and lit an Export Light. "Soon as Carny can talk, he'll tell them. He'll remember the guy." She leaned across the table, lowering her voice.

"Now you tell me where I can score."

Vanessa turned her head slowly, meaningfully, towards the door.

"Shane?" Vanessa shrugged. "Oh no." Tyah shook her head violently. "No way. No fuckin' way. You're right — I've been straight three years. You're absofuckinlutely right. I'm gonna go home, drop a couple of Valium, forget the whole thing, right?" She looked over at the door again to confirm her decision, but Shane was heading for the stage where a little man in a dirty windbreaker was waltzing drunkenly with the featured dancer. The audience began to shout encouragement, clapping and egging him on.

"It's Horace!" said Tyah. "The flower guy!"

"In here all the time now, drinkin'. Me don' know where 'im get the money."

They watched Shane pluck Horace from the stage and drag him away. "Poor little fucker. He used to love Carny, you know." Tyah stubbed out her cigarette and stood up. "Thanks for the shoulder, Vanessa. Sorry to hear about Hyacinth. Hope it works out okay."

"You want me to look around for you?"

"No thanks."

Horace was where she had expected to find him, on his hands and knees on the sidewalk. He was trying to pick up the loose change that must have fallen from his pockets when Shane threw him out.

"You okay?" He was very drunk and smelled terrible, but otherwise seemed all right. Tyah squatted, picking nickels and dimes off the concrete, trying not to smell him.

"You seen Carny?" Horace slurred. "How's he doin'? Terrible thing, them poor little girls. Terrible thing..." On all fours, solemnly shaking his head, Horace looked like one of those nodding dogs people put in the backs of cars. Tyah hauled him to his feet and poured his change into his windbreaker. She spotted a cab coming on the other side and whistled; the driver pulled a U turn with a whinny of power steering.

"Where do you live, Horace?"

"My ticket." He cast bleary, anxious eyes over the sidewalk. "Lose my ticket..."

Was he that pissed? "It's a cab, Horace. Where do you live?"

"Lansdowne. Forty-two."

Tyah knew the street. Rooming houses, the worst kind. Ten dollars would cover the fare and a tip. She pulled a ten from her wallet, opened the back door and gave it and the address to the driver. Horace insisted that he couldn't get in until he'd found his ticket.

"Jesus! You don't need a ticket, Horace, this is a goddamn taxi okay?"

He tottered on the sidewalk, fumbling intently through his pockets. "There!" He beamed, holding up a crumpled piece of green paper. "Thought she'd blowed away!" He thrust it under Tyah's nose.

It was indeed a ticket, from a pawn shop called Ivan's Trading Post on Church, telling her that Horace Haywood had pledged one Leica camera against seventy-five dollars. Tyah stared at the wording. She knew nothing at all about photography yet "Leica" rang a bell. Odd that he would be in possession of a camera at all.

"Where did you get the camera, Horace?"

"Find all kinds things onna street...money, tickets for the game once. Phone booths is best...umbrellas, gloves..."

"Where did you find it?" Tyah moved closer, heedless now of his beer-breath. "Can you remember?"

"Night them little girls was murdered, eh? Had a few with Wayne, couldn't find a cab three inna mornin'. Coulda stayed at Wayne's 'cept his old lady's working days again, she don't like me. I seen all them p'lice by the Doyle, went up that alley in back, see what all the fuss. Me and Wayne had one or two beers, eh?" He gave Tyah a sheepish, drunken grin. "Almost pissed on it!"

Tyah's voice was suddenly urgent. "Let me get this straight. At three a.m. the night of the murders, you found a camera behind the Doyle?" She remembered now. Carny had been mumbling about a camera when she pulled him from the alley.

"Finders keepers," whined Horace. "Just lyin' in the gutter. Nothin' wrong with that. Finders keepers, eh?"

"Sure, Horace. Was there film in it? Did you mess with it before you pawned it?"

"Didn't touch it!"

Tyah stood for a moment, staring at the paper. She pushed Horace into the cab and jumped in after him. "Ivan's Trading Post, Queen and Church," she told the bemused driver. "Step on it!"

CHAPTER
18

The news from the Doyle, horrible as it was, had come at the right time. It had galvanized Kate into action. With the lease problem between Midland and the Doyle presumably solved, the restoration would go full speed ahead.

The *need* for action had brought her here today, in a borrowed red Toyota sports car, ten minutes away from a rendezvous that could still make dreams come true.

Unsure of her direction at first, Kate had been researching the company itself, gradually losing her fear of tough-sounding words like "leverage" and "land consumption," collecting anything at all on the Midland Development Corporation.

There wasn't a whole lot. A prosperous, independent, low-profile company that had been around for fifteen years earning a healthy but not inordinate operating profit. A lot of subdivision housing, a string of mid-size suburban shopping malls, some low-rise office buildings, a trade centre in Richmond Hill, an arena in Ajax. Dull reading.

She changed direction, focused on the Vanguard and immediately hit pay dirt in a small, bi-monthly magazine called *Canadian*

Heritage, a three-year-old issue in which Midland first announced future restoration plans for their historic King Street building.

It was a scholarly, tedious article, but sandwiched between four pages of erudite waffle was an interview with Alistair Crawford, then, as now, President and Chair of the Board of Midland. Kate had already met him in her research: born in Scotland, immigrated to Canada in 1975 to set up Midland, having spent most of his working life in Indonesia in the rubber trade. In his early seventies, Crawford was more or less retired from the day-to-day running of the company, living a secluded life in the country near Port Hope. He kept himself well out of range of the media, even now that his King Street property was making the front page.

But in one obscure, long-forgotten interview at least, Alistair Crawford had let it be known that the restoration of the Vanguard Building was one of the important things in his life:

'There are certain times when even sound business sense should be tempered with other considerations. Did I pay too much for the Vanguard? I will never say I paid too much for a commercial building in Toronto! But I will say that I am prepared to pay a great deal more, whatever it takes, to raise it from its present neglected condition to the status of landmark.'

'So it's a prestige venture? A pet project?'

'Perhaps. Yes, I do have a personal interest in this one. At my age you start thinking about posterity, progeny if you like. Who's going to remember a few hundred detached homes in Halton? But the Vanguard — as I said, it will be landmark.'

The interview went on for another page in the same vein — Crawford sketching his ambitions, not for a spruced-up Vanguard but for a completely rejuvenated enterprise, paying its way with shops and restaurants and offices. Not a museum or a monument — "a living landmark."

At last Kate had a strategy. The Vanguard meant a lot to Midland's president; his prestige venture represented an upmarket image for an otherwise dowdy company. Granite Club respectability. But more than that, it sounded very much like an old man's swan song, his last shot at immortality.

Well, she would find him, this old man. If Crawford was unaware of the plan to cheat her husband, she would *make* him aware, make him undo it. If he was one of the planners, she would threaten to expose them all, let it be known to anyone who would listen how the Midland Development Corporation went about creating landmarks!

It might work. Obviously Crawford was still hot on the project. How much had Midland lost in potential revenue, stubbornly waiting for the "Doyle Diehard" to back down from his lease agreement? How much had they offered Danial to vacate? Probably hundreds of thousands.

And now these murders, the Vanguard threatening to become a ready-made landmark of a very different sort. Crawford would be highly sensitive to another smear coming hard on its heels, however slight by comparison. Would it matter to him which architect took charge of the restoration in the end, as long as he was competent?

It wasn't much of a plan, but Kate felt angry enough to run with it. Better than sitting back and being a victim. She wasn't angry with Hal, not anymore; her husband was focused on one thing: buildings, specifically old buildings. Not career goals, not money, and perhaps it was that narrow focus that made him good at his work. But he needed someone to light his fire, someone with ambition, drive, the things he lacked, and she was it. They were a team, and right now Kate was up at the net — up to her to smash this difficult volley through.

Kate twitched the Toyota's leather wheel towards the Port Hope exit. Five minutes later she was in the town centre, stopping for a traffic light at the crest of the hill where the steep main street began. She knew it well from the time Hal had worked here: the high-fronted shops he had restored, the Victorian streetlamps, the sidestreets of Gothic beauties.

She pulled down the sun-visor and checked her makeup in the vanity mirror, rounded up a stray smear of lipstick, fluffed her hair. Sweet of George Reathkin to cover for her at the magazine and lend her his brand new MR2; she would make a much stronger impression in a red sports car.

The light changed and Kate surged forward, gratified by the car's willing power. Now she had a view down to Acorn Antiques beyond the bridge and could see that Crawford wasn't there yet. That didn't mean anything, it was only just two o'clock.

Mid-afternoon, mid-week in a sleepy country town. There were a few tourists, middle-aged ladies in cotton prints and straw hats passing in and out of the craft and antique shops; the usual teenagers were loafing around; there was a drunk waiting to sober up outside the liquor store, a long wait by the look of him; there were pickups double-parked outside the feed mill, weathered men in tractor caps, running down the farm-loans manager at the CIBC.

But there was no Alistair Crawford outside Acorn Antiques. Not at a quarter past two. Nor half past.

At a quarter to three, hope began to fail her.

Kate started to feel ridiculous, *sounded* ridiculous to herself as she replayed her morning phone call to Crawford's residence: "My name is Kate Sebastian. I have some information for Alistair Crawford." She had kept her voice low on the phone, cloak and dagger. "I assure you it will interest him if he cares about the reputation of his company."

God! She had sounded like something out of the worst soap opera. And she hadn't even talked to Crawford himself, who had been (what else?) unavailable. She had played to some assistant, or maybe it was the man who cleaned the billiard room — she'd never found out because, in true soap opera style, she'd rung off after naming a time and place to meet. A wonder she didn't throw in some heavy breathing!

Kate stood on the sidewalk, staring at the window of Acorn Antiques, at the reflection of the red Toyota. Far from enhancing her image, the car seemed to mock her now, a bright red reminder that she herself owned a clapped-out Chrysler Valiant and would never have a car like this, would never live anywhere but in one half of a water-damaged slum on Grace Street, growing old pasting up pictures of her dreams and other people's realities in *T.O. Time*.

Kate stole another glance at her watch: it was five to three. With downcast eyes she began a dull inspection of Acorn Antiques' window, a display of the usual overpriced tourist bait: a few more or less antique items, some hand-painted wooden decoys, jars of pot-pourri, old-people dolls with sentimental, dried apple faces. Had she expected Crawford to be like that? Not from his photographs, which showed hard, predatory intelligence. What on earth had made her think he would bother himself with a piddling matter like this?

The shop door chimed and Kate looked up as two cotton-print ladies came out. Then something just inside the doorway caught her eye.

"Lovely day," greeted the shopwoman, "we've been so lucky, haven't we? Is there something I can help you with?" The woman came to her side, plump and friendly. "Birdseye maple. You don't often see a maple harmonium. Nice, isn't it? I love the stool." In needlepoint, on the cushion of the matching stool, Kate read: ABIDE WITH ME.

"It's local," chattered the woman. "That makes it even more special, I think. Been in the church basement for years gathering dust. Got themselves an electric organ but they lost their flock just the same."

"Wesleyville…" murmured Kate.

The woman suddenly realized that Kate was close to tears. "Oh dear, I hope I didn't say the wrong thing? You're not from there, are you? Of course the whole village has gone really, hasn't it?" Getting no response, she rambled nervously. "The keys are real ivory. Do you play? Have a go if you like. It works like a dream, all except the one F sharp."

Like a dream.

Kate left the shop. She found George's keys, unlocked his car. It was time to go back.

The dream was over.

"Mrs. Sebastian?"

Just a dream. She opened the car door.

"Mrs. Sebastian?"

This time she looked, across the road where the voice seemed to be coming from. She saw a man walking across the bridge towards her, crossing the road now. A young man — tall, deeply tanned, a powerful, limber body under his summer suit.

"Are you Kate Sebastian?"

"Yes?"

"You wanted to see Mr. Crawford. He's waiting."

Butterflies, swarms of butterflies quickening in the pit of her stomach, shimmering into her throat.

"Follow me please," said the tanned young man.

Kate shut the car door and followed him on rubber legs — over the road, across the bridge and into the municipal parking lot towards a dark green Jaguar Sovereign. The Jaguar was perhaps fifty yards from Acorn Antiques although the shop, and her sports car, remained in full view. At last Kate found her voice: "How long have you been here?"

"Since two o'clock."

"I don't understand."

The young man kept his eyes averted as they crossed the lot. "Mr. Crawford is not used to dealing with strangers, Mrs. Sebastian. Especially strangers who introduce themselves with phone calls like yours."

"You've been sitting here watching me?"

"Mr. Crawford values his privacy." They were almost at the Jaguar. Through the heavily tinted windows she could make out a dark shape in the back of the car. Kate's escort turned to her. "May I see your bag please?" She met hard, steel grey eyes. She had recognized his voice immediately — the man who cleaned the billiard room. But he didn't, did he? Kate got the feeling she could be just as much afraid of this young man as he wanted her to be.

She tried to smile, an antidote to her jangling nerves: "You don't really imagine I've got a gun do you? A flick-knife perhaps?" He waited with icy politeness. Kate shrugged and unshouldered her black Roots bag. "Just like the movies!"

He glanced in the bag, handed it back. "This side please." He led her around to the rear driver's side door. The dark shape in the back of the car shifted, and Kate's butterflies swarmed again: had she bitten off more than she could chew?

Then the door opened and Kate was engulfed by the sweet, nostalgic aroma of Connelly leather.

"Good afternoon," said the shape inside. "I am Alistair Crawford."

Her first impression was of a huge, raw-boned man filling the rear compartment. He wore a dark blue suit with a triangle of white handkerchief in the breast pocket, an old-fashioned touch.

Because he is an old man, came the second, subordinate thought, although the eyes regarding her with keen interest — pale blue with startling black pupils, as piercing as a bird's — Alistair Crawford's eyes were anything but old.

"I believe you have something to discuss with me. Please get in."

For a second Kate seemed unable to move, his eyes holding her, hypnotically. Then a thin smile touched his mouth. "You hesitate. Perhaps your mother warned you about getting into cars with strange men?"

Kate came to her senses. "But I invited *you*, Mr. Crawford." She climbed in, greeted by the butter-smooth caress of the Connelly hide.

"Thank you, Greg." The heavy, precision-fitted door thumped shut. Through the tinted window she watched Greg start across the parking lot towards the street. When she turned to Crawford again, his slight smile was gone. "What do you wish to tell me that concerns the reputation of my company?" His voice was as seduc-tive as his eyes — educated English, its edges smoothed by life abroad.

Kate steeled herself against him. "I'm here on behalf of my husband, Hal Sebastian," she said tersely.

No reaction.

"I didn't come here to play games, Mr. Crawford. Hal is one of the architects competing for the restoration of your property on King Street — the Vanguard Building."

"Mrs. Sebastian," he said evenly. "You should know that I very seldom involve myself in the preliminary stages of development projects."

"But this is the exception, isn't it? 'Posterity, progeny if you like.' Sound familiar?"

The eyes watched her. "What do you want?"

Kate looked stonily at him. "You're telling me you've never heard of Hal Sebastian?"

"I'm telling you nothing. *You* are telling *me*; I am listening." A trace of annoyance. "To a very resourceful woman by the sound of things. May I ask how you obtained my private number?"

Kate shrugged. "I knew you lived near Port Hope. When I found you were unlisted I called some of the retailers here, said I was phoning from the Crawford residence. I told them some calls had been going astray, I was checking to see that they had the right number. I got it third try, I think it was the drugstore."

"Extraordinary. And what do you do, Mrs. Sebastian, when you're not ferreting out unlisted telephone numbers?"

Kate ignored the question. "Do you know who Karel Lorenz is?"

Crawford gave a guarded nod.

"Then I imagine you've seen his proposal for the Vanguard — an atrium, cost efficient because the shell is there already, galleries on every level, shops and restaurants on the first two floors. Shall I tell you how I know that? Because it *isn't* Lorenz's proposal. My husband made those crucial discoveries at the Vanguard, then translated his findings into a brilliant proposal for the restoration, which he presented at your head office to a unanimously favourable reception by *your senior management*! Only to learn that the whole exercise was a sham!"

It was pouring out, all the frustration and anxiety of the last weeks. Kate could feel tears of anger scalding her eyes.

"Lorenz was your man from the start, wasn't he? You thought, for a few hundred lousy dollars, you could pick my husband's brain, then cheat him out of his rightful prize!" Kate blinked but her eyes filled up again. "Mr. Crawford...my husband is the best, the most intuitive restoration architect in this country. He deserves this chance and the Vanguard deserves *him*! He…" She wiped savagely at her eyes. "He…he can…dammit!"

Through the mist of tears appeared a white flag. Kate twisted away, glaring furiously through her side window, cursing her weakness.

"Please, Mrs. Sebastian." He laid his white pocket-handkerchief across her knee. "Truce?"

Kate rounded on him. "Everything I just told you, you knew already, didn't you?"

Crawford gave a slight nod. "As of this morning, after you called."

"Oh sure!"

"Kate…may I call you that?"

"Call me whatever you like, just don't bullshit me!"

"Shortly after ten a.m., Greg informed me of your call and gave me your name…Sebastian. I had never heard it before. I made inquiries with my people at Midland, told them about your extraordinary telephone call and mentioned your name. I immediately learned some interesting facts.

"I will be candid with you: although I was not involved in the selection of architects to compete for the Vanguard project, I had, as of a week ago, received the submissions; as you rightly pointed out, the Vanguard is of personal interest to me. I was therefore surprised to be told that Hal Sebastian had been among the competitors — surprised because I had not received his submission along with the others. I asked why not. I was then apprised of a situation much as you described to me."

Kate looked cynical. "Fine. What are you going to do about it?"

"First I would like you to understand that there is nothing…illicit about this. When your husband — any of the competitors — agreed to accept payment for their designs, they were surrendering ownership. The work then became Midland's property, to do with as we saw fit."

"That's not what my lawyer tells me. Anyway, you think this is 'fit' do you, to take one man's work and put another's name on it? You *did* receive Lorenz's submission, right? An atrium?"

"Yes. And it is for that reason as much as the principle of the thing — the fact that my subordinates neglected to inform me who the real author was — for that reason I had your husband's original design delivered to me at ten-thirty this morning. I dislike the sensation of wool over my eyes as much as you do."

Kate held her breath.

"Everything considered, I should be grateful to you for calling me. And I must admit, when I did finally see your husband's design, I liked it rather better than the 'revised' version."

Over the last few seconds, hope had begun to creep back into Kate's being. Crawford must have seen its colours on her face. He held up a steadying hand. "Of course I need more time to compare his work with the other submissions. As I inferred, other changes were made besides the name Sebastian being altered to Lorenz. But so far, your husband looks like the front runner."

Kate saw a different face now, a benign, smiling face. "I...I'm not sure what to say."

"I am: if Hal Sebastian is half as resourceful as his wife, we would be very foolish indeed to overlook him. Have you eaten lunch, Kate?" He chuckled at her surprise. "Ah...the strange man offers sweets!"

Kate resisted the smile tugging at the corners of her mouth. A moment ago, she had been hurt and angry. "It sounds like you think you're talking to a child, Mr. Crawford."

"Alistair."

Kate gave her smile half an inch. "Anyway, no restaurant will be doing lunch; it's a quarter past three."

"Is it really?" He watched her, amused, admiring.

"Really. In fact, they'll already be serving afternoon tea at the Cobweb on Bank Street." Kate allowed another half-inch of smile. "Real clotted cream imported from England. In tins."

"In tins!"

When Kate raised the white handkerchief from her knee and blew her nose, Alistair Crawford laughed aloud.

Kate took the lakeshore route out of Port Hope. She drove at a quiet pace, afraid that going any faster might use up her joy.

How could she have dreamed, a few hours ago, that this day would turn out so perfectly?

She had been acting at first, aware of delivery, gesture, timing — responding to his gallantry to further her cause. But after a while, she had begun to enjoy his company. The proprietor of The Cobweb pulled out all the stops — shrimp-paste sandwiches, scones with thick yellow cream and homemade strawberry jam, strong tea steeping in a Brown Betty; for nearly an hour they had celebrated their Englishness.

Kate talked about Worcestershire, told him she was an artist, that she worked for a magazine. She told him about Rain. She mentioned, since he was a developer, their millstone at Delray Beach.

He sketched for her his career in Malaysia, not in rubber as Kate's research had misinformed her, but in tin mining, like his father. Except for three years "swatting Japs," it had been "a supremely unexciting life." Eventually the ore deposits began to dwindle on his family's holdings, then on top of that, the market went soft. Having been a bachelor all his life, with no family ties, he got out.

It was hard for Kate to imagine any of it, beyond a typical Somerset Maugham picture of English colonials strutting around in pith helmets giving orders to little brown men, sipping gee and tee's on the veranda, playing endless games of bridge. "Somehow I don't see you doing anything 'supremely unexciting' for so long." Kate looked across the table at him, teasing. "Are you sure you haven't left something out?"

For a second Crawford's eyes had regained their first brilliance; watching eyes, dangerous, decidedly sexy eyes, even in an old man. "Believe it or not," he told her, "I was something of a sportsman in my time. Tennis, riding, hunting." He glanced sideways in disgust at the twin walking sticks leaning against the wall beside their table. "It's only the last few years that have...slowed me down."

That was as near as he came to mentioning his infirmity, which Kate guessed to be severe arthritis. She wondered how much pain he was in, whether it was pain that gave his face its strained, slightly unnatural look. He was profoundly crippled; Greg had practically carried him up the half-dozen steps to the Cobweb.

And Greg was there to assist him down again, though Crawford took Kate's arm across the sidewalk to the Jaguar. "I have enjoyed this afternoon," he said. "Don't worry about Hal any more, we're going to take care of that. And you're an artist you say. Do you by any chance paint portraits?"

"My specialty."

"Well, well!" He gave her arm a parting squeeze as he lowered himself into the car, irritably shooing Greg away. For the second time Kate noticed the Jaguar's highly unusual carpeting; not the standard Wilton but an Oriental that had been cut to fit. She had been admiring it on the way to the Cobweb.

"I like your Bokhara," she said. "I thought it a Pakistan but now I'm not sure. Is it Russian?"

Crawford was both pleased and surprised. "Turkoman Russian. You know something of Oriental carpets?"

"A little. I took a course at art college. I still like to browse, not that I can afford to buy anything!"

"Well, well," he said again, and shut the car door. A moment later the window purred down. "Perhaps you would care to visit me sometime."

"I'd like that very much."

"Then you'd better give Greg your telephone number...just in case you're unlisted!"

Kate was still composing a snappy comeback when the black window whirred up again.

It was four-thirty when the sign announced Wesleyville and Kate stopped to refuel her dream.

The church was still for sale. She had known it would be. She was certain now that destiny had arranged for that first lakeshore drive to discover it. Destiny had put a realtor's sign on the lawn...and a harmonium in Acorn Antiques.

ABIDE WITH ME.

Destiny had brought her together with Alistair Crawford today — from across oceans, across years.

She was relieved to see the church looking every bit as wonderful now, solidly real, as it had in her dream. Relief slipping into a higher gear as she walked around the building, trailing her hand along the rough bricks, her excitement growing until she felt she would burst if she didn't let it out.

"Yiiiiiiiiy!" Kate cried aloud as she hugged the wall.

She had won!

CHAPTER
19

Tyah went to the hospital gift shop where, as usual, she bought a single pink carnation. Six o'clock was peak visiting time at Saint Mike's; she rode up to Special Care on a crowded elevator that stopped at every floor to discharge visitors bearing flowers and toys and sadness and hope.

The nurses' station was empty, but Tyah visited every day so she didn't need directions along the terrazzo and cream corridors to Carny's room. As she walked, she patted the fat envelope in her pocket to make sure it was still there.

There had been an anxious moment at Ivan's Trading Post, where an obese, light-deprived creature showed her the Leica. It was out of Tyah's price range, but worse than that, it was empty. "Did you notice any film in it?" she asked the pawnbroker.

Ivan's pig eyes travelled up and down her. "You a friend of that hobo?" She had left Horace snoring in the cab. She put the ticket in the pawnbroker's hand, careful not to touch him. He looked at it, his lips curling into a lecherous grin. "It was fast film, far as I recall." His eyes slid over her breasts to her face. "Fast film is for low light. Anything I should see?" When Tyah had stared him down, he waddled along the counter, rummaged sullenly in a drawer.

"Next thing, someone's gonna pawn a banjo, come back for the friggin' strings!"

The pictures, developed in one hour at Yonge and Dundas, had told her a clear story. They had been taken with Hal Sebastian's camera, no doubt about it. There were a dozen shots of the Vanguard — the kind of artsy, detailed pictures a hippie-professor *would* take — obviously the reason he had it with him in the first place. There was also a dim, though perfectly recognizable, closeup of the Chinese man she had Maced in the alley. Somewhere, somehow, Carny had snapped this picture, then dropped the camera in the alley where it lay until Horace took his fateful piss.

What an amazing break! The Doyle Contingent had been down, but now they were coming back, on a roll, she could feel it! Next thing, Carny was going to come round the corner in his dressing-gown and slippers with an unfiltered Player's stuck in his face. John had rescued his big old Buick from the lot. She'd get a few of the girls together, show up in that big boat to take him home. He was going to wake up, no doubt about it. Guys like Carny didn't linger in fucking comas. They didn't call him the "Doyle Diehard" for nothing!

Carny's door was ajar. Tyah wondered why she couldn't see the cardiac monitor at the end of his bed or the tent of his feet under the blankets. She checked the number on the door and pushed through.

They must have moved him. The bed was made up, and all the cards and flowers were gone. Nothing but the hospital furniture throwing hard shadows on the flat green walls. She would just have to go back to the desk, find out where they had put him.

Special Care was on the second-highest floor of Saint Mike's. She could see the surrounding roofs and there was smoke or steam coming out of half-a-dozen stacks. In here, she could smell the sweet-sick hospital smell, somewhere between talcum powder and urine. She could hear the hospital sounds echoing along the corridor: the isolated coughing, the distant rumble of elevator doors, the rattle of a trolley, the squawk of crepe-soled shoes…growing louder, stopping now.

"Excuse me?"

Tyah turned from the window. A nurse was standing in the doorway, a very young girl with pink skin, like a doll.

"Were you looking for Mr. Danial?"

Tyah stood absolutely still.

"I'm very sorry," said the nurse-doll, and the funny thing was, she really did sound it.

They brought coffee to the lounge. It went cold on the formica table next to a heap of grubby magazines.

"You sit there as long as you like," the doctor told her.

She sat in an orange plastic chair while the cold coffee grew a skin. She had completely forgotten about the photographs weighing down her pocket. She distracted herself only with the terrazzo around her feet; it looked like a million tiny stones, all colours...like pebbles under water.

She was sitting in a river, waiting for it to carry her away to the sea. And if the river didn't take her — and Tyah doubted now that it would — then she knew another way to get there, quick and sure.

She left the pink carnation behind, on the table beside the coffee cup. After an hour in her hand, it had wilted.

PART 2

CHAPTER
20

Through the hoarding, the excavating machines looked like tanks manoeuvring in a storm of dust, the hardhats like infantry soldiers deployed behind the armour. It *sounded* like a battle — the crump of compactors, the yatter of jackhammers, the screaming of concrete drills. Overlooking the battleground, the generals high in their glass and steel towers ordered the razing of whole city blocks with a scrawl of ink, then reordered the landscape. It thrilled Kate to think how much power rested with her husband, that *his* vision would be superimposed here, changing people's lives.

"Let go of the fence now."

"See Daddy!"

Kate smiled, "Daddy doesn't make the buildings, Monkey, he draws pictures of them in his office, so these men know what to build. Come on, let go." Rain relinquished her grip on the plastic mesh and Kate plopped her down onto the sidewalk. "God, you weigh a ton!" She hefted her two shopping bags and took Rain's hand.

"See Daddy now?"

"Yep."

"Go cayshun?"

"Yes, Monkey. We're *all* going on vacation!"

A crisp autumn wind was blowing off the lake, hurrying storybook clouds across a blue sky. Kate could see them reflected in the downtown skyscrapers — it looked like a city of clouds.

Her feeling of well-being was undiminished by the twenty-dollar parking ticket flapping under the Jeep's wiper. She lifted Rain into the high cab and secured her in the car-seat. With the church winterized, they needed a vehicle that could make the journey safe in all weathers, with room for friends, furniture, Kate's canvases — whatever travelled regularly between city and country. Kate opened the back and put in the big carrier bag of art supplies and framing materials she had bought this morning at Grafix, the other bag with croissants for tomorrow's breakfast, fresh pasta and herbs, balsamic vinegar and virgin olive oil for salads, decent wine — things they needed for the week ahead that didn't exist in the country.

"See Daddy now?"

"Yes, darling."

"Daddy's office?"

"That's right."

Kate pulled out, took Adelaide east.

"Daddy cayshun too?" Rain persisted.

Kate didn't mind it today, answering the same question a dozen times; Rain's need for reassurance was genuine. The promise of Hal's long-awaited holiday, the three of them together for a whole week, had been made and broken twice this past summer.

Sebastian family life had changed in the year and a half since the Vanguard competition. There had been the cathedral restoration to fortify Hal's sudden reputation, a U of T extension to secure it. And now the Distillery, the town house development whose beginnings they had just observed — new building, not restoration. The second commission from Midland, it was Hal's biggest yet. With so much work, it was a rare night he made it home for Rain's story and her goodnight kiss, many times mother and daughter set out alone for the church on a Friday, Hal as often as not working straight through the weekend.

But Kate knew it wouldn't go on like this forever. Hal would hire more staff, free up more time. The early years of any successful business always meant intensive care.

The lunchtime traffic jostled them east through the downtown core, past the building that housed *T.O. Time.* "There but for the grace of God!" Kate told working women friends who expected her to be bored now. Bored? Finally she could use the magazine to *enjoy* her city!

They reached the Vanguard at one o'clock and found a lucky meter on Court. She let Rain feed it, then they walked to the Van's main entrance on King, around the corner where the striptease place used to be, where the dancers were murdered.

There was no unpleasant residue to be felt in the Vanguard. Kate was proud of Hal a second time as they entered the building and looked through to the atrium courtyard, filled with sunlight and greenery. It drew you in, made you glad to be there. As an ex-office drone, she could imagine what a difference that initial daily impression would make. Even Rain gravitated towards the courtyard, straining at Kate's hand as they waited for an elevator.

The vestibule had been recreated with warm red granite, in keeping with the sandstone exterior now scrubbed to a rich glow. Tunnel-vaulting through to the courtyard and round arches over the elevators created the peaceful mood of a Romanesque church.

They rode up to the sixth floor where Hal's new office occupied fifteen hundred square feet, soon to be increased by half that again. Right now, Hal and Julie were the only architects, with two full-time draftspeople and two students on a temporary basis. Like the Van's other offices, Hal's had a glass front wall looking over a wide, carpeted gallery to the atrium. Julie saw them coming and opened the glass door to greet them.

"Hal's still at his computer course, he should be back any minute."

"Still trying to drag him into the twentieth century?"

Julie smiled. "It'll be the twenty-first before he gets here!" She was always prettier than Kate remembered. Especially when she smiled.

Kate said: "We were just by the Distillery site. Seems to be all go."

"All go to hell if we don't settle our differences soon. Sawtrell's trying to play it safe as usual — stone lions and brass knockers — Georgian Junk! You want a cup of coffee or something?" To Rain: "Some juice?"

Kate declined for them both. The plan was to get lunch at the courtyard restaurant before they hit the road. Julie excused herself to field some data from the fax machine, a new Fujitsu with a mate at the church. Kate watched her transfer the data to the nearest terminal, her small fingers a blur on the keyboard. Such devices were second nature to Julie, one of the reasons Hal valued her so highly, that and her "useful skepticism" as he called it.

And her style, thought Kate.

She smiled hello to Don Wales and the other draftsperson whose name she could never remember. She would have been happy to wait for Hal in the office amongst the trappings of his professional existence, leafing through *Progressive Architect* and *Old House Journal* in the reception area, but Rain was hungry and restless. She pulled magazines onto the floor and made noise while Gloria, Hal's secretary/receptionist, tried to sound efficient on the phone.

Kate took her outside the office where she let off steam running laps around the carpeted gallery behind the tempered-glass barrier.

Kate folded her arms on the iron rail, dividing her attention between Rain and the people six floors below, lunching amongst the greenery. Midland had relinquished brass hardware and awnings but not the jungle in the courtyard; Kate had to admit (not, of course, to Hal or Julie) that she was glad.

It was gratifying to see her own rendition come to life. The traffic of businesspeople, the shoppers passing below with parcels from the smart boutiques and specialty shops that surrounded the courtyard on the first two floors. She watched a uniformed cleaner on the gallery below pulling a vacuum cleaner along, could hear its wheels chuckling over the new carpet as it trundled behind him like an obedient dog.

Rain came around for the second time, pausing just long enough to nuzzle her hot face against Kate's hand, then off again. Sunlight poured down on them through the glass roof; the air was good to breathe, enriched by the plants below, filtered and conditioned by benign, silent systems. A palpable sense of well-being spiralled up through the atrium, like a thermal of warm air, buoying Kate up. The feeling that order and security — the stuff of her present happiness — were being spun around her like a cocoon, not least by her circling child.

The feeling awoke memories from another time of comfort and certainty. The comfort of Grandy's lap, the spicy aroma of a leather-bound *Arabian Nights*, the buttons on his waistcoat, the ticking of his pocket watch at the end of its buttery gold chain, the warm weight of his big hands.

Rain came round again. "Chase me!"

"Not now, Monkey, I'm having a think."

"Why?"

"Because." Kate watched the scampering little girl, remembering how Grandy would fold up his pink *Financial Times* and exchange his leather slippers for one of twenty pairs of bespoke walking shoes that gleamed in ranks in the boot room. Their "perambulations" — around the kitchen garden, along the lupin walk to the dell, Kate's excited, darting sallies into rhododendrons and across broad lawns never taking her far from the rhythmic tap of his walking stick, knowing that running away only meant returning to the absolute, certain warmth of his hand.

She had wanted such security for Rain and now they had it. On a modern, smaller scale (which was as it should be), but at least they were...comfortable!

When Rain came around again, Kate knelt and swept her, laughing, into her arms. They were like that when Hal stepped out of the elevator.

Kate had a salad. Eating in the green, sunlit courtyard, salad heightened the pretense that summer was still here, that it wasn't really the first of October. Hal announced, over his second eight-ounce glass of red wine, that he wasn't going to call the office for a week, wasn't going to think about architecture for seven days. "We must drink to it!"

Kate fingered the stem of her glass, hesitating. "You're sure Julie can handle everything — for a week?"

"I'm not even going to talk about work." Hal took a big drink of wine, forgetting their toast. He beamed at his family. "What else can we talk about? Ever fly a kite, Monkey?"

"Of course she hasn't."

"Well, that's something we can do. There's a store right over there that sells nothing *but* kites. It's called *High As A Kite*, just like Daddy."

"Hal…"

"And on the other side they sell coffee machines, but remember not to say EXpresso — you have to say ESSpresso or they won't serve you. Aren't they silly?"

Rain laughed uncertainly.

"Stop it, Hal!"

He began, tipsily, to sing *Let's Go Fly a Kite*. People were looking.

"How was your computer course?" Kate said to distract him.

"Thrilling."

"Come on. Seriously?"

"You're right — it was serious. Serious stuff!"

"Forget it. Let's go." Kate pulled out her VISA card and signalled the waitress.

Hal's appearance had changed in eighteen months. The long hair was gone, the granny glasses had horn-rims now. The old Vyella shirts and the worn corduroys and the battered Harris Tweed jacket weren't allowed out of the closet except on weekends. Under it all, she liked to tease him, there had always languished "a body born for Armani." Glancing sideways as she drove, Kate was reminded how handsome he looked, even tired as he was, in a really good suit.

The church had been given a makeover too. A new roof, new eavestroughs and downspouts, new exterior woodwork and a whimsical, palest yellow paint job that thumbed its nose at historical accuracy.

As usual, Rain woke up as soon as Kate turned off the engine.

Hal let her out and she broke away, scrambling up the steps, dancing up and down by the front door.

"Does she need to pee?" Hal asked.

"Church mouse!" shrieked Rain, twisting the knob.

"What's she saying?"

"The church mouse," Kate repeated. "The church mouse always leaves something for Rain." She took a load up to the door. "What'll it be today, Monkey?" At the end of each visit, Kate surreptitiously left some small, indigenous item — a pretty leaf, a sea-gull feather, a nice pebble from the beach — to be discovered next time. Today it was a smooth stick of driftwood, pale as bone against the grey slate tiles in the vestibule.

Rain carried it off to add to her collection while Hal unloaded the Jeep and Kate put away in the antique pine kitchen, playing back messages on the answering machine.

The library in Orono, their local shopping centre, wanted overdue books back. No more than a book room really, but the limited choice somehow made it easier to use. Kate had imagined reading every single book on the shelves, those classics one was always meaning to get to.

The Activities Committee had called, wanting Kate to organize a painting bee for Farmer's Day, a backcloth for the produce display, "something harvesty — sorry about the short notice."

There was a call from Meredith Woolley, the local doctor's wife who knew they were down for the week. Sarah would love to see Rain, how about Wednesday, then Mrs. Boyd could watch the "*enfants*" and the moms could sneak off for lunch? Meredith had heard marvellous things about a new place in Kirby, a converted feed mill.

Raincheck, thought Kate. She would see enough of Meredith Woolley at the painting bee. The woman was a country snob; she had pounced on Kate the first week of church renovations, smelling a potential country snob recruit, homing in on Kate's correct English accent and her "How d' you do?" and her professional husband. On the plus side, Sarah was civilized company for Rain, and Meredith had let Kate have the incomparable Mrs. Boyd, who cleaned like a tornado one morning a week for five dollars an hour.

The last message was the most interesting.

"You won't believe this," she said to Hal when he came back with the last load, a case of twenty-four Black Label. "Jo Graves called to…"

"Who's Jo Graves?"

"Acorn Antiques in Port Hope. The harmonium's back in the shop, it's for sale again! Five hundred and fifty." Hal dumped the beer on the island, ripped open the case and began loading the fridge. "Don't put them all at the front, you're blocking the food!" He twisted open a bottle, gulped half of it. "What about me?" Kate said.

"You want one?"

She intercepted him between the fridge and the island, put her arms around his neck, smiling wantonly. "If we got a harmonium you could learn my big secret: I can play *Inn-A-Gadda-Da-Vida* with two fingers!"

"In other words, you want to spend five hundred and fifty dollars on a conversation piece."

"Creep!" She kissed him. "It's part of the past. It belongs here. I've got the perfect spot for it, look…"

The church was divided into two halves. The large kitchen/dining-room, the vestibule and Kate's studio occupied the south half, above which there was a loft for two bedrooms and the bathroom. They had left the north half of the building open to the roof, filled with light from the high gothic windows and added skylights. A woodstove gleamed where the altar had been; an antique Navajo rug covered the wide pine boards between two chesterfields, big as barges to keep scale with the wide-open space. Against the east wall an open-tread pine staircase, still in need of a rail, led up to the loft, which extended around the living space as a gallery. The walls at the back of the gallery displayed books and art — Kate's watercolours rescued from damp obscurity in the Grace Street basement, some bold acrylics painted here in her new studio.

She made him wait below while she hurried up the stairs and

around the north end of the gallery, above the woodstove. "Right here," she called down, forming a crucifix as she measured with her arms. "Then we can call it the minstrels' gallery!"

"Organ loft," he corrected her. "And your harmonium will look like a toy up there. A pipe organ would be more in scale."

"You think it's a cheesy idea?"

He shrugged and started back to the kitchen with his empty beer bottle.

"Will you come to Port Hope tomorrow anyway and have a look at it?"

"Sure. I need to get lumber for the stair-rail."

Kate heard the hiss as he opened another beer. He was drinking too much, she knew that, but once the pressure was off and the practice had gained its own momentum...

He was tense right now, preoccupied, but that was only natural. Working so hard, she couldn't expect him to change gears at the drop of a hat. They had a whole week to get to know each other again.

She lingered, enjoying her elevated view, feeling a reprise of her earlier contentment at the Van. She loved what they'd done to the church: such a lot of space, and what greater luxury could there possibly be than that? Enough space to hang glide in!

They bought the harmonium, five hundred with delivery. It could go in the basement until they decided where to put it.

"It's prim and Presbyterian," Hal said gloomily, heedless of Jo Graves writing up the bill.

Kate laughed to hide her embarrassment. "Prim and United! Anyway, all it's ever played is hymns; *Inn-A-Gadda-Da-Vida* should blow the cobwebs out!"

They were on their way out, Kate thanking Jo, when Rain twisted away. "Duck!" she cried, toddling towards a collection of decoys nesting in the pulled-out drawer of a Quebec pine dresser.

"Don't touch," Hal warned. Rain kept on going. "I said don't TOUCH!" The shout was so unexpectedly harsh that Rain stopped dead in her tracks and burst into tears.

Shocked, Kate gathered Rain up and carried her weeping from the shop. "That wasn't fair, Hal! She's really good about stuff like that, aren't you Monkey? She never ever just grabs things, she's very careful!"

Hal looked away down the street, muttered something inaudible. Then he was kneeling beside his daughter. "I'm sorry, Rain. Friends, okay? Want to go back and see the ducks?" He held out his arms but Rain only burrowed deeper into Kate's skirts. Kate saw the look of hurt on his face and struggled to unfold her.

"Come on, how about a hug for Daddy? You just have to get used to each other again, that's all. Come on Rain, that's enough!" But Hal was already walking away up the road.

"Hal…wait!"

Resolutely cheerful, Kate insisted they buy ice cream cones in spite of the cool grey weather, because they were on holiday. They stopped at one of the Victorian shops Hal had restored, really not that long ago although it seemed like a lifetime. "Such a pretty town," she said between licks. "If it wasn't for the cars, we could be back in 1800."

"And the ice cream and the parking meters and the video store and…"

"Alright, you've made your point."

"Anyway, it's 1850."

"Excuse me!" It was Kate's turn to be petulant. Except for an hour in Beaver Lumber this morning, choosing wood for the stair-rail, Hal had been a royal pain in the neck. At the bottom of the hill, the town clock chimed two. She saw Hal check his watch to confirm it, impatient to be back at the church with his building supplies and his power tools, a good excuse not to have to communicate. "I suppose you want to go back now."

Hal shrugged. "There's a lot of work to do."

"You can say that again!"

On the way back to the Jeep they passed a parkette with swings and a slide. Inevitably, Rain began tugging on Kate's hand. "Could the stair-rail wait ten minutes?" she said to Hal.

He gave her a scourging look as he hoisted Rain into his arms.

"Want to swing? Sure you do, all monkeys like to swing!" He tried to fit Rain under the sliding safety bar into one of the canvas swing-seats, difficult enough with a co-operative child. She wriggled free and fled towards the slide.

"Let her go," Kate said. She sat down on a wrought-iron bench, patted the place beside her: "Come sit with me a minute." But Hal remained standing beside the bench, tensed, watching Rain begin her ascent up the ladder to the metal platform at the top of the slide, ready to dash if she got into trouble. Kate smiled, reached for his hand and squeezed it reassuringly. "It's alright. She knows what she's doing. I bring her here all the time."

Hal withdrew his hand. "All the time...is that right? Looks like I've got a lot to learn. Maybe I should make a list so I don't boob again. What comes after the church mouse and touching things in stores and playground safety? What else don't I know?"

"Please, babe..."

"Mummy, look!" Rain shot down the slide, her hair streaming behind her like a flag. She landed on her feet and ran back to the swings, manoeuvring under the bar and into the seat with a single convulsion.

"Mummy, push me!"

"Daddy's going to push you," Kate shouted, and gave Hal a push.

"*Mummy* push me!"

For at least two hours each day, Hal faxed or phoned his office about the Distillery. Kate learned that Sawtrell had given them a deadline to come up with acceptable detailing for the town houses. The dimensions had all been finalized, excavation was going ahead, but Julie and Sawtrell were apparently still at loggerheads over the "Georgian Junk" — the stone lions and brass knockers.

The rest of the time, Hal worked on the church like a man possessed. When he had finished the stair-rail, he planed the doors and windows that had warped during the first year; he tiled a back-splash in the kitchen; he took his caulking gun and hunted leaks where Lake Ontario winds drove rainwater through impossible places; he removed the screens and put up the storms, working his way up to the roof where he battened down loose shingles with lead-head nails.

Rain seemed content merely to know that her father was near, reassured by the sounds of him working, impressed by his aura of sweat and sawdust at mealtimes. Kate accepted the fact that he needed the physical activity as much as the church did, accepted it even at bedtime when it brought him instant deep sleep. Whatever was eating him, it was best to let him work it out of his system.

She busied herself sketching some ideas for a mural for the big room — heading into their second winter, cool white had begun to seem a little too cool. Relishing the smoky autumn air, she put to bed her patch of garden. And as usual she filled her life with Rain.

There was the daily beach routine, feeding the quarrelsome geese massing for their winter migration — *their* holidays, Kate explained. They hunted amongst the beach pebbles for the bits of green, water-smoothed glass that were Rain's latest "must-have." They flew the Chinese dragon-kite they had bought at the Vanguard, calling it Puff, though Kate saw nothing of that sweet, gentle dragon in the way it darted and shivered and stabbed at the air.

On Thanksgiving morning she cooked a bumper turkey and at eleven, Hal's sister Elizabeth, her husband Bob and their three boys descended. Elizabeth and Bob generously added a Waldorf salad, two pumpkin pies and a gallon jug of last year's homemade wine to the clutter in the kitchen.

"Ye gods!' laughed Kate. "There's enough wine here to sink a battleship."

"You can bottle what's left," Elizabeth told her.

"Who says there'll be any left?" Bob said, already filling glasses. "Where's Hal?"

"Up on the roof."

Elizabeth raised an eyebrow. "You sound like he's been sent there for bad behaviour." Kate offered no comment. Elizabeth exchanged a look with her husband. "Is there…anything I can do in here?"

"You could lay the table," Kate said.

"Bob's specialty! Isn't it, darling? I'm going up to see my baby brother."

Kate always felt comfortable with Bob, the few times a year she saw him. He was VP at a big advertising agency in the city, media planning — nothing creative about roly-poly, red-faced Bob. But an amusing and amiable man; they chatted easily while Kate basted the turkey and Bob laid the table between trips to admonish the children. They had opted for Thanksgiving lunch rather than dinner to spare themselves over-tired kids; morning-fresh now, Rain and her cousins were howling around the gallery.

Elizabeth returned just as the microwave beeped, meaning the sweet potatoes were done and it was time to carve. Kate said: "Is Hal joining us?"

"Of course he is." Elizabeth lowered her voice confidentially. "Let's save an hour of daylight for ourselves, okay? Take a walk on the beach after lunch."

Kate looked at her, a question hanging in the air before it was swept away by a brawl of hungry children.

At last the family was installed in ladder-back and booster and high chairs, and feeding commenced around the long harvest table.

"Have you thought of a name for this place yet, or is it still 'The Church'?" Elizabeth asked.

"I want it to have a Welsh name," Kate said. "They always give their houses beautiful names."

"Welsh..." pondered Bob. "What is that, Gaelic or Celtic or are they the same?"

"Welsh is the tongue of poets and minstrels," said Kate airily.

Elizabeth laughed: "What's wrong with the tongue of architects and art directors?"

"I never was an art director. I was a paste-up girl and proud of it."

"You weren't proud at all. You hated it."

"Paste-up girl," repeated Bob. "Hmmn...sounds pretty sexy to me."

"Do you know where we get the word 'holidays'?" Kate said to the feeding children.

"Holy days," Hal said to his plate.

"And we're spending our *holy days* in a church!" Kate explained. "Isn't that neat?"

"It's not a church," muttered Hal. "Part of the value of a good building is its adaptability."

Kate and Elizabeth and Bob looked at him, waiting for the old smile, the Groucho waggle of his eyebrows to tell them all it was only his impersonation of a pompous ass. But Hal merely went on eating. Kate saw Bob about to challenge him, saw Elizabeth quieten her husband with a look.

The moment was never resolved — no more than any other grown-up business, attempted and abandoned under the onslaught of four young children, acting up now that the novelty of the meal had worn off, needing encouragement with their vegetables, to be hushed and applauded and scolded and comforted and mopped up and taken to the washroom and mopped up a second time. At three-thirty, Kate and Elizabeth settled the children down to naps and quiet-time amusements, left the dishes for the men and went for their walk on the beach.

So deep was the peace and quiet after their rowdy lunch that for some time neither of them could disturb it. They walked slowly and aimlessly amidst the soft clatter of pebbles, infinite shades of grey.

Eventually Kate said: "See those wet stones?" She pointed them out, at the very edge of the water, their dark gloss and rich patterns renewed with every wave's lapping. "The first time I came down here with Rain, we couldn't believe those stones. We went crazy for them, collected a whole sackful; we could hardly lug it home. It was so disappointing when we went to sort them out."

"They'd dried?"

"Just pale grey like all these others. All the shine was gone, all the colour."

"You could always try polishing them." They walked carefully for another few yards. Then Elizabeth stopped and gave her a plain sideways look. "Isn't that what you do to bring back a shine?"

Kate smiled warily. "Are we talking about pebbles here, or is this...*ta da*...a Metaphor For Life?"

Elizabeth ignored her flippancy. "I don't know, Kate. Is it?"

Kate dug her hands into the pockets of her bomber jacket and walked on. The first crack in the ice, now both of them waited for it to spread. At last Kate said: "Have you any idea how long and hard I dreamed about this, about this place, having time with Rain?"

"I think so. But did you dream about how much it would cost you? And you know I don't mean money. Remember that guy, that amusing, easygoing guy you were married to once?"

"He's got a new, successful practice, Biz. It takes time to get established."

"But how much? After lunch, when Bob suggested you guys go in on the winemaking this year, did you see Hal's reaction? It was just as if Bob had proposed a six-month safari!"

"You don't have to tell me this, Elizabeth."

"Don't I? Have you considered how long your relationship can stand Hal's sixteen-hour days, you coming here with Rain every weekend while he stays at Grace Street? You're apart so much it's becoming a habit you can't even break when you're together!"

So this was what they had talked about. It annoyed Kate to think that Hal had shared so much with his sister on the roof. "You think this is new to me? I am his wife, you know!"

"Yes you are. For richer for poorer."

"Fuck off! How dare you." Kate marched a short way along the beach, whirled around. "This is actually very interesting. What else has he been saying to you?"

Elizabeth spoke evenly, riding Kate's anger: "That he isn't very happy. That he's forgotten how to relax. You know why he's been working on the house all week?"

"It needs work."

"You know that isn't the answer. And it isn't just to keep a wall up between you either. He's starved for dirty work, Kate; he says his business is all administration and networking now. Says he hardly even *draws* these days."

"They're expanding. When he gets more staff…"

"It doesn't work like that. The more people you hire, the more new business you need, the deeper you go. It's a vicious circle."

"Hal said that?" There was a faint note of alarm in Kate's voice.

"Yes." Elizabeth took a deep breath. "And he said something else.

149

I'm not supposed to tell you but I think you should know. He wants to cancel the office expansion. He wants to cut back, do some teaching, get some smaller jobs for a while. Get his hands dirty again."

Kate uttered a hard sarcastic laugh. "I see. Fine. And I suppose that's going to mean 'adjustments' to the way we live. Or should I say readjustments? By the way, has anyone told Rain all this? Sorry, darling, we can't live by the lake any more and Mummy can't take care of you, isn't that too bad, have a lovely childhood at Mrs. Giaraldi's. Ciao!"

"Katy..."

"Shut up!"

Kate turned away, staring out at the lake, her eyes burning, bitterly dry. Halfway to the horizon a sunbeam penetrated the cloud cover, forming a circle of light on the water. Kate had seen the phenomenon before; it looked like a spotlight for some aquatic show — dolphin riding, synchronized swimming, formation water skiing. She watched the hole in the sky close up, the spotlight die, show cancelled. Grey October water again, grey like the pebbles on the beach.

When she spoke again, her voice was very small. "What am I supposed to do, Biz?"

Elizabeth was silent for a long moment. "You must be honest with each other for a start." She bit her lip, gathering fresh resolve.

Kate looked at her cautiously. "What now?"

"Are you seeing someone else?"

Kate stared. "What? Oh this is good! This is bloody incredible, this is. Was that part of your little chat on the roof?" Her voice grew shrill with indignation. "Is that what Hal thinks?"

"I don't know; we didn't discuss it."

"I see. It's what *you* think."

Elizabeth said calmly: "Do you remember a couple of months ago, I told you I was looking for a sitter and I asked you if you were still using Mrs. Giaraldi?"

"Vaguely. What of it?"

"You said you'd found a teenager on Grace Street for three-fifty an hour, that you'd hardly spoken to Mrs. Gee in a year. You said she reminded you too much of the bad old days."

"Okay. So what?"

"Last week I happened to be on Harbord and I remembered the Italian cheese shop you've always raved about. I bought a pound of asiago and some olives and I was on my way out when I met Mrs. Gee coming in with Rain."

Kate felt her cheeks burning. "Which day was that?"

"Wednesday afternoon."

"There you go. I used Mrs. Gee in a pinch last Wednesday afternoon. Big deal. I can't even remember..."

"Every other Wednesday, Kate. Every other Wednesday afternoon."

"Huh?"

"I said to Mrs. Gee it must be nice to see Rain again after so long, and she said oh no, she takes care of her every other Wednesday afternoon. I asked how come, and she said you go to drawing class at Central Tech, which I know for a fact you don't. They haven't held life drawing classes at Central for five years."

"I suppose you checked that."

Silence.

Kate stared at the horizon for a long time before she said: "Hal doesn't know?"

Elizabeth shook her head. She looked at Kate with a mixture of sadness and expectation. Kate wandered a little way away, sketched absently in the pebbles with her toe, then turned back.

"It isn't how you think."

CHAPTER
21

Shane dropped Tyah at Les's high rise at eight p.m., then gunned the Continental around the turning circle with his usual yap of tires. He only waited if it was a new client; Les was a steady date.

During the year, she had needed to page Shane only once for assistance — the time that guy had wanted to put his foot inside her. Tyah thought he was joking, said: "Only if you're size thirteen, ha ha."

"No, no…it's okay, really," the guy reassured her. "I'm a nine. And I cut my toenails."

"You want me to leave right now?"

"Just try. Please?"

"No."

"Come on. Just try."

"You don't hear good? I said no!"

"TRY!"

The worst part was having to be grateful to Shane for almost killing him: "Wanna foot-fuck, guy? Fuck this! Wanna fist-fuck?"

Tyah crossed the lobby, the kind a lot of high rise buildings have, with the seating area no one ever uses — like a living room suite except the lamp and the vase and the fake oil paintings are all screwed down. She walked into a vacant elevator, her eyes flickering over the control panel as the doors dragged shut, locating the red alarm button. Elevators made Tyah nervous. Everyone thought about being stuck between floors and needing the bathroom, but for a junkie, imprisoned in the dark, maybe for hours, needing a fix...it was about as clear an idea of hell as Tyah could get. She was feeling buzzed out anyway from the speedball before she left, Shane's treat because she was a good girl, ready on time.

At the fourteenth floor the doors opened on a corridor carpeted in threadbare turquoise. From the apartment at the far end, she could hear the inevitable vintage Zeppelin. She followed the music, clicking her fingernails in time. It was the speed working on her, nerves not nervousness; there would be no surprises with Les.

The forty-two-year-old man who was paying two hundred for the next hour with Tyah had never found anything in his life to replace Led Zeppelin. His bachelor apartment was papered, floor to ceiling, with posters of "the only rock and roll group in the fuckin' world, man!" As a younger fan, Les had travelled six times by plane to hear them, twice across the Atlantic, though he never got to meet the band. The nearest he got, Les figured, was balling a chick who claimed to have balled John Bonham the week before he died. Les drove a delivery van and may or may not have been in a bar band once, but he was definitely going to play air-guitar for her tonight, smoke up and turn on his red mood light and "play the fuckin' *sap* of it!" And at the point where the hard rocking part began in the otherwise mystical *Stairway to Heaven*, Tyah was going to for sure get to suck Jimmy Page's cock.

Les Zeppelin. Ha ha.

Shane picked her up at ten after nine in the Continental. It wasn't his car, it belonged to Sam Wexel, the owner of the French Quarter where Shane had risen to manager in the last six months.

Two events had spawned Tyah's present relationship with Shane: first, Hyacinth got busted a second time and went down to Kingston to the P4W, just around the time Tyah's addiction hit two hundred dollars a day. Then Shane told her about his moonlighting idea.

He said he was working it for a number of girls at the Quarter, like this: it was mentioned to certain regular and reliable customers at the club that some of the girls were "special," meaning that Shane could arrange for a private appointment and yes, you could touch. As long as it was handled discreetly and he got his forty percent, Sam Wexel was only too pleased for his club to be used as the showroom, happy to lend Shane his Lincoln and give him time off to chauffeur the girls to and from their appointments. Shane heard Tyah had a big jones, that she was hard up. Why not let bygones be bygones? Why not come and dance at the Quarter?

"You awake?" Shane said outside Les's. "Nine-fifteen now, you got eleven o'clock — Burgess, Jarvis Street and Richmond."

"Me and who else?" In his seventies, Norbert Burgess normally required a stag show, two girls in school uniform, best friends, "curious" about each other.

"Just you tonight, must be love. You got less than two hours. You want I drop you home or what?" His fingers flittered through Les's crumpled bills. "Make up your mind, Tyah, I need to get back to the club." He leaned across and stuffed Tyah's fifty into the space between her thighs. The quarter/three-quarter split was unfair but it still meant fifty bucks tax free for an hour's work, and she was getting her dope at a discount.

"Hey!" Shane flicked her thigh, stingingly, with the backs of his fingers. "Wake the fuck up!"

Tyah roused herself from the deep leather seat. She wanted to be alone, to walk home, as if walking could get the Les taste out of her mouth and the ringing out of her ears. "You don't have to drive me anywhere." She made a move for the door handle and felt little steel fingers digging into her arm.

"I'm protecting my assets. Anyway..." He released her, reached into the breast of his silk jacket, tossed a nickel bag onto her lap. "I'm a nice guy, right?" He started the car and squealed out of the circle, wringing the leather wheel as a temporary substitute for the rubber ball in his pocket.

Tyah said: "You're not a nice guy. You're an asshole in a pimpmobile thinks he's tough shit."

"Asking for a smack mouth, Ty."

"Smack away, asshole. I don't need teeth in my line of work." It really wasn't that funny, but Shane laughed half way to Dowde Street.

Like a lot of people, Tyah had looked in the directory after Bell installed the phone, just to see her own name and address in print. After the initial indignity of finding eleven other people with her last name, she was able to appreciate the anonymity of a phone book listing.

No one chancing upon "**Whiteside T 39 Dowde**" would ever see the naked bulb swinging in the drafty, littered hallway, the parched linoleum flaking off the stairs. They couldn't hear the crackpot in the room next to Tyah's arguing with the walls. Best of all, the phone book had no smell — of stale laundry and hot-plate cooking and one filth-speckled bathroom per floor. When Shane found the place, all that mattered was the low rent. Now she dealt with her situation by staying high and eating out and plain getting used to it. She was getting used to a lot of things, bit by bit.

Tyah kicked the thin door shut behind her and took Shane's freebie to the table, a Formica relic on drunken chrome legs. She licked her finger and sampled, identifying the ingredients of another speedball, the heroin-amphetamine cocktail that is one of the few ways a habitual user can party with heroin. Not that Shane's motives were anything but selfish — he knew that a speedball would tempt her away from a straight fix, from nodding off and missing her eleven o'clock appointment.

Tyah called for a cab for a quarter to eleven, then prepared her injection in the usual way, dissolving the powder in water in a spoon heated over a stub of candle. Shane kept her busy enough that she didn't have to dance much these days; when she did, her costume included long evening gloves to hide the tracks on her arms, which were almost played out now.

She tied off her right leg above the knee and sat on the edge of the plaid sofa bed, resembling a hurdler with her left leg tucked under and her right stretched out. She steadied her fingers, then slipped the hard needle in, booting blood and drugs back and forth, in and out of the syringe to prolong the rush. Good music.

When the music died, Tyah found herself with some surplus voltage of amphetamine energy and about forty-five minutes before her cab was due. She turned on the TV, which was snowing on both available channels, snowing in Miami on Crockett and Tubbs, still wasting Colombians in rerun limbo. But she kept it on for company while she used up energy tidying — something that didn't get done in the normal course of coming home and fixing and going on the nod. She tidied in decreasing circles around the table — clothing and *People* and sticky glasses full of cigarette butts and balled-up tissues. She left a sealed brown manila envelope in full view on the table, a reminder to post it tonight on her way to Burgess.

Apart from the sofa bed and the table and a chair, the only other furnishings were a plywood dresser and a sour-smelling cardboard closet of the type moving companies use, both holding her costumes. There were two appliances, the TV and a countertop refrigerator balanced on a milk crate in the absence of a counter.

The fridge was a problem; Tyah had unplugged it a couple of months ago, unable to bear its racket — a sizzling sound like stinging insects. There had been a meatball submarine in it at the time, which meant there was one there now (a meatball mutant by this time), but there was no way she was going to open the door to see. One of these days Shane was just going to have to take the fridge somewhere and dump it.

Everything else was long gone. The Chevette first, the sewing machine and the serger, the cutting table and the judy, her stock of leather and fabrics — Hyacinth had found new homes for all of it, part of the service for a steady customer. Tyah hadn't lost Fletch until the day he came home and found the big cactus gone. That was the day he gave up his bid to turn her around, to keep them together — Fletcher's bid for sainthood. He wasn't angry, she could have handled that. It was as though something in him, the devoted part that sustained them both, had quietly and suddenly failed. Maybe the hardest part was knowing she could not have expected anything else.

He called once, months later, from Honolulu of all places. Tyah was pretty stoned. Fletcher cried on the phone when he realized she was having physical trouble talking to him. Since then she had tried to keep him out of mind, like the rest of her former life. Out of sight and out of mind, like the contents of the fridge...like the photos ought to have been.

The packet of photographs in the manila envelope on the table should have been in a shoe box at the bottom of the dresser — would have been there had not Tyah's cowgirl outfit (which she never wore anymore) slipped off its hanger last week, and had not Tyah accidentally dipped into the vest pocket and found a slip of paper with a name on it.

Hal Sebastian. Not that she'd ever really forgotten about him. But actually seeing his name made her do a foolish thing, which had been to go to the shoe box and take out the photographs for the first time in the year and a half since Carny died. Foolish because that same night last week, Tyah had started having the dream.

She was on a roller-coaster at night, sitting behind Felice, Nicole, Suzanne, Lena DiMaio, Mary Jo Korenycky and Sandra Dell. In the last car, way behind, was the young Chinese man that had killed her friends — the face that she had been unable to evoke for Sergeant Hamray that was, perversely, so terribly clear in her nightmare. The roller-coaster only went down, hurtling faster and faster, everybody screaming their heads off, and every time Tyah looked back, the killer was another row nearer her, immune to the gravity that was pinning her to her seat.

Now she woke up every night drenched with sweat, smothering and struggling in the heavy, flickering curtain of the dream. Then she would lie awake for hours seething with guilt. But what was she supposed to do? She was a junkie. It was her job to stay away from police, from surveillance and interrogation — from anything that took up more than six hours maximum between one fix and the next. Look what happened the last time over a lousy roach. Carny was dead, Christ knew where Horace was these days...*fuck* the police.

Although Tyah couldn't bring herself to destroy or throw away the photograph of Felice's killer, neither could she bear its presence in her room any longer. Her compromise was the sealed manila envelope on the table, addressed to Hal Sebastian at 361 Grace Street, the address that matched his number in the phone book. Right up until she was licking the envelope, Tyah had imagined she would only send Hal Sebastian his Vanguard shots, eighteen months late. Tossing that other picture in at the last moment was an irrational impulse, she had tried to tell herself, but she knew that wasn't so. She was leaving the door open, if only a crack. And one day, if she ever got it together...

The phone rang. It was Shane with her wake-up call. There had been a change, Burgess wanted a show after all. She'd be playing doubles with Patrice, which was too bad: Patrice had the worst breath and she couldn't act worth shit.

CHAPTER
22

Hal's office was electric with Monday morning energy. He was waylaid by Gloria with a deck of messages three inches high, the Canon rep caught him with brochures and prices on a new stepless zoom colour copier, the Bell technician wanted to know if she could go through the drywall to trace the glitches in the multi-line system. And finally, Don Wales needed approval on the mechanical drawings for the expansion, which Hal withheld.

It was ten-thirty before he was able to get to the main business of the day. Julie had been out at a site meeting, but now she marched in with the roll of new Distillery drawings shouldered like a rifle. Hal could feel the displacement of air in his office, caught the disturbing fragrance of her hair, which was out of its pony-tail, long and glossy black.

She dropped the drawings on his desk and gave him an appraising look: "I dunno Hal, guy goes on vacation for the first time in a year and a half, he's supposed to come back looking all rested up."

Hal frowned. "How do I look?"

She turned and began smoothing the drawings across his desk, uncharacteristically tidy after a week away. "Like something the cat dragged in," she said casually, then glanced round at him and laughed, full of fun. "I am about to show you some very critical drawings; you wouldn't want me to try and soften you up!"

Hal raised his eyebrows. "Wanna bet?"

Julie's elevations for the Distillery houses were exactly what Hal would have done given *carte blanche*, evidence of how close their thinking had grown in the last eighteen months. The houses took their cue from the distillery at the hub of the development — a functionally grand, thick-walled, five-story building with a proliferation of shuttered windows. A fine, plain building. Julie's houses were plain, too: no bay windows, no safe wrought-iron railings, no carriage lamps or stone lions or brass knockers...no bankrupt Georgian Junk.

He came to the end of the drawings and sat quietly, his fingers monitoring the pulse in his temple. He eased himself back in the chair, made a mask of his hands and drew it down over his face.

"They're wonderful," he said. "You must have burned a few gallons of midnight oil."

"So did Don and Gloria."

"When's our deadline on this?"

"Monday. A week from today."

Hal nodded slowly, chewing his bottom lip. "Could you leave them with me for half an hour?" Julie looked surprised. "Please Jules?"

At noon, he still wasn't taking phone calls. However much he scrutinized the drawings on his desk, nothing became clear except the problem.

Midland wouldn't buy them. Sawtrell would take one look and the shit would come down in big warm lumps and bury them.

Did he want that to happen? Ron Allis had faded into the woodwork after his Vanguard defeat, making Midland the kind of client most architects could only dream of. Already they were talking about a third job, twice as big as the Distillery. Whatever he may have said to Elizabeth on the church roof, there were other factors to consider before committing corporate suicide.

Julie would be okay — twenty-four, unattached, with a talent like hers. But what about Gloria bringing up three kids on her own?

What about Don Wales with an ex-wife who took him to the cleaners first of every month?

What about Kate and Rain?

These town houses at six hundred thousand a crack…a lot of people working a lot of hours to buy into the Distillery, to send their families first class. But of course they weren't like him, were they? These guys were robots, or congenitally happy idiots. These guys came muscling up the garden path every night at eight o'clock with happy, fulfilled grins behind their eight o'clock shadows: *Whistle While You Work*, swiping up the evening edition, patting the dumb dog, ruffling Junior's hair — "Mmmm…smells good, honey!"

Or were they just regular guys keeping their end up, unselfish enough — mature enough — to face their responsibilities?

Good guys.

Hal was still looking for an answer as he parked the company Pontiac on Grace Street at seven p.m. He had taken the train from Oshawa this morning, leaving Kate with the Jeep till Wednesday. Busy with her painting bee, she said. True or not, she had every right to eschew his company after last week: he'd been a major jerk.

He plowed a thick drift of mail with the front door. He gathered it up and carried it to the kitchen, opening windows along the way to release the stale smell of a house unoccupied for ten days. In spite of a local dope crisis, the ice and crack with its attendant crime explosion, the house was just as they had left it.

Hal and Kate owned 361 Grace Street now, having made the landlord a solid offer one week after Breakers II rented. Kate had given her excitement full rein, a dust-shrouded, pickaxe-wielding fury as she smashed the walls that had confined them for eight years. The result was a spacious open-plan on the ground floor, with three upstairs bedrooms plus a converted attic. The Boys must have been happier on the second floor than anyone thought — they had maintained a cool silence since their departure. Hal felt badly about that.

A search of smooth kitchen drawers and pastel cupboards produced sardines in tomato sauce, which Hal ate out of the tin with Ritz crackers. He was no stranger to this scene, here alone, like a bachelor, with Kate and Rain out at the church. Sometimes he walked up to the San Lorenzo for a Caesar, listened to twenty-year-old Italian guys arguing about soccer and old guys about bocciball, doing take-home work by a candle in a lumpy red glass. He didn't want to go there tonight; it would remind him that he was going to be thirty-eight in a couple of weeks — maybe not bocci yet, but he wasn't soccer any more was he? There were things he hesitated to lift now, times he realized, in disgust, that he had tuned the car radio to an easy-listening station. And all those times Rain's lovely eighteen-year-old babysitter called him *Mister* Sebastian:

"Goodnight, Mr. Sebastian."

"Goodnight now, Andrea."

Jesus…he sounded like Fred MacMurray!

Hal felt lonelier tonight than usual. He missed Kate and Rain. Especially Kate. How long since they had opened a bottle of wine, put something schmaltzy on the stereo — Antonio Carlos Jobim — and danced slow? He found his heart beating faster at the thought of making love with his wife…shy, uncertain lovers because it had been so long.

He pushed away his plate and picked miserably through the heap of unopened mail. Bills and begging letters, nothing interesting except the October *Esquire* and a brown manila envelope addressed to him in big, unsteady capitals. He was about to open it when a sudden, surprising impulse took him to the cupboard under the sink where he found a plastic shopping bag, which he brought to the table and excitedly stuffed with mail.

"Hit the road, Jack! Truckin'!"

He knew about the construction on the 401 eastbound, a last gasp before winter. He would open all this mail, even pay some bills for something to do if he hit a jam.

Why was he here? He didn't *want* to be here! He wanted to be at the church with his family. He wanted to see Kate, to dance with Kate, to make love with Kate.

He wanted to say he was sorry.

The transition from city to country did not become a reality until Hal shut off his engine and lights. The silent darkness was a wonderful shock. The thump of the car door, the crunch of gravel, the scrape of his shoes on the church steps — every sound isolated and crystal clear. He stood in silence on the top step, inhaling cool clean air touched with woodsmoke. He saw only a sprinkling of stars at first. Then, gradually, his eyes adjusted after the highway glare and he saw a heavenful.

It was warm and new wood-smelling inside the church. A soft orange glow spilled down the stairs. He dropped the bag of mail on the kitchen table and followed the light, taking pride and pleasure in the solid smoothness of his pine stair-rail. Halfway up, he called out so as not to frighten Kate, but the portable TV was on in their bedroom and she didn't hear.

He looked in on Rain. As usual, she was lying across the bed, legs dangling over the edge, duvet in a heap on the floor. He very gently placed her lengthwise, covered her, then knelt by the bed. He brushed a stray curl off her forehead and laid his head on the pillow next to hers where he could feel the gentle blush of her heat, get the clean milky smell of her. Her face had started to mature, to find definition, but not a lot. The baby was still there in the roundness of her cheeks, her button nose. Little clown. Down here, so close, he could almost imagine himself into an innocent, magic world where everything was new and simple, every problem fleeting. Who was the guardian of that world if not himself? He whispered: "Goodnight, baby," and kissed her tender, slightly smiling mouth.

Kate was lying outside the covers in her grey Nike sweats, dozing. He quietly spoke her name. She became aware of him slowly, through half-lidded eyes. Drowsily she reached for the remote and turned off the television.

They looked at each other without speaking. Kate propped on her elbow now, Hal standing by the door. At last he toed off his shoes and went to her, lay down and took her in his arms and kissed her, a gentle remedial kiss. He slipped his hand under her sweat top, around to the silky small of her back. He quickened, pulling her against him, withdrawing when he felt her resistance.

Kate said: "Julie called."

Hal sighed his disappointment, rolled onto his back and looked up at the ceiling. "Was it so important?"

"I thought you'd want to know: Midland called your office after you left — the Distillery deadline has been moved up to this Thursday."

"Jesus."

"A brick shortage or something; Midland has to place its order as soon as possible. Julie wants to know if you've come to a decision on the drawings, whether she has to re-do them. She said she'd start tonight, although it's getting a little late now."

"Did she tell you what re-doing them means?"

"Brass lions?"

"*Stone* lions!" he snapped. "Stone lions and *brass* knockers!" He swung his legs off the bed, plunged his face into his hands. He sighed deeply. "I'm sorry, Kate. I came here to be nice to you."

Kate said anxiously: "Is it true you could lose Midland over this?"

Hal stood up. He walked slowly towards the night-black window, towards himself reflected in its panes: face to face with a nearly thirty-eight-year-old husband and father. "Don't worry," he said quietly. "That's not going to happen. I'm not going to let it happen."

He saw Kate's reflection get up, grow in the black window. He felt her hands on his shoulders. "Let's go down and have a drink," she said. "There's something I want to tell you. Something I should have told you before, but now may be the best time after all."

Kate filled two blue Mexican glasses with Bob's wine and brought them to the woodstove, where Hal sat waiting on one of the big chesterfields. Kate sat on the Navajo rug at his feet, drew her knees up to her chin and looked at the fire. After a moment, she said: "Do you remember when I went to Port Hope and met with Alistair Crawford on your behalf?"

"How could I forget? You got us the Vanguard."

"Your design got it. But I helped." She took a sip of wine. "Maybe I can help again."

Hal frowned. "You mean see Alistair Crawford again? About the Distillery?"

"He listened to me once."

"Of course he did. The Young Turks were getting too uppity for the old man's liking; you provided him with the opportunity to slap them down."

She looked crestfallen.

"Don't get me wrong. It was wonderful what you did, Katy...all that research, meeting with him; you were amazing. But this is different. No one's withholding information from Crawford, Allis has gone, there's no axe to grind with Sawtrell. It's straight business this time and architects' wives simply do not meet company presidents in parking lots and force multi-million-dollar business decisions." He gave her an apologetic smile. "Not twice!"

"He will listen to me."

"I appreciate the offer, Katy." He took her hand. "Is this what you had to tell me?"

She gave him a level stare. "No."

Hal let go of her hand. "What, then?"

"Alistair Crawford will listen to me because I've seen him *since* that day in Port Hope. In fact, I've seen him every other week, more or less, for over a year."

Hal stared. "I don't understand."

"Of course you don't, and I should have told you when it started, but..."

"When what started?"

She almost smiled. "Don't worry. It's nothing like that."

"Like what?"

Kate growled. "Why don't you let me *tell* you?"

"This is amazing!"

She took a deep breath. "That first time, in Port Hope, he mentioned that he would invite me out to Mead End — that's the name of his place. A couple of months later, I hadn't heard so I called him up and invited myself. I wanted to see the house and garden, which is fabulous by the way — like stepping into another world, a little piece of England. We got on famously, just like the first time, and he told me to come back whenever I liked. So I did. I do. Whenever I like. I leave Rain with Mrs. Gee and go, every other Wednesday. He's a perfect gentleman, good company, charming..."

"Lonely."

"Yes, but he never plays it up. Feeling sorry for him is not why I go there."

"Why, then? And why the hell didn't you tell me?" He looked at her, hurt and angry. "Is he Grandy? Is that what it's about?"

"I thought you might say that."

"Well? Back to the secret garden, Kate's lost childhood? Why else would you have to sneak away there by yourself if you're not screwing him — what's the opposite of cradle snatching by the way? Grave robbing?"

Kate jumped up, spilling wine. "Don't be obscene! I'm telling you tonight because I want to *help* you! Who do you think got you the damn Distillery in the first place?"

He stared. "What did you say?"

"Wake up, Hal! If you had one grain of business acumen, you'd have made sure you stuck to Midland like glue after the Vanguard! But oh no...one job at a time for dear old Hal. Except the real grown-up world doesn't wait for the dear old Hals. You have to *push*!"

His astonishment raced with sudden, blinding anger.

The anger won. "I see. And now you want to push dear old Hal again, so you decide to tell him about your little liaison with Sugar Daddy." He couldn't help the sarcasm dripping off his voice. "Because you want to help? How considerate! Of course it wouldn't be because of any sudden little urge to be straightforward with your husband! Dear me, no. Honesty doesn't count that much with you, does it? Honesty wouldn't be enough of a motive for Grandy's girl! Who are you helping here, anyway?" Hal suddenly shouted. "Me? Or *yourself* as usual?"

Kate stared at him, her eyes huge, glittering with tears. He turned and walked away to the kitchen with his empty glass.

Shocked and trembling, he filled it with wine and gulped it down, then filled it again. He heard Kate going upstairs, heard the bedroom door close firmly behind her. He felt the urge to go up after her, to learn more, but he was still too hot — there would be more ugly words, which he didn't want. He needed to cool down. Some objectivity.

Hal returned to the big room and turned on the television, blipping from one inane talk show to another while he drank his wine. He turned the TV off and went back to the kitchen and poured himself a finger of brandy, then set himself the therapeutically mindless task of going through the mail. The outbound traffic had been moving after all on the 401, slowly but steadily enough that no bills had been paid. He saw to them now — hydro, gas, telephone, taxes — all of them in duplicate, one set for Grace Street, another for the church. Triplicate if you counted the office. Two cars to pay for and maintain, and Kate was talking about a boat next summer. They owed VISA over five thousand dollars for September, a conspicuous part of it for restaurants and clothing stores Hal had never heard of.

Hal felt his anger rising again, fresh and hot. *Kate and Crawford...every other Wednesday..."Who do you think got you the damn Distillery in the first place?"*

Hal tore distractedly at the big manila envelope, which he had saved until last — his carrot for getting through the bills — and shook out a packet of photographs, a Kodak pack from a one-hour developer in Toronto. He picked off the sticky-tape closure and emptied about a dozen colour prints onto the table. His mind still blurred by anger, he had looked at more than half the photographs before he realized they were his.

The Vanguard shots, the ones he had taken with the Leica — *lost* with the Leica nearly two years ago!

Mystified, he retrieved the manila envelope, turned it over; there was a week-old Toronto postmark but no return address. The inner envelope bore, along with the Kodak logo, that of a familiar one-hour service at Yonge and Dundas, downtown.

He went back to the pictures, all pre-restoration Vanguard until the very bottom of the pile. This one wasn't his. An underlit closeup of an Asian man, Hal guessed Chinese. A round, pale, slightly smiling face — a conceited smile. A strange face and yet...vaguely familiar. Could he have taken it? Hal had no recollection of doing so; he didn't *know* any Chinese apart from Julie and her family.

He examined the manila envelope again. Who had sent it? Was it possible he'd removed the film that day before he lost the camera? Maybe Kate had found it and dropped it off at Yonge and Dundas, then forgotten. Maybe the store was clearing out unclaimed orders...

He picked up the Kodak packet and turned it over, and now he saw a name — "T. Whiteside" — on the order form, and a phone number with a Beaches prefix. Whiteside...Hal racked his brains but came up blank. The order was dated a year ago last May.

He returned to the picture of the Chinese man. Maybe T. Whiteside wasn't ringing any bells but *something* was. Something about his face...whispering...something just out of reach.

Hal glanced at the clock on the microwave: nearly eleven-thirty. Too late to call T. Whiteside now. The mystery would have to wait till tomorrow. He stood up and went to the wall phone anyway, because wasn't he supposed to call Julie about the Distillery, because

I want to hear her voice.

The clear, unbidden thought caught Hal so much by surprise that he almost dropped the phone as he put it smartly back on the hook, like something too hot to touch.

Stupid. He'd just had a fight with his wife and he'd been drinking. Double stupid. Julie was his friend and his employee.

Nothing more.

Hal's cheeks were burning as he called her apartment and got her machine. Then he called the office and got Gloria on tape. Julie was close to her family, spent lots of nights at home. Just because he couldn't reach her at eleven-thirty on a Monday night didn't necessarily mean she was with...

Hal terminated his foolishness, disgusted with himself. He took a last hard swallow of brandy and put his glass in the sink. On his way out of the kitchen he lingered for a parting look at the photographs, thinking what a pity about his camera; it had gone relatively unmourned in the shadow of darker events at the Doyle. The Leica had always taken beautiful pictures.

Not that this face was beautiful, this Chinese man. Quite the opposite, Hal thought, although he had no real reason for thinking it — there was nothing about the features that could be called ugly. Why the whispering? Where had he seen it before?

He could feel the answer close by, only just out of reach. It would come to him. On the other hand, he was having more trouble than ever with his memory these days — another dismaying symptom of approaching middle age. Or was it just that he had twice as much to remember?

Exhausted and quite drunk, Hal turned out the lights and went unsteadily up the stairs, grateful for the support of his new stair-rail.

Kate was sprawled in the middle of the bed. Hal gently moved her arm and lowered himself onto the available narrow shelf of mattress. He turned his back to her, nudging her over with subtle pressures.

"Mmmnn?"

"Hi Katy," he whispered. He wanted her to wake up. In spite of what had happened tonight, he wanted her to know that he would stand by his word on the Distillery, that he was ready to try and understand her reasons for secrets…Grandy or whatever. That he was sorry for the things he had said in anger. He turned to her, reached for her hand but her breathing had already fallen back into the rhythm of sleep, her fingers lying cool and still in his.

Crash…one of those computer words they were trying to teach him, like "interface" and "handshake." But of course they used to say "crash" in the old days, didn't they? In the good old days it used to mean going to sleep.

Hal shut his eyes and waited for the peaceful picture he often conjured up when he needed to sleep: the Ancaster house with its cool, quiet rooms, fragrant with the scent of new carpentry. He waited to be transported to the shade of his kindly oak, to gaze out over a summer lawn at a white gazebo glowing like a shrine.

But sleep came only fitfully, a half-sleep of bad dreams, a steady, relentless delirium of fearful images: an old-fashioned elevator counter gone haywire, its pointer blurring clockwise, anti-clockwise; a steel fire door banging off its hinges, wrenched by some invisible force; waves running onto the shore, never breaking or receding, only gaining, gaining; an unmoored kite, darting, stabbing the whispering air, its string trailing just out of reach...a dragon kite with a familiar face.

CHAPTER
23

As soon as they were in the door, Rain made a dash for Mrs. Gee's living room. The furniture was plastic-covered but there was plenty of china on low shelves, far from Kate's taste, but no less breakable for that. She took a firm hold of Rain's hand and tried to lead her out.

"Jesus!" exclaimed Rain.

"*What*?" Then she looked back where Rain was looking, at the hippy Messiah over the mantle, long-haired, bearded — sexy! Maybe Mrs. Gee's taste wasn't so bad after all!

She squatted in the dark hallway, the zipper of her open jacket rattling against floral ceramic tiles as she kissed her daughter goodbye. "Mummy'll be back at five o'clock to take you home." She looked up at Mrs. Gee hovering behind Rain. "I'm sorry to keep landing her on you for lunch."

"Sorry nothing!" Mrs. Gee scolded, shooing her out. They waved from the porch, Mrs. Gee hugging Rain from behind, patting her tummy. "I make a special lunch, cappelli di pagliaccio. You pick up Rain tonight, you gonna need a truck!" Clown's hat pasta, Rain's favourite. Thank God it's not every day anymore, Kate thought as she unlocked the Jeep; Rain would be a chubby *bambina* by now, with a gold crucifix and cheap little earrings.

Kate hit the inevitable construction on the eastbound 401. She took advantage of the slow going to look in her bag, to check that she had remembered the Vanguard shots for Alistair, pinched from Hal's mystery package.

But it probably wasn't a mystery at all; ten to one he'd unloaded the Leica before he lost it, taken the film into the One Hour at Yonge and Dundas and forgotten all about it. Some good soul at the developer's had been clearing out unclaimed orders, sent them out with the right mailing envelope but someone else's order form. Kate had pilfered the best shots of the Vanguard and the negative strips in case Alistair wanted enlargements — some good "before" pictures of his favourite building.

Kate braked for the hundredth time behind a smelly, hissing tractor-trailer. It was eleven-fifteen; at this rate she'd be late and Matilde would be stroppy when she served lunch, clattering dishes and muttering. Frustrated, imprisoned in the car with nothing to do, Kate delved into the side-pocket of her bag for the cellophane sheath of negatives and held it up to the windshield.

Still no bells rang — no idea who the Chinese man was, as she had told Hal. The Beaches telephone number on the order-form was no longer in service, so T. Whiteside had been a dead end. But there was probably a simple explanation for the Chinese picture, too, which Hal had also forgotten. He was chronically absent-minded, and it *was* nearly two years ago.

Things were still strained between them after the blowup on Monday night. Hal had made a show of reconciliation, had given her a copy of Julie's original drawings for the Distillery houses to take to Mead End today, with which to petition Alistair. But he was still angry, proving it by his decision to go ahead with revisions anyway, the stone lions and brass knockers for tomorrow's meeting. Insurance, he called it, but Kate knew it was more than that: it was his way of showing his disapproval, of rejecting her help.

Fine. If Hal wanted to look a gift horse in the mouth, that was his problem. But it would be hers too if he ended up having to compromise on the Distillery. Whatever he promised now, he might think twice about taking on Midland's next big job — at the very least, he would be hell to live with, like last week at the church.

Eventually the traffic began to flow and then the sun came out. She made good time after all and was able to enjoy the country road that wound prettily through the hills north of Port Hope. Fall had been early this year and the colours were at their zenith — it looked as though a sea of fire had parted to make the road, billowing red and gold on either side. She saw a hawk skimming the treetops, menacing grace, hovering for a few seconds in the deep air, passing like a shadow.

It was five to twelve when she turned in between Mead End's tall stone gateposts. She maintained a sedate pace along the driveway, relishing the luxurious crunch of gravel beneath her tires, the stately parade of maples on both sides, anticipation mounting as she waited to glimpse the house. Eventually, the maples gave way to fat cedar hedges, a forty-year-old planting, clipped into restrained topiary spheres and obelisks.

And there it was. A mansion by any standard, yet in tranquil agreement with its setting, Mead End was simply the most beautiful house Kate had ever seen outside England — probably because it *was* English in everything but location. It was built of imported Hornton stone (richer even than its Cotswold relative), soft and golden like sponge toffee. A real Edwardian, reminiscent of a Voysey or a Lutyens house with its tall, dreaming chimneys, the roofline lowered like benignly serious brows over deep, leaded windows.

Still fifty yards from the house, the main driveway forked and Kate took the smaller, secondary drive, parking just outside a high-walled courtyard between the rear of the house and the stable block, now converted to garages. As she climbed down from the Jeep, Greg opened a side door.

"Good afternoon, Mrs. Sebastian."

Kate managed a lukewarm smile. "Is it?" She glanced at her watch: exactly two minutes after twelve. "Yes, Greg, good afternoon."

Greg was always icily correct. He was wearing another of the sleek suits she had first seen in Port Hope when he had summoned her outside Acorn Antiques. She had never seen him without his tan, as deep in February as in August. Kate imagined that Greg had a tanning parlour set up in his quarters, could picture him in his off-hours, leafing through *G.Q.* while he slogged away on that tan.

"Mr. Crawford is on the west terrace. The courtyard gate is open. I assume you know the way by now."

"Yes, thank you."

His insinuation, clear and ironic, followed her into the courtyard. She pulled her leather jacket close, aware that the side door hadn't closed, which meant he was probably standing there watching her. Was he protecting his boss, she wondered, or his own turf? Like Matilde, Greg had been with Alistair for several years; he would no doubt be hanging on now, expecting the moon when his elderly employer died.

Kate cleared her mind of such gloomy thoughts with a deep breath of fresh air as she strode through the courtyard past the converted stable, now home to four thoroughbred motor cars, including the green Jaguar. At the far west end of the courtyard she opened a wooden door set into the wall and joined a mossy stone path through the bountiful kitchen garden. Kate must have helped herself to bushels of fruit over the course of last summer, telling herself she was saving it from the squabbling birds. Who else was it for?

Beyond another high garden wall, the tennis court begged the same question. Its net was strung tautly at competition height, its playing surface immaculately maintained. For whom? Obviously not Alistair. Either it was for weekend guests or he kept it up as a reminder of past glories. Knowing his sporting history, one could have forgiven him keeping a tack or gunroom with Hemingway-esque photographs of himself on safari or shark fishing, to say: "Look at me in my prime!" But apart from his Oriental carpets, she couldn't remember seeing *anything* from his past, as though he'd severed it when he left the East. Perhaps all that stuff was in some upstairs room she'd never seen, like a shrine. The house was certainly big enough to keep secrets.

She reached wide, semi-circular steps, climbed them to the west terrace. He was turned slightly away from her in a weathered-silver teak chair, his face tilted into the sun. His wheelchair, a kind of three-wheeled, battery-powered scooter, was parked beside him. The arthritis had worsened in the last year, so much so that Kate had not seen him walk, other than between chair and wheelchair, for six months.

Kate could tell from the slow rise and fall of his overcoat that he had dozed off while waiting for her. It touched her, producing an unexpectedly warm, protective feeling, like she sometimes had when she watched her sleeping daughter. Unwilling to wake him, other than by the small sounds of her presence, she walked quietly around his chair until she reached the stone balustrade at the perimeter of the terrace.

The west outlook was over the rose garden. Bereft of roses now, it was still impressive with its intricate gravel walks converging on a goldfish pond. At the edge of the black water was a beautiful and unusual fountain: two slender Arabian jars, one standing, the other lying artfully beside it, issuing gently and unceasingly into the pond. The perfect symbol, Kate used to think, for all this bounty. But was it? Winter was coming, the sun already south west at noon, getting lower and weaker by the day. Winter was coming, and when it did the pond would freeze white and that fountain would dry up.

Her view swept across the park-like south gardens until she was turned, facing him. Without the benefit of his mahogany voice, with his extraordinary eyes closed and his intellect dormant, there was nothing to distract her from the fact that Alistair Crawford was seventy-four years old…the same age as Grandy when he died. He was still a big, broad-shouldered man — even his stricken legs had retained their bulk — but now he was the prisoner of his physique, wore it like a heavy restraining suit, a painful burden. Whatever he might have looked like as a younger man under an eastern sun, age and Ontario ordained a pale, wax-like complexion. The tight features that Kate had once ascribed to arthritic pain were the result — she was almost certain now — of plastic surgery. Forgivable, of course, but surprising in a man of an otherwise modest, even re-clusive, disposition.

Kate glanced at her watch. Twelve-fifteen — he would be disap-pointed if Matilde rang the gong before they had had a chance to enjoy their customary pre-lunch sherry. She left the balustrade, went to a teak table beside Alistair's chair where she filled two glasses from a crystal decanter, allowing the heavy stopper to strike a sweet chime as she replaced it. But there had been no need for that gentle alarm because when she looked up she saw that he must have been awake for several seconds, his eyes were wide open, watching her.

She grinned foolishly. "Caught me red handed!" She went quickly to him, bent down to kiss his cheek. "How are you, Alistair? It's lovely to see you."

"Lovely?" He grunted and sat up. "I highly doubt that. Had my mouth open, did I, drooling like a baby?"

Kate laughed as she fetched him his glass. "Not even snoring, I promise. Cheers." Kate took the chair beside him and sipped her sherry, feeling the sweet amber liquid warm her insides.

"Of course," he said, hauling himself upright, "I could always feed you a line about old habits dying hard. Out east you were a damn fool *not* to catch forty winks at noon."

"I thought mad dogs and Englishmen…"

"I'm a Scot. Not the same thing at all. So tell me…" He subjected her to a moment of amused scrutiny. "What's happening in the land of the living? How is that clever husband of yours?"

"Fine."

"Fine, is he?"

There had been only the minutest lack of enthusiasm in her re-sponse, yet his eyes were instantly, irresistibly at work. "Is he go-ing to give me a decent Distillery? How's he getting on with Gra-ham Sawtrell? No more trouble there I hope." Watching her. Waiting.

Kate laughed thinly. "Not fair! I haven't even had my sherry!"

Alistair's eyes gleamed. He folded his big arms and hugged him-self: "I get the numbers every day you know, on my fax machine. And I'll tell you something: they always add up right. The numbers always tell me how very good we are at making money. Did I say we? Of course I mean Graham Sawtrell. He makes oodles of money for me."

"Alistair…"

"Hand over fist as they say." He pretended to be stern. "And now I suppose you want me to throw a spanner in the works."

Kate held her ground. "Since when did an idea of Hal's lose you any money? The Vanguard's one big cash register. It just happens to be a beautiful one, thanks to him."

"And Julie! That's her name, isn't it, the little Chinese girl? From what I hear we can expect some fairly…divergent ideas this time."

Kate was taken aback. "On the Distillery?"

He raised his eyebrows. "Isn't that what we're talking about?"

"But they haven't presented yet. How do you know…?"

He raised his eyebrows. "My dear girl, whatever must you think of me? There have been seventeen separate meetings, approximately fifty hours of boardroom time on this business. Site preparation has been underway for a month. I may not be physically present at these meetings but we live in an age of communication. Do you imagine that I sit here all day with a rug over my knees, dribbling into my warm milk?"

Kate felt herself stinging all over. Suddenly he reached for her hand. "Forgive me. That was cruel." He winced contritely. "A cruel, vain old man and of course you're right…your husband's instincts have been absolutely sound so far. I'm trying to get the name changed, by the way, from the Vanguard Building to Crawford Place, if those pansies at the Historical Board will let me. Crawford Place…what do you think?"

Kate withdrew her hand, pouting. "I brought you some very good photographs of it. Pre-restoration. Hal took them. But I don't think I'll give them to you now."

He chuckled. "I said I was sorry."

"No you didn't."

"Very well, I apologize."

"You *know* I would never ask you to consider anything unbusinesslike. Yes, there are differences of opinion about the Distillery design, but what numbers say you have to feed pablum to buyers of six-hundred-thousand-dollar town houses? Why should it be any different from the Vanguard? You could have *two* landmarks. I've got the drawings in the car, why don't I get them?"

As she rose from her chair, a gong thrummed in the house.

"Matilde summons us," he said. "We must both go. You can show me everything after lunch."

Kate helped him make the shuffling, agonizing journey to the scooter then turned back to drain her sherry glass, hoping it would relax her, give her back her timing, which had been badly thrown off.

"Come on, come on!" he called back as he propelled the scooter towards tall french doors. "Matilde gets furious if I'm late for meals. She thinks I'm going to drop dead at any moment and she'll have done all that preparation for nothing!"

He often made such references to his age, jokes at his own expense, a kind of defence against the march of years and ill health. A way, perhaps, of wearing the subject out or at least of monopolizing it so that no one else might raise it. As if anyone would, she thought, resting her hand lightly on his shoulder. He was a powerful, wealthy man, surrounded by lackeys and grateful guests; he played at self-effacement like a lonely game of solitaire, for lack of an equal partner.

That earlier deep, warm feeling returned, and on an instinct she leaned down and kissed the top of his head as she assisted him up a shallow ramp and into the house. Hal's wrong, she thought: Alistair wasn't Grandy, not anymore. Perhaps she had seen him that way in the beginning, taking his strong arm through the rose garden, aware of the warm mass of him beside her, hearing the rhythmic tap of his walking stick. But somehow the scooter had changed that, along with all the other small signs of decline. He was no longer her protector — if anything, Kate felt that role to be her own, at least it would be if he ever needed to cast her in it.

She followed him into the library and closed the long doors behind them. A fire crackled in the grate, adding a comfortable touch

178

to an already easeful room. A leather room, old and brown and fragrant. Smooth, wonderful-to-touch leather on the sofa and club chairs before the fire, a whole wall of leather-bound books in walnut cases.

Matilde appeared at the inner door, a compact, middle-aged woman with grey hair braided into a tight bun. She smiled in welcome as she helped Alistair out of his coat and took Kate's jacket. Unless she hid it very well, Matilde shared none of Greg's resentment of her; the housekeeper's occasional testiness could be provoked just as easily by her employer.

Kate took the packet of photographs and negatives out of her bag and laid them on the coffee table as a reminder for after lunch. As she followed them out of the study, she glanced above the fireplace at the oil portrait she had finished last summer. She would never be happy with it; Alistair's facelift had sorely tested her skill. She had used so much diplomacy to feather out the strained quality that the portrait had ended up as little more than romantic flattery. The real Alistair Crawford had eluded her.

His infirmity now forced him to use an elevator to reach the second floor, denying him use of a magnificent staircase sweeping up from the grand hallway. It was hung on both sides with antique Oriental carpets, halogen-lit even in the day. Clicking across the hall's parquet floor, Kate's shoes fell silent on another rug, a shimmering blue Peking, large as a squash court, not antique but worth a fortune merely for its size.

Her passing knowledge of Oriental carpets had been vastly broadened by her visits to Mead End. Alistair's carpets were his abiding passion. Biting back the pain, he had tackled the stairs time and again during the early visits, to instruct her in the twenty or so museum-quality pieces in his collection, jabbing with his walking stick until she knew each one by design, country of origin, region and tribe, dye composition, silk and precious metal content and knots per square inch.

He was already working around to his pet subject by the time Matilde brought the main course — pink, succulent liver dijonnaise —

to the dining table. Alistair looked at his plate and sighed with pleasure.

"I like it pink, don't you? The pinker the better. Some people nowadays would find that distasteful, or they'd feel guilty. Too much guilt going around if you ask me. Forget AIDS, forget cancer — guilt is the epidemic of our time." He grunted. "I should say *your* time, it won't be mine much longer, thank God."

"Don't be silly."

"I remember a day when a man could cut a straight line without having to question every step, without being told how many acres of rain forest have perished because he's done such and such, how many damn whales and elephants, about the hole in the ozone layer, how many disabled lesbians he has failed to accommodate." Alistair looked askance at her amusement, shrugged as he cut his meat.

"I saw one of those fur people on TV the other night, calling for a ban on the importation of Persian lamb." He chuckled. "I have to admit even I felt a pang of guilt when I remembered my little Karakuls." He saw Kate frowning, hastened to clarify. "The broadtail pelt required for Persian lamb — more correctly, astrakhan — is produced by slaughtering the lamb as soon as it is born."

"Oh dear."

"To get wool soft enough for a fine Karakul prayer rug, it is necessary to go a step further, to abort the fetus mid-term."

Kate stared at the pink liver on her plate.

"Quite," he said. "But I would still like you to see a Karakul — rather, to *feel* one, to feel softness *melting* in your hands."

Kate wasn't expecting any revelations. Intimate as she was with his collection, she had surely examined the Karakul and forgotten the name — east of the Bosporus there seemed to be a "k" in every other word.

She was surprised, therefore, twenty minutes later after coffee, to find herself following Alistair into a part of the house she had never visited before. The corridor led through a butler's pantry and past a cavernous kitchen. Through the partially open door, Kate glimpsed a different Matilde, a hank of hair swinging in her face as she savaged an oven rack with steel wool.

Kate was hard pressed to keep pace with him as he powered the scooter on ahead in eager spurts. At last, after a labyrinthine journey, the scooter whispered to a stop outside a grey door — a steel door, Kate realized as she caught up. He entered a digital code on a keypad and the door rolled smoothly aside, disappearing into the wall. Light from the corridor showed a few feet of bare floor, beyond which the room was pitch black — a temperature- and humidity-controlled, strangely redolent blackness.

"The light will go on automatically when one of us crosses the threshold." Alistair's voice was submissively quiet. When he gestured her to go first, Kate experienced an absurd thrill of fear, a vision of permanent silent darkness, a ton of steel rolling into place behind her. Nonsense, she told herself, as she stepped through the door and reeled.

She had entered a morgue.

In the first blinding dazzle of light, that was exactly how it looked. It took two full seconds to realize that the adult- and child-size forms stretched out on the floor or propped, drooping, against the walls were rolled-up carpets and rugs.

He entered behind her, scooting ahead now to enjoy her expression of amazement.

There were dozens of carpets — scores of carpets — all rolled for storage in a windowless, thirty-foot-square vault. Pathways had been retained so that every roll was accessible, paths along which Alistair now manoeuvered the scooter, caressing individual pieces as his voice caressed the exotic names:

"Kashan! Kerman! Herat! My antique Ning H'sia, only twenty-five knots to the inch but to look at it you would swear half a thousand! And here...a sixteenth-century Caucasian dragon...only five collectors in the world own one and mine is the best! And this..." He reached down to a carpet lying like a felled tree trunk, dwarfing everything else in the vault. "My Cairene Mamluk, *fifteenth century*! Twenty feet by twelve, while almost all other examples are *fragments*! How much do you think, at auction in

Paris or Geneva?" Whispering: "Let's just say stupendously valuable!"

He scooted on, in transports of pleasure, stopping now at a rug made miniature by the Mamluk. "Ah, the little Karakul. Feel it, Katy. *Feel!*"

Kate walked forward and fondled an unwrapped corner of the rug, a sensation like kneading double cream. "It's..."

But he had already moved on: Qum...Tabriz...Kazan...Shala-mzar...Isfahan...an exotic litany that conjured a spangling indigo night with a crescent moon, a winged horse sailing over palm trees and minarets, the distant cry of a muezzin, the clash of scimitars, the whisper of silk.

Magic carpets.

Eventually he brought her to an archway at the back of the vault, powering the scooter aside to give her an unobstructed view into a long, narrow inner chamber. Hanging lengthwise on the end wall of the chamber, lit by a battery of halogen floodlamps, was a carpet of radiant, paralyzing beauty.

"Hereke," he murmured in a voice of awe. "Pure silk. Six hundred and fifty knots to the square inch, pure gold and silver wefts. Not the most valuable piece, not the largest, certainly not the oldest. But look at it...*look* at the thing!"

The carpet carried a floral design, the central medallion exploding outwards into ten thousand perfect petals. Each tiny component was brilliantly defined, thanks to the fineness of weave and the precious metal threads. A kaleidoscope of colours embellished the soft, blue-grey field, yet the true, natural dyes created a spiralling, celestial harmony.

"It's wonderful!"

"Wonderful? It's a miracle. It's from the workshop of Hirant Derkovorian, the greatest master weaver ever to work in Central Asia. Unfortunately for him he was Turkish Armenian, one of the six thousand slaughtered in the August pogrom of 1896. Go nearer. Go on!" Kate advanced down the viewing chamber. "All right, stop there. Do you see the flaw?"

Kate frowned helplessly at the teeming design.

"Stop looking at the trees, look at the forest!"

"Do you mean…?" By half-closing her eyes she could see something, a faint shadow eclipsing almost half the carpet. "Do you mean that dark patch? Is it stained?"

He uttered a low murmur. "Derkovorian was killed at the loom together with his twenty weavers, all of them children between seven and sixteen years of age. The Turks smashed their heads with iron bars." He paused. "Fortunately for us they had just finished this piece."

Kate stared at the carpet. "My God. You mean…that stain is…"

"The price of all that beauty?" He smiled ruefully. "No, I suppose that isn't quite right." He smiled again. "Of course, Derkovorian and his weavers were especially unfortunate, but the finest carpets have always required children at the loom. Apprenticed at five, expert at nine, finished at sixteen when their fingers are too large to make the tiny knots, when their eyesight is ruined and their legs are puny from disuse." He gestured around the vault. "That's the real price of all this, as surely as the unborn lamb is the price of a Karakul. So…" He inched the scooter towards her, his eyes patient, amused, searching. "What are we going to do? Should we build a bonfire, have Greg take them all down to the bottom of the garden? Tell me, Kate, if all this was yours, what would you do? What would you do with all this stained beauty?"

Facing him down the chamber, she was mesmerized by his eyes, which had never before seemed so unbearable or so exciting. It seemed ridiculous, at this moment, to ever have thought of him needing her or anyone else's protection.

"You should know that apart from Greg and Matilde who must work here, I have never admitted anyone to these rooms before today. I would really rather you didn't divulge the…extent of my collection to anyone else, not even to Hal." He stopped the scooter directly in front of her. "Is that asking too much?"

Kate shook her head uncertainly. "No. I understand. To have something as valuable as…"

"Absolutely." He spun his vehicle in a tight half-circle then reached out and took her hand, propelling them both towards the main vault and the way out. "But of course I already know you can keep a secret, don't I, Katy?"

CHAPTER
24

"We did it! We *did* it!"

Julie gripped his arm so tightly, Hal had pins and needles by the time the elevator arrived to take them down from the twenty-third floor of the Midland office.

He wished he could share her excitement. But Graham Sawtrell having just approved Julie's original Distillery drawings without a single change was simply too hard to believe.

Kate's part in it, her influence on Crawford, was also incredible. So was the fact that Crawford had such a hold on his executive vice-president. How was that? The old man could never fire Sawtrell when every department reported to him. He was bound to be a major shareholder, his contract doubtless had a carryover provision to buy shares at a big discount, not to mention the severance agreement for a player like that — it could be up to five years' salary. Sawtrell could be as mutinous as he liked, knowing that Crawford couldn't *afford* to fire him. There had to be something else holding him, but what?

Hal felt a nudge as they rode down. "What's with the long face?" Julie whispered. "I never had you pegged for a sore winner!"

She was glowing. At close quarters in the crowded elevator, Hal could feel her heat against his skin; he braced himself every time she was jostled against him, terrified by his awareness of her strong, dynamic body, the smell of her hair, her excitement.

He had neglected to tell her about Kate's revelation on Monday night, the real reason behind their success today. He would have to say something eventually, but not yet; not until sweet Julie Lee had enjoyed her victory.

Then, as the elevator sighed to a stop and the bell chimed to announce the ground floor, Hal's disturbing thoughts of Julie were terminated by a sudden, unexpected bombshell.

Having ridden down from a high floor, they were standing at the back of the elevator. Julie was out of the door before she realized that Hal hadn't moved. "Hello? Earth to Hal."

He came out, walked slowly across the wide lobby towards the revolving street door. Halfway he stopped, turned, stared back at the twin banks of chiming, winking elevators.

"What is it?" Julie grinned. "Forget something else?"

"No I...I just remembered something."

She laughed. "Isn't that the same thing?"

Hal was still gazing at the elevators, his grey eyes narrowed behind his glasses. He turned to her, spoke with quiet intensity. "Do you remember that day we first presented here, almost two years ago now?"

"The Vanguard. How could I forget?"

"Do you remember after the meeting, I went back for my tape deck, and when I came down again you were still on the forecourt? You'd seen a man, remember? A Chinese man, the same man you'd seen at the Vanguard, the one who ran away when he heard us coming."

Julie pointed through the glass towards the Bay Street steps. "Out there. I remember very well. Creepy guy."

"Would you recognize him if you saw him again?"

She frowned. "Why are you bringing this up now?"

He took her arm. "Come on."

"What is this?"

He hustled her towards the revolving doors. "I want to show you something."

It took a few minutes to get through the hullabaloo when the rest of the office heard the good news about the Distillery. They had all worked overtime on the backup drawings, and Hal wanted to compensate them for two late nights of strong coffee and pizza; he told Gloria to phone The Amsterdam and book a table for seven for one o'clock.

Hal's desk looked like the aftermath of a hurricane, but at last he found the Kodak envelope. He took out the closeup and put it on the desk in front of Julie. "Is that the guy you saw?"

She reached down, lifted it carefully by its edge. "Where on earth did you get this?"

"Is it him?"

"Yes. No question. But how...?"

"When I first saw this face I knew it looked familiar — I thought maybe I'd taken the picture and forgotten, maybe he was a friend of yours that I'd met sometime. I was meaning to ask you but things got so crazy with the Distillery. Then just now, coming down in the elevator at Midland — *ding!* — it suddenly hit me where I'd seen him before."

Julie settled, frowning, into Hal's swivel chair. "I don't understand. You *didn't* see him. It was only *me* that saw him, both times. First at the Van, then at Midland."

"Ah...but I *did*! Right after that first meeting, when you were in the washroom and I was waiting for you by the elevators. He walked out of one, asked me where Midland was. Their name's on the door, I remember thinking he couldn't read English. Then I saw him again, just for a second when I went back for the tape deck. He was in an elevator, about to ride down, which must have been just before *you* saw him coming out of the building."

"Okay, but who took this picture? Where did it come from?"

Hal smiled. "One thing at a time. I don't know who took it but I know *when* it was taken. At least, I know it was after I lost my camera at the Doyle." He tapped the Kodak packet. "It was the same roll as the rest of the shots in here, which are the last ones of the Vanguard I took with the Leica." He reached for the packet, looked inside. "From the sequence of the negatives, you can see it's the last..." He rechecked both pockets of the envelope. "That's funny."

"What?"

"Doesn't matter. I must have left the negs at home."

"You still haven't told me where this picture came from."

Hal turned the packet over to show her the order form on the back, the name and phone number. Julie read aloud: "'T. Whiteside.' Who's T. Whiteside?"

"I don't know. I tried the number but it's out of service. I got as far as discovering twelve T. Whitesides in the phone book before Sawtrell moved our deadline up and things went apeshit here. It didn't seem all that important until just now."

Julie looked at him quizzically. "Why is it so important now?"

Hal sat on the edge of his desk. For a moment he was silent, chewing his lower lip. "That day at the Vanguard, when we surprised this guy. You cleverly went to the window while I was in the stairwell, and when I came out you asked me what he'd been doing. I couldn't tell you then, and maybe I can't now, but I do know something was wrong in there."

"Like what?"

"There was an emergency exit from the Doyle, right? It only opened *out*, into the stairwell, and yet I clearly remember an exit sign on the stairwell side of that door. Is that normal?"

Julie shook her head. "There'd be no point to it. If there was a fire, you'd head down the stairs, not into the Doyle, even if you *could* open the door, which you couldn't."

"Exactly. And that's not all: the sign was way below regulation height. In fact, it was almost down to the level of the opening mechanism on the Doyle side. Now just say you were somebody tampering with that mechanism, making it possible to open the door from the stairwell side; say you'd cut through the metal door — remember we heard a power tool — and say you needed a way to cover up your incision; a metal plaque would be a good solution wouldn't it?"

Julie looked from Hal to the photograph on his desk. "You're saying this guy wanted into the Doyle. Why?"

Hal looked at her intensely. "First we meet this Chinese person at the Vanguard, possibly tampering with the fire door connecting to the Doyle. A month later we both see him at Midland. That night, three people are horribly murdered — at the Doyle."

Julie looked incredulous. "You're trying to tell me the Chinese guy killed those three dancers?"

Hal shrugged. "Why not? And it gets juicier than that, doesn't it?"

"What? Midland is involved now? Come on!"

"Is it so outrageous? They certainly ended up profiting from the murders. The Doyle closed down, no more carrying an expensive unrented building, on with the restoration!"

"But it was public *pressure* that closed the Doyle. All those demonstrations."

"And Carny Danial popping off. Remember him...the Doyle Diehard? Died good in the end though, didn't he?"

"But Hal, everyone knows who did those murders at the Doyle, they simply haven't caught him yet: the Grafitti Killer! He'd already killed three strippers a year before the Doyle."

"How very convenient for Midland. When they realized they couldn't get Carny Danial off their back any other way, they had the perfect bandwagon to jump on — all they had to do was commit copycat murder and they would be free of the Doyle *and* free of suspicion! These are very, very smart people: they predicted how the public would react and they were dead right!"

Julie stared. "I think you'd better go have another vacation. At least break for lunch!"

"You think it sounds totally crazy?"

"Totally!" She was quiet for a moment, then gradually she smiled. "On the other hand, I'll never forget that first job in Port Hope, the first time I met you. I remember there was paint flaking off one of the shopfronts; one of the workers started picking away at it and you gave him hell. I asked why and you said there was an original commercial sign underneath all that paint, and I said how could you *possibly* know that."

Hal chuckled. "I remember. I knew you were trouble the minute I laid eyes on you!"

"You said you knew because the shopfront was 'whispering' to you! I thought you were crazy then, too."

"And was I?"

It didn't require an answer. The sign had been a beauty, pale mauve on a yellow ground — *PIANOS* — a ghost-sign preserved in the pores of the brick, ripe for retouching. The Port Hope Council had been sufficiently moved to convince a music store to lease the restored premises.

Julie did one complete rotation in Hal's chair, then leaned back, her hands clasped behind her head, gazing at him. "Do you hear whispering now, Sebastian-san?"

Once again Hal found himself achingly aware of Julie Lee. But this time there was a subtle, thrilling, terrifying difference: it was *their* closeness now, not just his awareness of it...it was *their* heat. Hal knew it from her soft, steady gaze, felt it, as though there was an invisible wire stretched between them, humming with a powerful current.

Hal blushed deeply and looked away, throwing the breaker that cut the power. He levered himself off the desk and turned away. He squatted, opened the bottom desk drawer and hauled out a phone book. "Why don't we call a few T. Whitesides before lunch?" he said, trying to sound normal, although his voice came thickly from his throat and his fingers trembled amongst the pages of names and numbers. "And let's hope you're right; let's hope to God I am crazy."

CHAPTER
25

Tyah was awakened by the sound of Shane's key in the lock. She knew by the depth of her craving that it was late, that Shane was here to escort her to her one o'clock appointment — she should have had her fix and been dressed and waiting on the doorstep instead of lying in bed. As he came in, Tyah drew up her knees, forming a protective ball under the bedclothes.

But Shane was in a rare good mood. The john had cancelled for one, wanted two o'clock instead. New guy, hadn't learned any fuckin' manners yet. Did she know Paulie Rozsas, came in the Quarter all the time, musician? Paulie was going to be a special customer from now on, even though he was a fuckin' smartmouth. For instance, Paulie said Shane's idea of using the club as a showroom wasn't original. Said they used to do the same thing in the sporting houses in New Orleans. Instead of the sound system, Paulie said, they had some guy playing piano while the girls stripped for the out-of-town customers. Paulie said one piano player, Jelly something, wrote a special song for the show, called *The Naked Dance*. The joke, according to Paulie, was that they used the exact same tune on a kids' TV show called *Kukla, Fran and Ollie*, used it for the theme song. Shane frowned at her: "You ever seen *Kukla, Fran and Ollie*?"

Tyah didn't think so.

"Nor me. Guess it must have been a pretty old show, eh?"

"I guess so, Shane."

He nodded, strangely gratified. "Yeah. So fuck Paulie, right?"

"Yeah, Shane, I heard you — two o'clock."

Shane liked that, stood at the end of the sofa bed and laughed and laughed. No one else cracked him up like Tyah, he said. Then he said he reckoned he'd maybe better fuck her today, right now in fact. When he started undoing his shirt, she reached onto the floor for her sweatshirt, slipped it on and threw back the covers.

"Where you going?" he demanded.

"I'm going to have a piss and then a fix. D'you mind?"

"Jesus, Ty, you're so fuckin' romantic!"

Halfway to the bathroom she heard the phone ring. Shane picked it up. It was most likely for him anyway, she was constantly taking his messages.

There were times, when he was relatively mellow like this, that Tyah could actually bring herself to feel sorry for Shane. Not so much Shane now, but the little boy with tiny, weird hands, dragged from one seedy, small-town hotel to the next in the days when Evelyn was on the road, before she started working for Carny. She thought of little Shane alone and afraid in one cramped, dirty room after another, missing years of school while his mother jiggled downstairs in the draft parlour. That had to be why he was so surprised he'd never caught *Kukla, Fran and Ollie*. At one time Shane was probably a world expert on every kind of TV show, must have watched constantly in those hotel rooms. To turn it off would have meant listening to the old men coughing through the paper walls, the dopers on bad trips, the biker shit going down in the corridors. But even the TV probably couldn't drown the fear of Evelyn coming back skunky with beer, of her shrieking abuse and unpredictable, stinging slaps.

Poor little bugger. No wonder.

She went back to the room and closed the door. He had finished on the phone, was sitting at the formica table, looking at it.

"Who was that?" she asked casually.

Shane shook his head. "Guess I must be goin' deaf." He had his rubber ball out, rolling it hand to hand across the table top. The ball was a bad sign: it meant his good mood was over. She watched him, cautiously, from the door. He looked up at her now, still shaking his head in mock-disbelief. "Couldn't've heard that guy right, could I? Tellin' me my lady been sending him photographs? *Could* I?"

Tyah stared at him, bewildered.

He shrugged. "Like...this guy was saying T. Whiteside sent him some photographs. Said his name was Hal. Said it was 'confidential.' I must've made him nervous after that, 'cause he said maybe he'd got the wrong T. Whiteside after all and hung up. What you think, Ty? Think he had the wrong T. Whiteside?"

The answer was all over Tyah's face before she could hide it. Without realizing it she started to back up, felt the door handle dig into her spine.

He got up lazily, pocketed his ball, came very slowly towards her.

"Please, Shane...it wasn't nothing like...Shane I can..." But she couldn't explain. And she wouldn't, she realized with sudden, surprising conviction. Somehow this thing had come back, like a boomerang. Something special now. Something in her life — maybe the *only* thing — that *wasn't* Shane's business. With every step he took towards her, the stronger became her need and her resolve to hold onto it.

"What are we talkin' about here?" he drawled. "What's this 'confi-DENT-tial'?"

The first slap bounced her head against the door frame. She wandered away, disoriented, but Shane was right on her, driving her, marking the rhythm of his speech with powerful, controlled slaps to her head: "WANN-a TELL-me what FUCK-ing CON-fi-DENT-tial MEANS?"

Tyah tried to guard herself, but Shane had been a boxer and each blow found a window.

He drove her onto the bed and there the slapping stopped. Tyah's eyes were still tight shut but she could hear him through the ringing in her ears, could hear him panting as he stood over her, aroused as only violence could arouse him, unzipping himself now, his belt buckle jingling, his Italian shoes clattering off across the floor.

Tyah vomited until she could produce nothing more than agonized groans. For five minutes she remained, draped across the cold, filthy toilet like a shipwreck victim clinging to wreckage. She was shaking and sweating because she had missed her fix, because he had taken her last tenth gram and she wouldn't get another taste until she had something to tell him.

Tyah stood up slowly, hanging onto the basin for support. When she came level with the mirror, her reflection drew an unexpected sob from the deepest part of her, a part she had almost forgotten existed.

She saw a hag looking back at her. It wasn't just the glaze of puke and the matted hair and the addict's gauntness. It wasn't the new-swollen lip or her livid, crimson cheeks. It was an older, deeper wound, a blunting of scar tissue from the months and years of "getting used to": the Shanes and the Sam Wexels and the host of lonely men who rented her, tits and a slit.

Tyah splashed her face with cold water and swilled the rancid bitterness from her mouth. She went back to the room and took her address book to the bed. She huddled under the covers to make her calls, but not even a sauna could have stopped the shivering.

She looked up Marc's number first, in Montreal. She hadn't seen Felice's brother since the funeral, but that wouldn't matter. Marc would open his door to her, at least long enough to see her through a four-week detox program. It would have to be Montreal; she already knew there was too long a waiting list for the Toronto program and if she stayed in town, Shane would find her.

She dialled the long-distance number, then slammed the phone down on a sudden thought: Shane paid the bills at Dowde; he would be like a bloodhound after she disappeared, certain to check the phone bill for a scent. She would have to call from Vanessa's.

She knew the number by heart, knew also that Vanessa was lonely with Hyacinth still a year away from parole in Kingston — Tyah and Vanessa talked a lot on the phone. She had just moved to Kensington Market and wasn't one of Shane's "special" girls — he probably didn't know her address. And maybe Nessa could score for her; when she saw Tyah was desperate, surely there were enough of Hyacinth's old contacts around that she could dig something up.

CHAPTER
26

By Saturday, exactly a week before Hal's birthday, Kate had thirty-three definites for the party.

There were ticks beside Elizabeth and Bob, Ross and Verity Ames, George Reathkin, Tim and Ann Millard and the Croydons. Jeremy and Glenda Parks were bringing Glenda's mum, visiting from Santa Fe where she was a fairly well-known potter. The Greenwalds were coming, Linda Constantine and her new man, Meredith and Dr. Woolley of course, and Hal's gang — Julie and Don and Gloria were firm, all of them welcome to bring someone. Julie kept her private life very much under wraps, but Kate imagined her bringing one of those perennially dark, intense boys with severe black clothes and radical tastes, the kind that had daunted her at Art College. Still, the more the merrier.

They needed this party — a focus for communication between husband and wife, which was still broken down after that awful night at the church. It didn't help that the office expansion was disrupting Hal's normal business hours, creating a backlog of work that kept him at the Vanguard till ten every night. Once again on a Saturday morning, Kate and Rain were at the church without him.

At ten-thirty, Meredith Woolley dropped Sarah off, staying long enough to dictate her dip recipe and give Kate unwanted advice on where to set up bar and where to put guests' coats so they didn't end up a mountain on the bed.

It was a cold, blustery morning, the sky busy with bruised silver clouds. They spent it indoors, Kate judging Rain and Sarah's fashion show, which as usual featured a layered look — underwear over bathing suits over pyjamas. She fed them easy beans on toast for lunch, assuaging her conscience by peeling crisp October apples for dessert.

They had just finished when the doorbell rang. Kate was expecting Meredith and let the children get it, surprised when they scampered back to tell her, in hushed tones, that it was "a man."

It was Greg.

"Mr. Crawford would like you to accept this with his regards," Greg informed her with his usual calcified politeness.

The tubular parcel was wrapped in brown paper, but Kate knew what it was even before she took the supple, crackling shape in her arms. Not waiting for a response, Greg turned and went back to the green Jaguar idling in the road. Kate watched, frowning slightly as he got in and drove away.

Her irritation was forgotten by the time she had laid the parcel down on the living room floor and the excited children began tearing off the wrapping.

"What is it, Mummy?"

"Don't you know? It's a magic carpet!"

It was a prayer rug, about three and a half by five feet. Kate had not seen its design in the storeroom at Mead End, but one touch was enough for her to identify the Karakul. "Stroke it," she urged the children. "Isn't it soft? Just like a pussycat."

Rain and Sarah soon lost interest and went to play upstairs. Kate took a pad and pen to the kitchen table to compose a thank-you letter to Alistair, scrunching her bare toes in Karakul wool for inspiration. It was a delicious sensation, as long as she didn't think about how the wool was produced. Was it really true that they still used child labour to weave Oriental carpets — used them up as Alistair described?

On the other hand, maybe he was right about there being too much guilt around. Maybe he would even condone the shameful, greedy thoughts that had been recurring since her last visit to Mead End. She *was* ashamed of them, yet there was always a moment before she remembered their inappropriateness, a moment such as now when her face grew hot along with her imagination and the questions bubbled up again: what was he going to do with it all? His fabulous house, the cars, the furniture. His carpets. There didn't seem to be any family, at least none that he ever spoke of; Greg and Matilde were nothing more than paid servants, surely. He was hardly the type to leave it all to the Humane Society. He didn't even seem to have any close friends.

Except Kate.

She was glad when the wall-phone rang, stopping her train of thought just as it became a guilt trip. When she heard Alistair's voice, the hotness stormed up through her neck and face once again, set her babbling: "I always thought you had ESP, now I'm sure of it! I was just trying to write you a thank-you letter and not having much luck. Can I say it now, will that count? It's *such* a beautiful rug, Alistair. You're very naughty."

"I'm glad you like it. Let me know when it needs cleaning; there's only one place worth using in the city, anywhere else will ruin it."

"I'll remember that."

"Listen," he said casually. "I think you left some photographs last Wednesday. A packet of photographs of the Vanguard."

Kate squinched her eyes tight shut. "God! I'm sorry. I wanted to go through them with you. I forgot all about them."

"Greg found them in the study."

"I know, I know. I left them there for after lunch and then...well, it *was* rather an exciting day!"

"Quite. Didn't you mention that Hal took them?"

"Right. I thought if there were one or two you particularly liked, I'd get them blown up. Then Hal could take the same angles again and you'd have before and after shots of the restoration."

"How thoughtful of you. It's going to be hard to choose, they're all so good. Did Hal take every one of them?"

Kate frowned slightly. "I think so. Why?"

"Nothing really. I was looking at the negatives and they're all Vanguard except one. Looks like — I'm not sure — it could be a Chinese face. I was simply curious about it, nothing very important."

For nothing important there was a distinctly expectant silence at the other end of the line. Kate said: "I'm afraid I can't tell you who that is."

"I beg your pardon?"

"No, I mean I haven't a clue *who* the Chinese man is. Hal doesn't know either."

"I don't quite understand. You told me Hal *took* the pictures."

"Not that one. At least he doesn't remember taking it. All the others but not…"

"Who did?"

Kate's frown deepened. "I haven't the faintest. Why are you so interested? Do you know this person or something?"

Silence from the other end.

"Hello? Alistair?"

"Sorry to be such a bore, but I must get this straight. You say the Vanguard shots are your husband's, yet he doesn't know who took this odd one."

"That's what he *says*."

"What do you mean?"

"Well, he says he didn't have any of them developed, either, but I wouldn't be at all surprised if he's forgotten. You see, he lost his camera a couple of years ago, supposedly with this film in it — actually it was just before I met you."

"Go on."

"Then about ten days ago the developed film arrived in the mail at our Toronto house. Hal thinks it's all very mysterious, but if you ask me, he took the film in to be developed and then forgot. I mean, how else would they have known where to send it?"

"*They*? Who is they?" His voice carried a peculiar urgency.

"The developers," she told him. "A one-hour place at Yonge and Dundas. Some other customer's order form got mixed in, but they had our mailing address right."

"What was the name on the order form?"

"Gosh…Whiting? Whiteway? Something like that. Nobody we'd ever heard of."

"Please try and remember exactly."

"I can't!" Kate laughed nervously. "What's all this about anyway, what's the big deal?"

Long seconds of silence. When he spoke, it was carefully, choosing every word. "I'll be absolutely frank with you. For reasons you already know, the Van…Crawford Place is very important to me. Certain events occurred around the time of its restoration, events that have given rise to…misunderstandings, which in turn have led to some particularly hurtful gossip." He paused. "As you know, Kate, for a long time I've thought of Crawford Place as my swan song; you can imagine how it upsets me to hear my song murdered by a gaggle of malicious geese."

"This man in the photograph, is he…?"

"Please just listen, because my reputation may be in your hands. Are you willing to help me?"

"Of course, but…"

"Will you help me find out how this photograph came into Hal's possession? I assume there is a print to go with the negative."

"Yes, I think it's at Hal's office."

"And the order form you spoke of — that is also at his office?"

"I think so."

"Good. You must call Hal immediately, and have him tell you the name on that form — Whiteway or whatever it is, with its exact spelling. Isn't there usually a telephone number on such forms?"

"Hal tried it; it was out of service."

"Never mind, I need it. I want you to call me back as soon as you have the information. And Kate?"

"What?" she answered, mystified.

"As my friend, my *special* friend, I must ask you two other favours: firstly, that you mention this conversation to no one, not even Hal. Secondly, that you inform me if Hal or anybody else has anything more to say on the subject of this photograph, who might have taken it, where it came from — anything at all. I'm not asking you to be disloyal to your husband am I?"

"If it's so important…"

"It is *vitally* important to me!" His voice softened. "Help me, Kate, and I will be so very grateful. And I don't mean another little prayer rug. In fact, you may consider the Karakul a minuscule token of my good faith."

The receiver had grown slippery in Kate's hand. Inside her, waves of butterflies shimmered.

"For heaven's sake Alistair, I don't want…"

"Call him now, please. Then call me back."

"What am I going to say? What reason…"

"Dear me!" The voice was smiling now. "A resourceful girl like you? You'll think of something. I have absolute faith!"

"Alistair?"

"What is it?"

She hesitated. "This malicious gossip: does it have anything to do with…with what happened at the Doyle, those girls that were murdered?"

There was a moment of deep silence on the line, then: "Please Kate, not now. I can't begin to tell you how much all this upsets me. Please just call Hal and call me back. Will you do that for me?"

Without being aware of it, Kate had carried the cordless phone back to the kitchen table and sat down. Once again she felt the luxuriant softness of the Karakul between her toes and suddenly, out of the blue, she heard an echo from the vault at Mead End, an expression he had used there, something about "stained beauty."

What would you do with all this stained beauty?

"Kate?"

And then the echo was gone and she said: "I'm sorry, Alistair. Of course I'll call. I'll call him right away."

CHAPTER
27

The night before his thirty-eighth birthday, Hal went to an exclusive private party. James Brown played, so did Jimi and Aretha and the Beatles, so did Creedence, Sly Stone and Tower of Power. The Doors were there, and the Dead, and the Band; so was Janis and a young, righteous Van Morrison.

Golden oldies: the first party tape Hal had put together since undergraduate days, the first time he had played some of these albums in twenty years. He was already hurtling down Memory Expressway when he pulled The Byrds' *Sweetheart of the Rodeo* from it sleeve and, with it, a brittle, flattened Baggie containing a palmful of khaki dust.

Dope days. Long ago and far away. The little off-campus pad he had shared with Ross Ames, fragrant with incense and patchouli and sweet, heavy smoke. A circle of hairy people passing the paraphernalia, smiling beatifically from wherever Panama Red or the Black Afghani had abducted them, constant arrivals and departures from the circle announced by Tibetan temple-chimes at the threshold.

Luckily, the dope days only lasted for the first year of college — a year of downward-spiralling marks proving just how hard it was, zonked out of your skull, to get those staggeringly fine ideas onto paper. But the music…had it ever sounded as good again? Did it ever again *belong* to you in quite the same way?

Hal drank brandy while he worked (in the absence of reefer) but his hand had lost none of its old, sure touch on the tone-arm as he cued up the oldies, then filled a second tape with newer music — Little Feat and Talking Heads and Ry Cooder — shocked to realize that "newer" already meant over ten years old.

By eleven p.m. he was ready to record the slow-dancing tape, only to discover that he had left the rest of the blank cassettes, a whole carton of the things, at Grace Street. He thought about recording over *The Best of Burl Ives* then reconsidered: he could probably get Rain into that spooky old guy. Manfred Mann? Melanie? Mott the Hoople? There were stacks of ancient tapes, but one hour away from his thirty-eighth birthday, on his third large brandy, Hal was a sentimental drunk; it was impossible for him to pass the death sentence on a single old friend tonight; at some point in his life, there would be time to visit with them all again. He decided to try his satchel, which had dogged him from the office as usual, in case there were a couple of old tapes lying around from the Sony portable.

The church seemed very quiet after two hours of non-stop music, with Rain asleep in bed and Kate back in the city. For once the roles had been reversed so that Hal could do the music and Kate could bring the party food same-day-fresh from its suppliers. It had been good to have Rain to himself tonight; he had read her five stories at bedtime (not that it made up for all the missed bedtimes), cradling her in his lap for half an hour after her eyes closed.

He found his satchel on the harvest table in the kitchen, pleased when his rummaging produced one lint-infested ninety-minute cassette. It was old, had no doubt been erased and rerecorded a dozen times; the sound quality wouldn't be great but no one was going to be auditioning the hi-fi tomorrow night.

It was slightly before one a.m. when Hal cued up the last slow song, Dylan's gentle *Lay Lady Lay*.

He danced close to the dying woodstove as he listened to the old sweet song, soaking up the last of the heat and thinking regretful thoughts of Julie. Poor timing on the part of Julie's ancient great aunt, living to ninety-six and then dying two days before his birthday. And in Sarnia! Chinese funerals were a big deal; Julie didn't think they would get back to Toronto until late Saturday night. If it wasn't *too* late and she could borrow her brother's car, she'd try and make it out, but it didn't look good.

Hal missed her already.

Lay Lady Lay was over, the next song playing by the time Hal realized it and stopped the machine. He tried to cue the unwanted song to erase it, but he was working on his fourth brandy by now and rewound too far. Then he went too far forward, so far that he was over the edge of the music and into a recording of an old meeting. Hal found himself listening, ironically, to Julie's voice.

At first he couldn't place the occasion — it sounded like Vanguard business — then he heard the supercilious voice of Ron Allis and he had it: the first Midland meeting, the Vanguard presentation. Three quarters of the way into side two of the tape, it had never been erased.

Julie's first meeting. What was it she had said that day? Something about a hard-on...giving Jack Haines a hard-on? Hal went fast-forward to find it, chuckling at the memory. The nerve of the girl...not that she'd changed!

Sipping his drink, mesmerized by the whizzing reels, he allowed the tape to run almost to the end before he remembered to hit the play button again, at which point he sat up, suddenly alert.

He adjusted the volume, bringing up a voice that was clearly not at the meeting table but further away, across the room. Its speech was not intelligible, but through no fault of the Sony, which had done an excellent job even at some distance.

The voice, male, quite young, *was speaking Chinese*!

He rewound, stopped, hit PLAY.

How are you at praying?

Rusty.

Then practise. Pray for Mr. Carny Danial's speedy demise. A falling brick, a runaway streetcar...anything like that.

Hal stopped the tape. He could picture the scene as if it were yesterday: Sawtrell the jovial, charming host, lounging in his office doorway after the meeting. Meanwhile, the Sony had been recording, unperceived beneath the meeting table.

Hal's alcohol haze was evaporating by the second. He put down his drink, plugged in the headphones and slipped them over his head.

He listened to a short exchange between Sawtrell and his secretary — Sawtrell wanted a corned beef on rye, plenty of mustard, from the deli up the street, not from the concession. The office door closed. Half a minute of silence and then Hal heard Sawtrell again, talking on the phone. A marked change had come over his voice; he sounded tense, anxious — none of the weekend-sailor's bluster now.

He sounded frightened.

Ho called me, he told the phone. *Yes here! In the middle of a bloody meeting. Said he was in the neighbourhood, wanted to come up if you please. I thought he had been given express instructions… exactly…today of all days! He's worried about getting paid, for God's sake. I understood everything like that had been covered with those people.*

A long pause, interrupted by the office door opening and closing. Sawtrell immediately exploded. *For Christ's sake! He's here! Ho is! Standing right here in front of me!*

Hal listened for a moment longer then stopped the tape in amazement…

…rewound…

…played again, still unable to believe his ears as Graham Sawtrell let loose a tirade of furious Chinese!

Now there was a second voice on the tape, the young male Chinese voice that had first alerted him, unquestionably the native speaker. The tone was swaggering, undaunted by Sawtrell's angry interruptions.

Then, in livid English, Sawtrell said to the phone: *Little shit says he won't leave until he has spoken to you. Says he must speak to Dei Gin Tai Wong! A short pause. Are you serious? No, the line's perfectly safe. No, I sent her out, but you'd better be bloody quick.*

The Chinese, Ho, said something.

Hear that? He wants a fucking conference call! Says he wants me to hear that Dei Gin Tai Wong is respectful to Ho Kwan Shing! Where the hell did you get this little...

A longer pause, then a chastened Sawtrell: *All right. If you insist.*

And now a third male voice, an older voice, coming over the intercom. *Have you got it switched over?*

Sawtrell: *Yes, go ahead.*

Good afternoon, Ho Kwan Shing. A cultivated English accent like Sawtrell's.

Hello, Dei Gin Tai Wong.

Now the older voice, too, lapsed into Chinese. Whoever he was, Dei Gin Tai Wong was perfectly at home in the dialect, more so than Sawtrell. He delivered a soft, reassuring monologue, interrupted only once by a few syllables from Ho. The voice was coming to Hal via a telephone intercom via the Sony via poor quality tape and in a foreign language, yet its authority was unquestionable. Dei Gin Tai Wong was a man accustomed to respect.

He required no response to his words. At the end of his monologue he simply rang off. There was another irritable utterance from Sawtrell, a short, disdainful laugh from Ho, then the sound of the office door as it opened and closed again.

Alone now, Sawtrell said: *Mother fucker!*

Two minutes of silence followed, broken by the secretary returning with Sawtrell's corned beef on rye. He thanked her, said he would take it with him. He would be out of the office for the rest of the day. He hoped she would have a good weekend. Yes, he intended to go sailing.

The next sound, five minute of tape-hiss later, was a click, Hal turning off the machine as he collected it from under the table.

Hal ran it back and listened to the whole sequence again. He listened a third and then a fourth time, trying to make sense from inflection and innuendo, cursing the fact that Julie had left for Sarnia, that he couldn't play it over the phone and get a translation tonight — assuming, of course, that the dialect was Cantonese.

At last he gave up in frustration and turned off the equipment.

He damped the woodstove and switched out the lights and went upstairs, his exhausted brain reeling. He checked on Rain, lying across the bed as usual, straightened her and tucked her in and kissed her. In the bathroom he went through a careful routine of washing his face and cleaning his teeth, brushing his hair and polishing his glasses ready for the morning.

None of these routine activities did anything to unwind him. He could evoke not a single image of the Ancaster house. A long half hour later he was still lying stiffly in bed, his mind churning helplessly.

There could be little doubt that Ho was the man at the Vanguard — the Chinese on the elevator. He was certainly neither maintenance man nor courier although he *was* involved with Sawtrell — was being paid by him.

For murder?

And whose was the voice on the intercom? Was it Crawford? The age was right, he was English, he was Sawtrell's boss — it would be natural for Sawtrell to be deferential. Hal had met Crawford only once, at the official opening of the Vanguard. Hearing this voice filtered through so many media, Hal couldn't be sure.

But Kate would know.

He looked across the cold, empty expanse of their king size bed, read twenty past two on the quartz clock. Kate needed her rest, he told himself; she had a busy day and a late night ahead of her. Too late to spring this.

Up to now Hal had shared none of his suspicions with his wife, with sound reasons for not doing so: in view of the current chill between them, partly brought on by Kate's special relationship with Crawford, it was hardly the time to go to her with dire speculation about Midland; she would see it as nothing more than reckless retaliation and the chill would deepen. Even when Kate had called his office last Saturday, wanting the name and number that came with the mystery photos, eager to find a simple solution to the mystery, even then he had told her what she wanted to know — T. Whiteside and the phone number — and left it at that.

By now he had eliminated all the T. Whitesides in the phone book except the Dowde Street listing. He had called the Dowde number several times since that paranoid and oddly familiar-sounding guy had answered, but there had been no reply.

Lying in the darkness, burning with frustration, Hal knew that sleep would evade him until he had called it just once more. He had never tried at this hour before — maybe T. Whiteside worked odd hours.

Hal turned on the light and dialled; he knew the number by heart now. It rang and rang and rang.

Kate didn't get to the church until one o'clock on Saturday afternoon, winded and laden down with supplies. The idiot fishmonger had sold half her order of calamari for the paella, none of the other retailers had any, she'd had to go to the wholesale depot way the hell out in some industrial wasteland — two precious hours wasted in Saturday traffic!

She was in such a state, Hal didn't consider mentioning the tape, didn't deviate an inch from his allotted tasks. He took the Jeep into Orono to pick up the cutlery and plates and glasses reserved at the Rent-All; he got beer, ice, paper serviettes and a hundred dollars' worth of white gladioli, the florist hovering uncertainly between solace and felicitation.

Elizabeth and Bob came at three to help get things ready. Rain stayed long enough to see the church decked with flowers, then Hal drove her to the Woolley's for the rest of the weekend, Rain bubbling with excitement at the prospect of her first sleepover with Sarah. He got back to the church at seven, with half an hour in which to change before the first guests arrived.

By ten o'clock everyone had shown except the Millards who called to say their sitter had fallen through ("Fallen through *what*?" wondered Kate) and Linda Constantine, whose latest flame was directing a TV commercial and the shoot had only just wrapped — they were on their way.

The Woolleys came and two other local couples that Kate had invited but Hal had never met. Jeremy and Glenda Parks came with Glenda's mum, Gloria got a ride with Don Wales, who also brought a sweet though plain girl called, incongruously, Carmen. Felix and Bonnie Croydon, Ross and Verity Ames, John and Isobel, Gary and Kay. The Boys — Murray and Tom — came after all, having declined on the phone last week, still piqued by their "eviction" from Grace Street.

"We've decided to forgive you," Tom said primly as Hal took their coats. "We want to bury the hatchet."

Murray added: "Preferably in your back!" Kate and Hal laughed and hugged them both.

Three quarters of the guests knew each other; many were old friends: the party barely sputtered before it caught and burned, fuelled by Bob, red-faced and getting redder, in his element behind the bar. Partying in a church seemed to develop everyone's thirst for impiety and a dozen different vicar jokes made the rounds, along with Hal's birthday things. He got a vacuum pump for preserving open bottles of wine from Bob and Elizabeth, the 1991 *Penthouse* calendar from Ross Ames (boos from the women, all the men looked), a book of Hans Holbein's drawings from Jonah Frayne and a Lyle Lovett CD from the Croydons, Felix describing it as "country for college kids." Glenda Park's quite-famous-potter-mother from Santa Fe gave Hal and Kate a corn dolly to put over the door of the church for good luck.

"Couldn't she have managed even a little quite-famous pot?" Kate said in Hal's ear as they danced on an already crowded floor.

"Now, now…she doesn't even know us."

"I'm joking!" She looked at him, mildly reproachful. "Happy birthday to you too!"

"That's the fourth time you've wished me a happy birthday."

She smiled easily. "Well, I have to…you don't *look* happy enough."

Hal gazed at her, holding tight to both her hands, slowing her movement, looking at her until her easy smile was gone and she was really seeing him — seeing all the anger and silence and hurt of the past weeks.

"Babe…" he said.

"Not now, okay Hal? Not tonight." Then she was looking past him, back in her party face. "There's Linda! My, my…check out the guy!" And she was gone, shouldering her way towards the front door where Linda Constantine clung proudly to her handsome, fifteen-years-younger director. They both had studded black leather jackets and damp hair.

"Is it raining?" enquired Dr. Woolley, who wasn't dancing. The question led into a ten-minute lecture on caulking from which Hal managed to extricate himself only when Kate's hard-won paella emerged from the kitchen.

He went upstairs. With Kate serving and everyone eating, he could count on a few moments of privacy. He closed the bedroom door and sat on the bed beside the coat-mountain. He felt absurdly nervous as he dialled on the bedside phone — guilty — as if Julie were there in the flesh with him, behind a closed bedroom door. Beyond the door, Steppenwolf slashed and burned their way through *Magic Carpet Ride*, probably giving everyone indigestion — he should have changed the tape, put on the slow...

"Hello?"

"Julie! You're back."

"Five minutes ago. Happy birthday!"

"Thanks. So how was it?"

"Just fine. Great aunt Mei Fung is on her way to join the spirits of our ancestors. My great uncle expects to be talking to her any day now. How's the party? Can I still come? Jimmy's right here — he says there's no problem with the car."

Julie was doing her best to hide it, but she was exhausted; Hal could hear the frayed edges around her voice. He said: "What about coming out tomorrow, Jules?"

"Tomorrow?"

"There's something I want you to hear. Actually, I want you to translate it. Something fairly interesting."

"Can't it wait till Monday?"

"You tell me. I found an old recording last night when I was making tapes for the party. Remember after that first Midland meeting, when I left the tape deck in Sawtrell's office?"

"Yes."

"I'd left it on. It was still picking up."

"So?"

"I found the tape. Guess what…Graham Sawtrell speaks Chinese!"

"*What*?"

"Julie, I have a recording of a conversation between Sawtrell and our Chinese 'maintenance man' and someone else — an older guy, I'm almost sure it's Crawford. There's a bit of English, but most of the time all three of them are speaking Chinese — the butcher, the baker, the candlestick maker!"

"Play it for me now!" Julie sounded breathlessly excited. "Play it through the Sony over the phone."

"I don't have the Sony. It's at the office."

"What about the main system?"

"There are a zillion people listening to Steppenwolf right now."

"Hermann Hesse at a birthday party?"

Hal laughed. "It was a rock band too, back in the Dark Ages!"

"What about the Jeep? It's got a cellular and a tape deck."

"No flies on you, are there?"

Verity Ames opened the bedroom door, letting in a blast of music, said "Sorry!" and shut it again, causing Hal another absurd flush of guilt.

Julie said: "Do you know if it's Cantonese? Can you remember any words? If it's Mandarin, I'm no good."

Hal chewed his lip. On mental playback he found he could lift almost nothing from the babble. "Only the names," he said. "The Chinese was called Ho. Ho called the older man Dei Gin Taiwan."

"Huh? That doesn't make any sense. *Dei Gin*…that's Cantonese, it means 'carpet.' But *Taiwan*? Taiwan's a place. Are you sure it isn't *Tai Wong*?"

"Could be. Why?"

"*Dei Gin Tai Wong* would mean 'Carpet King' — like a nickname. Come to think of it…"

"What?"

"I dunno. It sort of rings a bell. Hang on — I'll ask Jimmy." He listened for a minute as she spoke Cantonese to her brother. "Bells ringing everywhere!" she told Hal. "We're going to ask Dad tomorrow." Julie's father managed the Toronto edition of a Hong

Kong newspaper called *Sing tao jih pao*, with smart offices in Chinatown. Hal could hear more animated Cantonese in the background, then Julie came back on. "Jimmy says he needs the car tomorrow. I'll have to come on the Go Train."

"Runs every hour. I can pick you up in Oshawa. How does the two o'clock sound? Gets in around two forty-five."

"I'll come on one condition: that I don't have to help clear up the party!"

Hal laughed. "I promise. Only murder mysteries!"

A pause.

"Hal?"

"Yes, Julie?"

"Happy birthday."

Hal kept the warm receiver in his hand, pressed to his ear, listening to his heart beating, waiting for her to break the connection.

He waited almost half a minute.

"Julie Lee?" he said softly.

"Yes, Sebastian-san?"

Hal waited a few seconds longer and then, very gently, put down the phone.

CHAPTER
28

Tyah didn't mind being nice to Vanessa but it was hard work for a Sunday morning. Half an hour and nothing to show but a burning ache in her wrist and a sore spot on the tip of her tongue from the unaccustomed pH.

She rested again, her hand lying in limp defeat on Vanessa's thigh, while those enormous yellow and brown eyes scorned her from the pillow. Vanessa sucked her teeth: "No patience! Worse than a man. Quick now, before me lose prime!"

Tyah roused herself for another assault. She dipped her middle finger, coaxed slickness onto Vanessa's inflamed clitoris and began polishing again.

"Yeah…like that! Pussy sweet now…pussy readeee!" After five minutes, things were looking up; Vanessa began to jerk her hips and moan in a rich, fruity voice. "Faster…oh faster now!" Tyah lathered with all four fingers, tugging and twisting Vanessa's nipples with her other hand. "Come on Nessa…this time…yeah…"

"Faster!"

The ache in her wrist was so intense it was crossing over into some kind of pleasure.

"Bite me!"

Tyah took one black, stiff-as-rubber nipple between her teeth.

"Bite it!" Vanessa's narrow hips began to quiver, her thighs began to scissor, her moaning became a joyous, rising song.

Then, like an air raid siren, the phone rang.

Tyah ignored it, let it ring three…four…five times. "That's right baby, nearly there…" She picked up the pace. "Come on baby…you can do it!" But she knew it was hopeless.

Vanessa quieted Tyah's hand with a deep, shuddering sigh. She lay still for one more ring, then reached over to the bedside table.

"Who dat?" She listened for a moment, scowling, then rolled back to Tyah. "For you." She dropped the receiver into Tyah's slippery, aching hand and slumped back onto the pillow.

It was Marc, glad to hear Tyah's voice. He'd been out of town with the band, just got her message.

Tyah said it was good to hear him, too. For a couple of minutes she caught up on Marc's musical career, then she came to the point: "I'm going to be in Montreal, Marc. Think I could stay for a few days?"

"Hey…of course!" Marc told her. "We're going back on the road for a week, start tonight, then we're back in town till Christmas."

"I need to come right away. Tell you the truth, I'm in a bit of trouble."

"Yeah?"

Tyah hesitated. But Christ — the guy was a musician, he would understand. "I've got a drug problem needs solving. There's a detox program here but they've got a six-week waiting list. Montreal is taking day-patients right away. I need a base."

"I see." Now the hesitation was Marc's. He probably understood only too well: a houseguest with the shakes and the screaming meemies, throwing up. There was probably a girlfriend in there somewhere as well. Tyah swung her legs off the bed, away from Vanessa.

"I'm sorry, Marc. I shouldn't've…"

"Non," he said quickly. "It's okay. You were Felice's best friend. That's good enough. I'm glad you thought of me. You come down, stay as long as you want. You need money for a ticket?"

"No."

"Got a pen?"

"Do you still live on Saint-Denis?"

"Oui."

"Then it's in my book. Can I come tonight?"

Tonight was fine. Marc would leave the key with the concierge, and the number of his agent in case she needed to reach him on the road. There'd be food in the refrigerator. Tyah gave him relieved, heartfelt thanks before she hung up.

Vanessa lit two cigarettes and passed her one, letting her fingernails trail down Tyah's back. "You goin' then."

Tyah barely heard the resigned statement. She was staring at a trio of plastic shopping bags in the corner, frown-lines deepening in her forehead. She stood up, covered the distance in two long strides. She tore out the bags' contents — shoes, costumes, make-up — those things, along with the portable television, that she had brought from Dowde Street.

"Christ almighty it's still there!"

"What 'happen?"

Tyah concentrated fiercely. "I got back into bed, didn't I? I was in bed when I called you. Goddamn it, I must have left it on the *bed*!"

"What you talkin' about?"

"My book! My *address* book!" Tyah sank down amongst her stuff. "Shane's going to find it if he hasn't already. He's going to tear that room apart and he's going to find it. And then he's going to go through every name and address. I *know* him."

Vanessa looked alarmed. "My number in there?"

Tyah jammed her cigarette between her teeth, rummaged for a pair of underpants and pulled them on. "I've got to go get it. Right *now*."

She had a fix before she left, the trampled-on Chinese Red that was all Vanessa had been able to score over the weekend. There were rumours on the street about some bad China cut with strychnine, but junkies would always gossip and there was always risk;

hell, you could pop a spiked painkiller from a drug store these days and die horribly.

The heroin wasn't poison but it was garbage compared to Shane's product. When Tyah left Vanessa's apartment at eleven she felt terrible and must have looked it; the cab driver, who had four NO SMOKING signs and air fresheners back and front, kept his nose in the air all the way to Dowde. When she asked him to wait, he said he had another call and drove away.

Tyah felt suddenly alone and vulnerable as she entered number thirty-nine and climbed the dark stairs. On the second floor she could hear the crackpot pacing the floor above, in the room next to hers. She knew his name from the mail boxes — Libby, like the beans. She should have been more thorough, should have called Libby from Vanessa's and asked him to check her room, make sure no one was there — should at least have called her *own* number.

Tyah considered going back down and calling from the pay phone on the corner, then dismissed the idea as paranoia. Besides, she didn't have any change.

She went up the last flight as quietly as the creaking stairs would allow, pausing every few seconds to listen. When she reached the third floor, the pacing stopped and a shadow appeared under crazy Libby's door — nosy as usual.

She waited a full minute, taking advantage of the quiet to look and listen. No shadows under *her* door, no sound from inside. Of course Shane would have been there. What there was behind the door would have been junked. Not that she cared, as long as he'd missed her little book. Oddly enough, what she dreaded most, apart from not finding her address book, was seeing the refrigerator open, the weeks-old submarine looking like some mutant caterpillar with blue fur. In the back of her throat she caught the fume of mould, dry and sour...

Cursing her inflamed imagination, Tyah unlocked the door and threw it open.

There was no smell beyond the usual staleness. Surprisingly, everything *looked* exactly as she had left it, not that she believed her eyes.

It was impossible to tell whether or not the bedclothes had been searched — she had left them in a rumpled heap. She snatched up the pilled blanket and shook it, then the sheet, flushing a small, fluttering object into the air.

Tyah's breath escaped in a hiss of relief. She retrieved the notebook, riffled the pages to make sure it was intact, then hurried out to the landing with her prize. She was closing the door behind her when her telephone blared, bouncing her heart into her mouth.

Shane? Oh what a gift of timing that would be. A golden chance to deliver the fond goodbye she had rehearsed a thousand times over the last twelve months.

She opened the door and went back inside to the phone, mustering all her dignity as she lifted the receiver.

So long, Scum of the Earth!

"Hello?" she said.

"T. Whiteside?"

"Yeah. This is Tyah Whiteside."

"My name is Hal Sebastian. This might sound a little strange but...somebody called T. Whiteside sent me some photographs in the mail and I'm trying to contact that person. You're the last T. Whiteside in the phone book, which kind of makes you my last shot!"

Tyah fumbled behind her for one of the chairs and slowly sat down.

"Hello?" said Hal Sebastian. "Are you there?"

"Yeah, I'm here."

"So...*did* you send them?"

"That's right, Hal."

She could hear him trying to suppress his excitement. "How did you know they were mine?"

Tyah took a deep breath. "We met once — at the Doyle Hotel. You'd lost a camera. You gave me your name and number." She gave a short, dry laugh. "I used to be a cowgirl."

A second's pause. "That's right! I remember! So you did get my camera back. You must have if you had the film."

"It's a long story. I can't get into it now. I'm going to have to call you back on this, Hal."

"No! Please don't go yet. I'm not just calling about my camera. It's much more important than that."

"What is?"

"They *weren't* all my photographs in that envelope. There was one odd one. A Chinese guy. Do you know which shot I mean? Do you know who he is?"

"I really have to call you back."

He sounded desperate. "*Please* tell me if you know about this — *please*, Tyah!"

"Okay, Hal, so I know who he is."

"Then tell me one more thing: did he have anything to do with what happened at the Doyle — the murders at the Doyle Hotel?"

"How the Christ did you know that?"

There was a moment of silence. She could feel his excitement burning up the line. "Why did you send me his picture, Tyah? *Why?*"

"It's... hard to explain."

"Do the police know about him?"

"I'm not goin' near the fuckin' police! I already told the police everything I know. I seen him at the Doyle, I was *there*, right? I seen him go for Carny Danial, I seen..."

Hal sounded incredulous: "If you were a witness...if you saw this Chinese guy at the scene of the crime, how come the public was never informed? The police never said..."

"Welcome to the world, Hal. I'm a stripper, right? Been in a little trouble before. They found some stuff in my car. My testimony wasn't reliable or some shit."

"Did you show them the photograph?"

"I didn't have it then. But it's not going to make any difference now. Not unless you've got a whole lot more fuckin' charisma than me!"

"I've got *one* thing."

"Oh yeah?"

He hesitated again. "Do you know who the Midland Development Corporation are?"

"Sure. They own the Vanguard Building. They owned the Doyle."

"Do you know anything about this Chinese guy working for Midland?"

"What?"

"I have reason to believe he was. That's an even longer story. We have to meet. This is way too…"

"I can't meet you," she said. "Not now. Not for a few weeks. I'm going out of town."

"Please, Tyah! You *have* to see me."

"I don't have to do a fuckin' thing, pal."

"Don't you want to get this guy?"

"The cops aren't going to…"

"Listen!" Hal interrupted. "I have a tape recording. I have a recording of the Chinese man in the photograph in conversation with the president and the executive vice-president of Midland on the night of the murders."

"You *what*?"

"His name is Ho Kwan Shing and he's on Midland's payroll and I can *prove* it! Tyah, listen…I don't know why I ended up with this photograph or why you had my film in the first place or a whole lot of other things; but you must have wanted me to help or you wouldn't have sent me that envelope."

"I…I don't…"

"Look, it doesn't even matter. I'm here and I *can* help. But not until I know what *you* know. You're on Dowde Street? I can be there in an hour."

"No! You can't come here."

"Okay, then you come to Grace Street. I'm out of town right now, but I'll drive in. You know where Grace is? It's in the west end."

"Where's out of town?"

"I'm in a place called Wesleyville."

"Where's *that*?"

"East of Toronto. About an hour away."

She thought a moment. "Is it anywhere near the 401?"

"Right off it. Ten minutes at the outside."

Tyah wound the telephone cord until it was a tight black tube around her index finger, making it throb. "I'll come to Wesleyville, okay? If it's east, it's on my way. I guess it won't hurt to talk for an hour. How do I get there from the highway?"

He told her to start looking for signposts after Bond Head, where the highway first narrowed to two lanes. Wesleyville itself was tiny, she couldn't miss the church. There would be a white Jeep Cherokee parked outside.

It was only after Hal Sebastian had rung off that Tyah became aware of the resonance on her line — a kind of hollowness to the amplified sound of her own breathing — something she had never noticed on her phone before.

The kind of sound you got if someone were listening on an extension.

Tyah realized she was being paranoid again. She called a cab to get back to Vanessa's — little chance of pulling one on Dowde Street on a Sunday morning — and settled back to wait for it. Vanessa had agreed to lend her the bus fare on top of what she had already shelled out for dope and food over the last few days; she wouldn't appreciate having to increase the loan to cover a rental car, but she knew Tyah would be good for it as soon as she was working again.

In the next room, Libby resumed his pacing, back and forth. Tyah knew it was dangerous to stay here. In a moment she would get up and go and wait for the cab outside, but just now she needed to sit quiet for a few minutes longer. Hal Sebastian's phone call had made her dizzy. She was feeling slightly sick and sweating a bit — cold and sticky — telltale signs that the poor-quality smack was no longer sustaining her.

Craziness! How in hell did he know to call her? She had deliberately put no return address on the envelope. Was he right, had she called for help when she threw in that last photograph? Right or not, there was one thing Hal Sebastian was going to have to understand straight off the bat: no way was she going to talk to any cops until she was back on her feet. No fucking way on earth she was going cold turkey for Metro Homicide. A month, maybe six weeks from now she might feel different. Even then she'd have to worry about Shane Pilch.

Tyah surveyed the gloomy hovel that had been home for over a year. She wasn't going to do this ever again. She wasn't even going to dance again. As soon as she was through detox she'd get some other kind of job, find a place and buy another sewing machine. Take it from there. And maybe some day — maybe one fine, clear day she'd give Fletcher a call. Just for old time's sake.

She felt ready for the stairs now. She stood, walked a little shakily out onto the landing. She held her breath, blaming her sick imagination when she heard a footfall on the staircase when it was only a creak in a creaky house.

She closed the flimsy door behind her, firmly and forever.

And heard it again: a long, stealthy creak…someone placing their weight slowly, trying not to be heard.

Bullshit!

She tiptoed to the top of the stairs, hesitated, then took the first one. She went down another, then another, then three more in quick succession until she had reached the half-landing where the staircase doglegged.

Nobody there. No way. Just an old, rickety rooming house.

But her rioting imagination was immune to reason. Shane would do something just like this, it told her. Shane would tease her like this, cat and mouse. She could hear him in her mind, just as plain as if he were really there below, creeping up the stairs.

Hello, Tyah.

Soft and insinuating, a travesty of politeness. She could feel the pain of the introductory blow, perfectly timed and regulated, not that he would care this time how badly he hurt her. No minor transgression this time, like missing an appointment or looking sideways at him — if he caught her now he would do her real and permanent harm. He might kill her.

Tyah swooned on the half-landing, unravelling, fighting for a spark of courage to stop herself bursting into tears. Unable to bear her foolish misery any longer, she spoke his name:

"Shane?"

No reply. Of course not. She was going to get away clean this time. Forever!

Emboldened, Tyah leaned over the inside rail and looked down into the stairwell's central shaft to confirm her foolishness.

Her eyes literally bulged from her head.

For a second she stood rooted, honestly believing he was an hallucination — a new visual dimension to her terror. Her feet didn't come unglued until he was half a flight away on the second floor and then she whirled to face back the way she had come.

For a paralyzing second, the six steps reared before her like the sheer face of a mountain, and then she was scrambling up, *crawling* up the last three, then along the corridor, past the bathroom towards the dented steel fire door at the end.

Tyah hurled herself against the crash bar but the frame was warped and the door stuck and her momentum slammed her into the metal surface with a sickening explosion of pain. She waltzed away, disoriented, far enough back from the door that she was once again level with the bathroom by the time her vision cleared and she saw him down the corridor, the pale moon-face from her nightmare, the glittering hand.

She fumbled her way inside the bathroom and threw her shoulder against the door, ramming home the bolt with less than a second to spare before the Chinese slammed against it. Unlike the room doors it was solid-core, original to the house, and it held.

"Help! Help me!" But even as she screamed, she knew that no one would come, not at thirty-nine Dowde Street.

Another crash shocked the room, but still the door, and the bolt, held fast.

"Libby! Call the cops! Libby!"

He hit the door again, savagely, and this time the bolt assembly jumped a half-inch from the door frame as the screws pulled out.

When Tyah saw that it was about to let go, her anger flared in a pure, white hot jet, burning off terror and confusion. She turned from the door and cast about the bathroom for anything — a glass mug, a toilet-brush — *any* kind of weapon, settling on the only possibility — a pitted chrome towel-bar beside the sink, already half out of the wall. She yanked at it with desperate strength and it came free, plaster dust spurting at either end.

The door shuddered again.

One more. The next one would be it.

Tyah was standing well back when the door burst and he came through. She saw the scalpel and his little, premature smile. Felice's killer had less than half a second to mime his surprise as Tyah painted a chromium rainbow in the air above his head.

The towel-bar bounced off the top of his skull, ringing like a bell. He threw up his hands and the scalpel flew, stinging Tyah's cheek, skittering ahead of her as she followed him through the open door into the corridor and swung again. He crashed against the far wall with blood sheeting down his face, shrieking in rage and pain. He was groping blindly, pawing at the blood in his eyes, stumbling towards the fire door when Tyah hit him a third time on the back of his head, dropping him like an empty suit of clothes.

For a minute she stood swaying, powerless, battered by a tidal wave of adrenalin, gazing at the prone, bleeding figure on the floor of the corridor. As soon as the wave began to subside, she dropped the towel-bar and ran.

CHAPTER
29

Since her telephone conversation with Alistair just over a week ago, Kate was no longer able to suppress her fantasy.

Mead End at Christmas, its deep sills pillowed with snow, fires blazing in every hearth, a shimmering tree grazing the hall ceiling. Christmas plans — plane tickets for Aspen or Saint Moritz.

Summer visions of swirling green flecked with brilliant colour. *Sounds* of summer...the *pop pop* of tennis racquets, the languid murmur of a garden party, the chuckling of water flowing — *endlessly* flowing into a goldfish pond from a bottomless Arabian jar.

She dreamed Conelly hide and premium gasoline and beating wings as a helicopter skimmed the lawn, like a dragon-fly.

She saw a villa on a mountainside above a crescent of white sand beside an azure ocean: the Caribbean, California, the South of France, a Greek Island...open the atlas and stick in a pin!

She dreamed schools with famous names where her child would befriend the children of the rich and powerful...and be on her way. And the network would work for Hal too, if he wanted. If he wanted to, he could restore the Taj Mahal!

The *ping* of the toaster-oven returned Kate to the aroma of warm croissants and fresh coffee. She collected two mugs, the cream jug and a pot of strawberry jam, put them on a tray with the croissants and the coffee, and carried them up. She avoided looking down at the party mess as she climbed the stairs in her dressing-gown, humming one of Hal's golden oldies from last night. It was almost noon; passing Rain's empty room, she couldn't help feeling smug to think that the Woolleys had started their Sunday morning five hours ago, up to their ears in Cheerios and peanut butter! Her overdue heart-to-heart with Hal was going to have to wait a little longer — after a late, lazy Continental breakfast in bed, she was going to screw his brains out!

Hal was propped up against the pillows, staring at the tent of his feet and chewing his upper lip. He looked tired in spite of the late hour; she had been aware of his wakeful tossing in the night, his getting up in the small hours and going downstairs.

"Room service, monsieur!" She put the tray down on her side of the bed. "Did I just hear you talking to someone? The Woolleys?"

Hal shook his head vaguely. "No...no, I didn't call them. Should we?"

Kate perched on the edge of the bed, poured cream then coffee. "Who *were* you talking to?"

Hal suddenly came to life. He threw back the duvet and got out of bed. "I want you to listen to something, Katy."

"Right now?"

"It won't take a minute." He got his robe from the closet, pulled it on. "I simply need you to listen to a couple of seconds of tape and tell me whose voice you hear."

Mystified, Kate followed him out to the gallery. "If I get it right, do I win the matching luggage or the dinette suite?"

"Wait there, you don't need to come down."

Kate frowned as she watched him go down the stairs to the stereo. "You still haven't told me who you phoned."

"I'll tell you in a minute. Just listen, okay?" The speakers crackled to life, a spurt of something unintelligible as he cued up a cassette. Then a voice she recognized, resounding through the church:

Have you got it switched over?

Another voice: *Yes, go ahead.*

The voice she knew again: *Good afternoon, Ho Kwan Shing.*

Hal stopped the tape. "Do you recognize anyone?"

"What is that, Hal?"

He came to the foot of the stairs. "Don't worry right now. Just tell me: do you recognize either of these two voices? I can play it again if..."

"It's Alistair Crawford. What's going on?"

He came up the stairs, took her by the hand back to the bedroom. "Let's have breakfast and I'll tell you everything I know so far."

Kate had one sip of coffee. After that, their breakfast lay cold and forgotten on the tray while Hal told her, starting one day eighteen months ago at the Vanguard.

He told how, with Julie, he had surprised a man on the fire stairs, possibly tampering with a door connecting to the Doyle Hotel. A second encounter, at the Midland offices on the night of the Doyle murders, Hal thinking nothing of it, assuming that the man belonged to Midland's maintenance department, until Tyah Whiteside sent him the photograph.

Hal looked gravely at his wife. "The link with Midland was tenuous, nothing more than speculation on my part...until two nights ago."

"Two nights ago?" Kate could feel cold perspiration all over her body.

He told her about a tape recording no one had known existed, made on his Sony in Graham Sawtrell's office: a taped conversation between the Chinese and Sawtrell and another man. "Last night I suspected it was Alistair Crawford but I couldn't be sure."

"And now I've confirmed it."

Hal paused uneasily. "I'm sorry, Kate. I know he's your friend."

Kate spoke in a hard, flat tone. "What are they saying on the tape, Hal?"

"It seems to be a dispute about payment to the Chinese man. But most of the time they're *speaking* Chinese — Sawtrell and Crawford! So I called Julie. I asked her to come out here this afternoon to translate it. If there's anything incriminating — even if there isn't — I think we should discuss what we're going to do about it."

"*Do* about it?" Kate couldn't hide her alarm. "You mean go to the police?"

"Don't you see the possibility we're facing here? You remember the first 'Graffiti' murders, in the summer of 1988 — Lena DiMaio, then the other two in September? The serial murder of strippers, right? Absolutely tailor-made for Midland when they needed a way to shut Carny Danial down, when they realized mere money wouldn't get him off their back. Hitting Danial would bring them under immediate suspicion, so they killed some more dancers. As long as they exactly copied the Graffiti Killer's style — the pink spray paint and the mutilation and his choice of victims — they had the perfect scapegoat!"

Hal's eyes burned with excitement. "The horrible thing is, it's brilliant! They knew *exactly* the kind of monster they would be creating with a triple-mutilation murder at the Doyle. They *knew* the publicity it would generate, the public pressure that would be brought to bear to close the hotel down."

He was on his feet now, hands thrust deep into the pockets of his robe, pacing the bedroom.

"I don't know where the whole Chinese thing comes in, but I'm not sure that it matters right now. Assume they *have* a Chinese underworld connection: they hire their assassin to commit copycat murder, and what happens? Midland comes up roses — hero of the people, defender of public morality! Even if the police d*i*d suspect Midland's involvement — and they must have at some point — they couldn't say or do anything without proof, especially when Midland had overwhelming public support to restore the Van. Carny Danial did end up dead, yes, but from a heart attack at the scene of the murder — he wasn't actually murdered."

Hal came back to the bed. "What Midland *doesn't* know is that Danial — or *someone* — managed to take a snapshot of their Chinese killer!" He reached towards the bedside. "This!"

Kate stared at it. The photograph Alistair had called her about: a man with the power to hurt him. To hurt Kate.

But now Hal had that power too, didn't he?

Hal was saying: "I was up half the night thinking all this out. I was also looking for the negative to this but *all* the negs seem to be missing, along with the best shots of the Vanguard. Have you seen them anywhere?"

Kate dropped the photograph on the bed and stood up. "No, I haven't seen them." She went to her closet for her clothes. "You're *still* speculating really, aren't you?" she said. "Until that tape is translated, you don't have proof of anything."

Hal looked at her. "There's one thing I've left out. That call I made just now? It was to Tyah Whiteside. She was in a hurry — I still don't know how my camera came to be used, or how she knew where to send the developed film, but she *did* confirm one thing on the phone, Kate: according to Tyah Whiteside, the Chinese man in this photograph *did* murder three strippers at the Doyle Hotel eighteen months ago."

"Who the hell *is* this mysterious Tyah Whiteside?"

"She was a stripper at the Doyle. She..."

"A stripper!" Kate laughed mockingly. "So a stripper has confirmed it, has she? Well in *that* case!"

He looked at her, confused by her reaction. "You can judge her integrity for yourself. She's coming here this afternoon."

Kate swallowed. "Is that right? Quite the little party. Seems I'm the last to know everything!"

Hal came toward her. He was diffident now, picking his words carefully, reacting to the hard rime on her voice, the stiffness of her movements as she pulled on her sweatpants and top. "I didn't want to come to you with pure speculation, Kate. That's why I waited to tell you any of this."

"But you told Julie, didn't you?"

"Kate...Julie was *with* me when I..."

"What? When you lost your camera in the Doyle Hotel? You've never taken *me* to a strip club! Did it turn you on to watch naked women with Julie?"

His eyes flashed angrily. "That's absurd!" He followed her to the bedroom door. "Jesus, babe...Look, I know this is a lot to take in.

Especially hard for you because of your relationship with Alistair Crawford."

"I thought you had one too! Don't you think you've done all right by him?"

He shouted angrily down the stairs after her: "What's *that* supposed to mean? Are you saying I should *ignore* all this? Is that what I should do?"

She didn't turn round. "Get dressed, Hal. There's a lot of cleaning up down here."

Kate demanded loud music while they worked, which Hal gladly supplied; it eliminated the need for anything but basic, task-related dialogue. He rinsed and boxed the rented things and stacked the boxes in the vestibule while she washed their own dishes and glasses, emptied ashtrays and wiped up crumbs and coffee rings. Hal left for the station at two-fifteen.

Kate watched from the kitchen window as he drove away. He had taken the tape, which was a pity, but only to be expected. They would want to listen to it on their way back from the station, wouldn't they? Hal and his fucking slant.

Was he fucking her?

Probably. Why not? They did everything else together.

Bottles of party liquor crowded the kitchen counter. She pulled the nearest one to her and unscrewed the cap. Without looking at the label she took two gulps from the neck.

It was light rum. Kate braced herself against the counter, breathing steadily to keep the liquor and the howling anger down. She took another gulp and breathed again. As soon as she felt the alcohol humming into her bloodstream, she pushed the bottle away, picked up the photograph and got a matchbook from the drawer. She would have to destroy the tape later. The tape was the most important thing but this would do for a start.

She held the print over the sink to light it, turning it this way and that until the flame had licked away everything but the corner between her fingers, which she dropped at the last moment. It made a tiny hiss as it landed in the wet sink.

CHAPTER
30

Hal parked the Jeep near the station exit. As Julie emerged from the terminal, he got out and walked to meet her. Their tentative greeting was a clear reference to their intimacy on the phone last night, an awkwardness they both recognized, then rejected, then smothered with a safe bear-hug. They walked to the Jeep arm in arm, their breath trailing, blending in the cool, damp air.

"You don't *look* a whole year older," Julie teased him.

"I sure feel it. I didn't sleep a whole lot last night, thinking about the tape."

"Did you play it for Kate?"

Hal nodded. "It's Crawford all right. Did you and Jimmy ask your Dad about the Carpet King?"

"Oh yes."

Hal climbed in behind the wheel and shut his door.

Julie slammed hers. "Are you ready? Alistair Crawford *isn't* Alistair Crawford. His name is Reginald Fairbairn, also known as Dei Gin Tai Wong — the Carpet King — to certain residents of Ko Shing, which is the warehouse district of Hong Kong."

Hal frowned. "I thought Crawford's background was Malaysian."

"You thought wrong. So does Customs and Immigration." Julie's dark eyes glittered. "Ko Shing, by the way, is where forty percent of the world's raw heroin supply is processed and packaged for sale and export."

"You mean...he's a doper?"

"Was," corrected Julie. "Although 'doper' is hardly the word for someone with top Triad connections moving kilos of processed heroin every week."

Hal gazed at her. "How on earth did you find this out?"

"From Dad. Listen, you want to know Fairbairn's favoured method of exporting his product? *Eviscerated babies.*"

"What?"

"Gutted babies full of heroin that appear to be asleep in their mother's arms through customs and on the plane. What kind of asshole wakes a sleeping baby, right?"

Hal closed his mouth and swallowed. "God in heaven!"

"Nice, huh? Then in 1974, Fairbairn got busted. The Royal Hong Kong Police had him on conspiracy to murder, five counts, plus kidnapping, extortion and, of course, trafficking in narcotics."

Hal had gone slightly pale. "*Eviscerated babies*! Mother of God..."

"But they didn't get him in 1974. He used his underworld connections and his smuggling expertise to smuggle himself out." She glanced out of the window. "How long are we going to sit in this parking lot?"

"Until you've finished," Hal said. "This is utterly incredible. So what's with this name...this 'Carpet King'?"

"I'm coming to that. The RHKP inquiry calculated that over the years Fairbairn had accumulated drug profits to the tune of two hundred million dollars, which he had been quietly investing abroad — the Hong Kong police were never able to find out which countries. But we know, don't we Sebastian-san? We know where." Julie was smiling luminously.

"Holy shit!"

"Exactly. In 1975, after a year hiding out somewhere in the Golden Triangle while things cooled down, Fairbairn came here after his money. He had a new face — he could afford state-of-the-art plastic surgery — and a new, RCMP-proof identity. Enter Alistair Crawford, tin-mining magnate from Malaysia. He immediately began consolidating his substantial Canadian real-estate holdings into…"

"The Midland Development Corporation."

"Now…the name 'Carpet King' was the thing that triggered my memory, except it didn't go off. Dad's *did*. His paper covered the Fairbairn story exhaustively at the time, all the Hong Kong papers did. I was only nine, but I remember the talk — an Englishman with Triad connections, the business about the babies — it was a big deal, the whole Hong Kong Chinese community was talking about the Carpet King.

"The name means just how it sounds. Fairbairn's cover was the carpet trade, and we're not talking broadloom here — I mean, ten-, twenty-thousand-dollar Oriental carpets. Apparently he's a world expert, pioneered two-way trade in the Far East — importing Persian carpets, exporting the finest Chinese and Tibetan pieces. He was legitimate for years, but all the time he was getting more and more addicted to his own stock. He was like a junkie trying to deal heroin — which is exactly what he finally *did* do in order to finance his carpet habit. It was perfect for him. He was already in the import/export business: heroin was the same game with different players. The inquiry found that on top of the two hundred million in drug funds, Fairbairn had shipped out a carpet collection worth anywhere up to *ten million dollars!*"

"All wool, huh?"

Julie beamed. "That's it. We were at the paper all morning, going through the microfilm library. Once you get my old man going…"

Hal looked concerned. "Did you tell him why you wanted to know?"

"Uh-uh. I told him I'd read something in a magazine and I was interested. Did you bring the tape?" When Hal nodded, she reached across to the steering column and twisted the ignition key. "I'll listen while you drive."

"One last revelation before we go," Hal said as he put the Jeep into gear. "I finally got hold of T. Whiteside."

"You're kidding!"

"T. is for Tyah. She was a stripper at the Doyle Hotel. And a witness to our Chinese friend being there the night the three dancers were murdered."

Julie frowned. "A witness? I don't understand."

"Join the club. She was reluctant to talk on the phone, but she *did* agree to come out to Wesleyville…this afternoon!"

Julie nodded slowly. Suddenly she seemed uncomfortable. "Hal…does Kate know why I'm here today?" It had rankled as well as surprised Julie to learn how the Distillery battle had been won.

"Yes she does," Hal said soberly. "I can't say she was thrilled when I told her what we suspect."

He drove towards the exit. All the other traffic connected with the two o'clock train had long since departed, leaving the parking lot Sunday-empty except for the employees' rank and the Jeep and a dark green Jaguar at the far opposite end.

Hal wheeled out of the lot, took the 401 on-ramp at Park Road and joined the quiet highway. He waited until they were settled in the fast lane at cruising speed, then reached down to the cassette deck and touched PLAY.

The dialect was Cantonese. He let Julie listen all the way through, glancing sideways now and then to monitor her reaction, his excitement rising as he watched her expression change from curious to absorbed to appalled. He waited until the part where Ho had left the office, until Sawtrell's "*Mother fucker*!," and then he could wait no longer. He stopped the tape.

"There's nothing much from here on in," he explained. "Sawtrell's secretary comes back, Sawtrell leaves, then a lot of tape hiss, then me coming back for the Sony." He took a deep breath. "So tell me, Jules."

When there was no reply he glanced sideways, found her staring at the dashboard. "Julie?"

"I think you better stop the car, Hal."

"Are you all right?"

"I'm okay. I just don't think we should get into this while you're driving."

"I can listen and drive."

"No, Hal. This is not something to listen to with distractions."

"I *can't* stop," he grumbled. "I'm on the bloody highway!"

"Get off it then!"

A quarter mile produced the Bond Head exit and Hal took it. It was the same road Kate had travelled that day of discovery eighteen months ago, with her sleeping family in the Chrysler. Spring then, but now it was November and the maples no longer made a green canopy over the road; now they twisted worried black fingers in the watery sky. The pretty Cape Cod cottages were shuttered, their driveways empty. At the end of the long straightway, Lake Ontario had lost its sparkle and its clean horizon, lake and sky merging grey.

Hal rounded the corner onto the lakeshore, brought the Jeep to a halt on the gravel shoulder and shut off the engine. Behind them, across a narrow channel, the crew at the Bond Head Marina were aboard the Travelift, plucking the last sailboat from the choppy water, alerted by the weather warning of a freeze and high winds.

Julie had been stubbornly silent since the highway. Now Hal shifted sideways to confront her. "Okay, we're stopped. So tell me...they did it, right? Crawford and Sawtrell via Ho Kwan Shing...they killed those three dancers at the Doyle in order to get it closed down, and used the Graffiti Killer as their scapegoat. That's right, isn't it?"

With the slightest motion Julie shook her head.

"Come on..."

"No, Hal." She spoke very quietly, defying his exuberance. He suddenly realized that Julie was angry — deeply so. "What you've just described, that would be bad enough. But the truth is much worse." For the first time since the station, she looked him in the eyes. "It's beyond belief."

Almost reluctantly, she cued the tape to the point at which Ho Kwan Shing entered Graham Sawtrell's office. Once again Hal heard Sawtrell's livid outburst:

For Christ's sake! He's here! Ho is! Standing right in front of me!
Again Hal heard Ho Kwan Shing assaulted by Sawtrell's flawed but
fluent Cantonese. At the end of the tirade, Julie stopped the tape
and translated in a flat, undramatic voice, a clear sign of how much
she was affected; Hal had to add his own emphasis and exclama-
tion marks.

Get out! Sawtrell ordered the Chinese man. *You were forbidden
to come here, especially tonight. Are you insane?*

Julie then punched in Ho's cocky response, and translated: *We
must speak of the payment now. Maybe after, you won't want to
pay very much.*

Sawtrell: *Don't be ridiculous! You know the arrangement. It was
explained to you with absolute clarity.*

Ho: *I must have the word of Dei Gin Tai Wong on this matter.
My uncle assured me I would have the Carpet King's word.*

Sawtrell: *Out of the question!*

Ho: *He is there! On your telephone! I will not leave until I have
spoken with him.*

Sawtrell: *I'm warning you, Ho.*

A derisive giggle from Ho: *What are you going to do? Throw me
out, make a big scene?*

Next came Sawtrell's livid English into the phone as he spoke to
Dei Gin Tai Wong.

Then Ho again: *We will have a conference call. You will hear that
the Carpet King shows respect for Ho Kwan Shing!*

Julie fast forwarded over Sawtrell's fuming, punching back into
a long pause as Crawford-Fairbairn-Dei Gin Tai Wong chewed
Sawtrell's ear off. Hal could picture Ho waiting with an impudent
smile, the favoured nephew. But where was the surprise? Everything
Hal had heard so far only confirmed what he already suspected;
there was nothing to challenge the copycat theory. Also, there was
a dismal lack of anything solidly incriminating.

Julie must have sensed that he was about to say as much and held
up a quieting hand. "Just listen."

Sawtrell came on again: *All right. If you insist.* And now came the sequence Hal had played for Kate this morning, Crawford asking: *Have you got it switched over?*

Sawtrell: *Yes, go ahead.*

Crawford: *Good afternoon, Ho Kwan Shing.*

Ho: *Good afternoon, Carpet King.*

Crawford's soft dialect flowed from the Jeep's stereo. "He speaks better Cantonese than my father," Julie said bitterly, then began to translate.

I would not tolerate this, Ho, were it not for the high esteem in which I hold your dear uncle. And I concede that you have completed two successful jobs for us, for which you have earned my congratulations and my reassurance: if everything goes well tonight, you will be paid in full, as agreed. There. You have my word. You will under no circumstances make contact with us again — any future communication will be initiated by myself or Mr. Sawtrell. Is that absolutely clear? Your payment, as in the past, will be generous. He chuckled dryly. *Too generous, I might add, for six little whores!*

Ho, with a smile in his voice: *Striptease artists, Carpet King.*

Crawford: *There's a difference? Yes, I suppose there is.* A regretful chuckle: *At my age, alas, one is liable to forget such differences.*

Julie stopped the tape. She had lost all trace of her skeptical good humour. Her attitude, bent forward with her hands clasped in her lap, seemed almost one of grieving.

Hal, too, felt stricken. He understood now why it had been necessary to stop the car to learn the meaning of this tape. Only now, in grey silence, could the enormity of the truth be grasped.

He spoke at last in a near-whisper: "They...they copied *themselves*. They had already killed and mutilated those three strippers in 1988. They knew...Jesus Christ, they *planned* — a year in advance — to slaughter those girls at the Doyle if they needed to. So they killed the first three to...to set a precedent. *Insurance*! They created the Graffiti Killer in case Danial continued to hold out. Imagine...the cold-bloodedness."

Julie nodded sadly. "I can imagine. It's no worse than transporting heroin in babies." She sank back into her seat. A gull skimmed in front of the Jeep and melted, shrieking, into the grey. "Can we get out of here? I'm getting bummed out. Let's go play this for Kate and call the cops on these assholes."

Hal reached for the ignition then paused. "If Crawford is Fairbairn, who is Sawtrell?"

She shrugged. "A businessman. A jaded ex-colonial like Crawford doing what his kind has been doing since the Opium War — putting a dollar-value on human misery." Julie gave him the first flicker of a smile since the station: "Just so you don't think I'm prejudiced, the Triad bosses are undoubtedly worse; I'm sure Ho Kwan Shing's 'dear uncle' eats monkey-brain soup and has people slaughtered every day."

Hal shook his head in disbelief. "To think we've been doing business with these people for nearly two years! You know something? Even after the Vanguard fiasco, I almost *liked* Graham Sawtrell!"

Hal started the engine and inched away from the shoulder, glancing left before pulling out, looking back the way they had come. One of the swank cottages had a visitor now — a sleek, dark-coloured car was parked a hundred yards up the road. It was hard to be sure at this distance, but it looked to Hal like another Jaguar. A lot of money about these days, came the wry thought.

He said: "We're going to lose our biggest client over this, you know."

"Good."

Hal smiled. "Yes. Isn't it."

It was after four o'clock when they reached Wesleyville. The flat, merging grey of lake and sky and road was breaking down into grainy dusk. The wind was up, stirring the long sugar maples around the church; without foliage to clothe their smooth, slender trunks, they looked serpentine, swaying to a charmer's music.

CHAPTER
31

It was dusk inside the church, too. Hal thought Kate had gone out for a walk until she startled them by appearing suddenly in the vestibule. She greeted Julie with a friendly smile as she turned on the lights. "It gets dark so early now, caught me out. We were so sorry you missed the party. Here, let me hang up your coat."

Julie removed the cassette tape from her pocket and gave Kate her coat. She walked through into the big room, Kate following close behind, turning on more lights.

"Does it feel cold in here?" Kate asked them.

Julie said she couldn't tell, having just come in from outside. She commented on the flowers. Kate offered them tea but they both declined.

Kate said: "You know, I think it really is chilly in here." She looked at Hal. "Be a dear and bring in some logs, would you?" She turned to Julie. "Is that the tape?" Julie nodded. "Good," Kate said brightly. "I can give it a first listen while Hal gets the wood." She held out her open hand for the cassette. "Is it cued up?"

Julie frowned. "Yes, but..." Kate took it from her hand.

"Hold on a minute," Hal interrupted. "There are a lot of things you should know before Julie translates this. It isn't as simple as we thought. For one thing, Alistair Crawford isn't even..."

Kate put up her hand. "I don't want to hear another word right now." She held the cassette behind her back. "I want to listen to this tape just the way it is, just the way you first heard it. I want some idea of what's being translated. When you come back, I'll make us some tea and you can tell me everything. Go and get the wood before we all freeze to death."

Hal shrugged. "Fine. I'll set it up for you." He started towards the stereo but she blocked him, steering him firmly towards the log-basket. She gave Julie an exasperated look. "Men! Honestly, they think we're incapable of pushing a couple of buttons!"

Hal frowned as he lifted the empty basket. "That's odd. I could swear there was wood in here this morning."

"Oh, Hal!" Kate laughed. "Maybe you'd better give him a hand, Julie, in case he forgets what he went out for!"

The firewood was stacked under a lean-to behind the building. Hal set the basket down and they started filling it, the small, dry logs knocking together with a musical sound.

"Is Kate all right?" Julie said. "She seems kind of...on edge."

"I know. We're going to have to be diplomatic about this. Crawford was Kate's friend, perish the thought. Thank God she never took Rain out there!"

"Exactly how much did you tell her this morning?"

"Everything I knew at that point. I don't think she believed me. But she'll have to now," he added grimly.

When the basket was almost full, they heard a car on the road, going slowly past the church. Hal stepped out of the lean-to but the car had gone. He realized that the Jeep's lights were still on and made a mental note to turn them off after they had carried in the wood. "I thought it might be Tyah Whiteside," he said as he stepped back inside.

"Think she'll come?"

"I don't know. She sounded pretty rough on the phone." He tossed in a final log. "I'm not sure that it really matters, considering what we already have. When the police hear the tape, they won't waste any time finding Tyah Whiteside."

They each took one end of the basket and carried it to the back door. He reached for the knob, then stopped. "We're going to leave out the part about the babies, okay? It's going to be enough of a bombshell without that."

"Yes, I agree."

He opened the storm door, blocked it with his shoulder and pushed open the inner door. They stepped onto a landing halfway down the basement stairs. Hal was surprised to hear no sound from the main floor. "I thought she wanted to listen to the tape."

"Maybe she's got the headphones on."

The door opened at the top of the stairs. Hal glanced up to see his wife looking down at them, shamefaced. "I've got a little confession," she said.

Without quite knowing why, Hal felt his insides go chill. "What do you mean?"

Kate looked sheepish. "I realize I'm going to look like a perfect idiot after what I said just now, but I can't seem to get the tape deck to work."

Hal felt an inexplicable measure of relief. "It was working fine this morning," he said, lugging his end of the basket into the living room. Kate shut the basement door behind Julie and followed them to the woodstove.

"The tape's going round all right," she said. "There just doesn't seem to be any sound coming out."

They set down the basket. Hal started across towards the stereo. "Have you got the selector in the right position? Maybe the speakers..."

For a frozen second Hal merely stared.

"*Jesus Christ!*"

He dove for the machine and stabbed — missed — stabbed again to stop it.

Julie hurried to his side. "What is it?"

"Christ!" Hal's eyes darted over the settings. How long had they been out at the wood pile...how long?

He held his breath, then pressed PLAY.

...it switched over?

Yes, go ahead.

Good afternoon, Ho Kwan Shing.

Good afternoon, Carpet King.

Hal remembered the translation perfectly, would probably never forget it:

I would not tolerate this, Ho, were it not for the high esteem in which I hold your dear uncle.

Hal stopped the machine. "We're all right." He was breathing heavily, as though he had dashed across a playing field to save the tape. "There's enough left...the most important part...but the rest is gone."

"Did I damage it?" Kate's voice, brittle and false, left no doubt in Hal's mind. It was a moment before he was able to turn and brave his wife.

She was standing by the stove, opening her mouth to speak. She closed it again when she saw the look on his face. To Hal she seemed somehow distorted, at a great distance. His own voice, too, slow and incredulous, sounded a long way off.

"You know perfectly well how to use the tape deck," he said, measuring each word. "I *know* you know how to use it. You...you erased the tape before you'd even listened to it. Why?"

For a few moments Kate seemed under a spell.

"Why, Kate?"

The spell broke. She took a bold step towards him, her face contorted by a leering smile. "Well, well...Hal the Dragon Slayer! Got a cause at last have you?" Another step. "Quite a change for you, isn't it? After all these years plodding quietly along — nice, safe, boring old Hal finally has something to get steamed up about!" The smile twisted away, her anger rising. "Alistair Crawford goes out of his way — *twice* — to hand you the chance of a lifetime, and this is how you thank him. Not content to look the gift horse in the mouth, you want to pull out his fucking teeth! A fair, generous, altogether decent man who never wished you anything but good. Jesus Christ — you don't even *know* him!"

241

"It's you who doesn't know him, Kate."

Julie cut in: "Alistair Crawford isn't his real name. He's not what you think he is."

Kate rounded on her. "No? But I'll bet you are! Fuck around with your *own* life, Julie. Not to mention your own man!"

Julie started angrily towards her, stopped when she felt Hal's restraining hand.

"Crawford's a murderer," he said in a still-even voice. "He's a drug dealer and a murderer and we can prove it. You want to know who Alistair Crawford is? He's the Graffiti Killer. He killed those girls at the Doyle and he killed the other three the summer before but the killing starts way before that. Killing people is how he does business, Kate, and he's been in business a long time."

For a moment he thought he had reached her. She was standing very still, staring at the floor, shaking her head in a slight, unconscious gesture of denial, like that night two years ago when he came home from the Doyle and told her Karel Lorenz was getting the Vanguard.

He went to her, laid his hands gently on her shoulders to guide her down onto the sofa but she was immovable, rigid as a mannequin. "Katy, listen, I wouldn't be saying any of this without proof. The Chinese in the photograph is the man Alistair Crawford hired to kill those strippers, plus the three the summer before. That's his voice on tape telling..."

But then she looked up and Hal saw the hard, cold light, heard the tinny, stranger's voice. He let go of her shoulders and took a step back.

"You're so clever, aren't you Hal? Still looking for your precious negatives by the way? I'm afraid you won't find them. Alistair has them. And you won't find the print of your so-called assassin either because I just burned it." She laughed at his stunned expression. "It's a *smear campaign*, you idiot! You're a pawn. You're simply being used by people who want to hurt him. But you know what I can't get over, you know what really pisses me off about all this? It's how fucking happy you are to oblige them. Why should it matter to you who killed a bunch of strippers? You think you can change

242

the past? Let me tell you, the only thing you're going to change is our future. You're going to fuck up our future like you wouldn't believe if you don't drop this whole thing *right* now!"

Hal's voice was only just audible. "Does he know where the pictures came from?"

Kate frowned. "You mean your little stripper friend? Of course he does."

"How long has he known?" demanded Julie.

Kate shrugged. "About a week. That's right, the day he sent over the carpet."

Hal exchanged a glance with Julie. "What carpet?"

She smiled. "You see? You don't know the first thing about Alistair. You don't have any idea what's important to him." She squatted in front of the sofa, reached for something underneath. "Did you know, for instance, that he has probably the finest private collection of Oriental carpets in the world? This is a very small sample. I didn't want people partying on it." She was dragging out a soft, tubular shape that she now sent unfurling across the floor, its fringe slapping the pine boards an inch from the toes of Hal's shoes.

She beckoned him: "Come here, feel it. Feel how soft this is." She spoke with a spurious brightness, the way a filament burns just before the bulb blows.

Neither Hal nor Julie made any move, watched her lay her hand flat on the rug to demonstrate how it should be stroked, petted, how it should be caressed with the back of the hand as well as the front. She stroked and stroked, her movements slowing now until finally her hand was still. When she looked up at him, her eyes were large and vulnerable.

"He can make dreams come true, Hal. Don't screw it up now. Please, babe."

"Hal?" Julie said urgently. He turned to her. "We have to call the police. Right now, Hal. He knows."

"Yes. Of course." He had barely started towards the kitchen when Kate was on her feet and running past him into the vestibule, into the kitchen to the wall-phone, blocking it, rounding on him.

"Let me have the phone, Kate."

"No."

"For God's sake, if Crawford knows, we could be in the gravest danger. That includes Rain." Hal heard Julie behind him, slipping by on her way to the front door to the cellular phone in the Jeep.

"Call the Woolley's as well," he shouted. "Number's in memory. Tell Meredith..."

"Don't you DARE!" Kate rushed for the door, but now Hal blocked. She flailed wildly, striking his face, catching his glasses, which sprang across the room. Then he had her wrists.

"Go!" he ordered Julie. "Tell them to keep Rain there, they mustn't bring her here now!"

"Bastard!" Kate's knee shot upwards for his groin, but he twisted aside so that they looked, for an absurd moment, like dancing partners.

Locked with Kate, minus his glasses, Hal failed to see Julie open the door and start backwards, didn't see the gun pointed at her head until Crawford and Greg were inside the vestibule with the front door closed behind them.

CHAPTER
32

It had taken them two hours to locate a rental car on a Sunday afternoon, a few seconds to find out that Tyah didn't qualify to rent a skateboard.

Vanessa signed the agreement with Budget, naming Tyah as an additional driver. Being a Sunday, there were no compact or even midsize cars available, but the guy let them have a Ford LTD Crown Victoria for a midsize price. The last car Tyah had driven was her little Chevette; with its chrome and fake wood and red velour seats, the LTD felt like a big chintzy living room on wheels.

Tyah drove it back to Vanessa's to collect her things. Tyah kissed her goodbye on the doorstep, a chaste, grateful kiss — for sanctuary, for the ackee and salt fish, for the dope and the cash loan. And the gun.

It was the gun as much as the car rental that made her late — Hyacinth's little .22 calibre Smith and Wesson. Vanessa insisted she take it in view of what had happened at Dowde Street, first priming Tyah with everything she had picked up from Hyacinth: how to drop out the cylinder and load the chambers, how to throw the safety and take aim using both hands.

It gave Tyah a measure of badly needed comfort to know that the gun was in the glove compartment along with her last tenth — a survival kit for desperate times. She was still shaking as she drove east on the 401 — from delayed shock and low-grade heroin and nervousness at driving for the first time in over a year, on the highway, in a big unfamiliar car.

The worst part of it was knowing that the shakes hadn't even started yet. Tyah had been through detox before and remembered only too well; you felt like the coyote in the Roadrunner cartoon, trying to cross an eight-lane highway and getting flattened by a Ford LTD and dragging yourself into the next lane and getting flattened by a tractor-trailer; lane by lane, day by day, taking a bigger, meaner beating each time.

She turned on the stereo, which was tuned to a classical music station; not her natural choice but she left it there, and soon, soothed by slow music, warmed by the heater, she began to relax a little.

The attack at Dowde Street had strengthened the need to see Hal Sebastian in Wesleyville, to warn him. Whoever the Chinese was working for, Hal was obviously in peril because of what he knew. But if he was right about Midland, where did that leave the Graffiti Killer? She thought of the roller coaster that still blurred through her dreams, and of the nightmare-riders — Felice and Nicole and sloppy Suzanne, and Lena DiMaio and Mary Joe Korenycky and Sandy Dell. Could all that death have been part of a business deal, some kind of investment?

Of course it could. A year of the Shanes and the Sam Wexels and the Burgesses had been a comprehensive education. It had given Tyah her own little jerry-rigged theory: that life was like the Limbo. Not the Catholic place full of unbaptized babies — the Limbo *dance* where people bend over backwards in order to wriggle under a pole. She had tried it once, on her first and only Caribbean holiday; striptease had been good training, and for a while she was right in there for the free water-skiing lessons. But someone went lower, and someone else went lower than that, and then one of the smiling locals moved the pole down six inches and turned into a rubber man. So life was like the Limbo: there was just no limit to how low people could go.

It was deep dusk now, when the hard outlines of day or night driving grow soft and out of focus. Even the road signs were shadowy and difficult to read, agitated by oncoming and following lights. She nearly missed the Bond Head sign, which, according to Hal, meant that Wesleyville was next. Tyah slowed right down; she didn't want to miss the exit.

At Bond Head the road had narrowed to two lanes, as Hal had said it would. It was tricky now, watching for signs and trying to keep the big, loose-steering LTD on a straight course. Unattended, it wandered several times across the centre line into the fast lane. On the last excursion, Tyah found herself blocking a vehicle coming up fast behind her. She steered back into the slow lane, expecting the car to accelerate past, but instead it moved over with her, on her tail, its headlights dazzling in her mirrors, making it harder than ever to see ahead.

Tyah swore and slowed to a crawl, tapped lightly on the brake pedal to flash her brake lights, but the car stuck.

"Give me a fuckin' break!"

All this grief because she had held the asshole up for less than five seconds! She had forgotten, in a year, how many shit-for-brains were out on the road. The possibility that it might be a police car didn't occur to her until she had powered down the window and given him the finger, long and hard, at which point Tyah's rearview mirror got a transfusion of pulsing maraschino red.

"Fuck!" she yelled at the top of her lungs. "FUCK!"

They were by the Wesleyville sign when the Ontario Provincial Police car slid onto the gravel shoulder and stopped in front of the LTD. Twenty seconds since he had flagged her, but enough for Tyah to reach into the glove compartment and, with as little body language as possible, drop the gun and the smack under her seat.

The OPP officer got out and came to her window, a large, middle-aged sergeant. "See your driver's licence please?"

Tyah handed it through. The sergeant looked at it for ten seconds. "Insurance and registration please."

Tyah tried to make her voice cheerful: "It isn't my car — it's rented."

"May I see the agreement?" He took the document.

"Is anything wrong, sergeant?" A truck roared by, buffeting the Ford, ruffling the papers in the cop's meaty hand. Any second now, thought Tyah, he'll be off to his car for the complete picture — the busts, the probation. Back with his flashlight and his *Step out of the vehicle please* and his *Well, well...got some interesting hobbies here Tyah, shooting and narcotics...*

By some miracle the documents reappeared at the window. Her licence was on top. His clean fingernail clicked against the plastic film. "You're almost expired, Tyah." She had been made aware of that at Budget. Now the cop's full face appeared in the window, his trained eyes flicking over the interior. Significantly, he had not yet given back any of the documents. "Headed for Montreal?" He must have read the drop-off point on the rental form. "Where are you hiding Vanessa Jones?"

Shit.

"I'm going back to Toronto to pick her up. I'm visiting someone in Wesleyville." She smiled apologetically. "Never been here before, I was afraid I'd miss the sign. That's why I wasn't driving too good back there. I guess you noticed, huh?"

"Who'd you come to see in Wesleyville?" It was none of his business but Tyah was in no position to tell him that.

"Name's Hal Sebastian."

The sergeant nodded. "Yes, I know him. Fixed up the church over there. Pretty nice job, eh?"

"I wouldn't know," Tyah said pointedly. "I've never *been* there, have I?"

The cop grinned, satisfied at last. "That's right. That's what you said." He handed back the documents. "Matter of fact, it's on my way. You tuck in behind me, I'll take you in." He chuckled. "To Wesleyville I mean. I'll show you the short cut."

He drove far too fast for Tyah's comfort; maybe his way of punishing her, she thought, in lieu of a ticket for poor highway driving. The short cut soon became a dirt and gravel road; on the loose surface the LTD felt about as agile as a mobile home. Rods of tension socked up into her neck every time she touched the power brakes, fully expecting the back end to come unstuck and swing her into the ditch or up against a tree. She was a city driver at the best of times, and right now was anything but the best.

Tyah was cursing him by the time he crossed the CN tracks three hundred years ahead of her. She was barely ten yards from the rails when the double light started to flash red and the bell started clanging; she could easily have made it across before the wig-wag came down, and at any other time she would have gone for it, impatient like most city drivers. She only waited now to make *him* wait — Jerkoff — way up the road, showing his brake lights for the first time since the highway. Tyah smiled when she heard the train's mournful bellow and saw the long beam from its cyclops eye sweeping around the bend.

It was the longest train she had ever seen. And the slowest. Eastbound box cars and refrigerator cars and flat cars and tankers, chemicals and frozen meat and sections of giant pipe, automobiles from GM Oshawa — Pontiacs and Chevys heading for dealerships in Montreal and Moncton and Halifax. She timed it on the dash clock: seven minutes from loco to caboose. When it was gone, she threw the Ford into gear and wallowed across the double track, her eyes still strobing from the parade of railcars.

When her vision cleared, she saw that the OPP was gone too.

CHAPTER
33

A monster, thought Hal. A monster out of Grimm, an insane, crippled giant with the head of a bird and wicked bird's eyes. His forward-tilted mass was pointed alertly over two ebony canes; the effort of the church steps must have cost him — he had been pale and perspiring when he first appeared, a shade paler now as he listened to the tape. He was silent, the brilliant eyes were turned away, but still he was riveting; not even Greg, pointing the heavy, silenced pistol, was any kind of distraction from Crawford.

They waited, lined up against the west wall of the big room, Kate near the south corner beside the kitchen hatch, Hal in the middle, then Julie.

When Crawford had heard enough, he signalled Greg who stopped the cassette, ejected and pocketed it. For several moments the old man remained silent, using the rubber tip of his cane to fuss with the fringe of the prayer rug.

"Obviously you have translated this." He looked up suddenly, examined Julie for a second, then the piercing eyes were on Hal. "And yet so much is erased." He sighed. "So many questions — far too many to ask here and expect truthful answers, so…" He shrugged his massive shoulders. "I will restrain my own curiosity and satisfy yours before we go. How did I know about this tape? A simple transmitter, costing a few dollars at a standard electronics shop; small enough to hide in Tyah Whiteside's phone, more than powerful enough to transmit to the room below. Thirty-nine Dowde Street has a transitory clientele — it was easy to install Mr. Ho on the second floor with a receiver." A whiff of a smile at Julie. "He has assimilated very well in the last eighteen months; his English is vastly improved."

"Where is Tyah Whiteside?" Julie sounded more concerned for Tyah than herself. "How did you know about her?"

Crawford caught Hal's dark glance at Kate, and smiled. "There! We *all* have a lot of questions. Don't worry about Tyah Whiteside. You'll be seeing her soon enough."

Hal's mouth was so dry he could barely swallow. It seemed impossible to launch defiance, but he had to try. "We had a party last night. My lawyer was here. I gave him a copy of this tape and told him everything I know. If anything happens to us, anything at all, you're…"

Crawford waved his cane dismissively. "Please stop. You are lying. And if you are telling the truth, I could hardly cause more trouble for myself. What have I to lose? You talk as if there were still a line to be crossed, but you would do well to remember, Mr. Sebastian, that Greg and I have already crossed it a number of times…as you know much too well."

"Alistair…" Suddenly all eyes were on Kate. She took a desperate step away from the wall, fetching an immediate reaction from Greg. "Hal hasn't told anyone and he isn't going to! No one knows but us, no one will *ever* know!" Her hands clenched and unclenched at her sides, her eyes were enormous, imploring. She took another step. Greg started to move in, but a small gesture from Crawford stopped him. "I've already burned the photograph," she said breathlessly. "That tape…most of it is erased because I erased it!" She turned to Greg, reached out an eager hand. "Give it to me, we'll destroy it now, together! There's no copy, no one will say anything, I'll see that they don't. I'll…"

"What?" Crawford's brilliant eyes transfixed her, grew round with mock anticipation. "You'll what? Do tell me, Kate; I had no idea you were so concerned about me." His voice carried a glaze of irony, sticky and deadly sweet. He moved around her, clambering on the black, bumping canes, as if she were a curiosity to be examined from every angle. Movement seemed to be a sensual agony for him now; Hal saw a deep, voluptuous shiver pass through the giant body. Crawford was looking at Kate, yet he addressed Hal:

"Your wife disapproves of me, Mr. Sebastian. I disgust her, if you want to know the truth." He sighed theatrically. "Aaah…but how she does *love* my house, my garden, my…" He raised one cane like an antenna, waved it to describe the room. "…my ability to *change* things! The genie in the lamp!" He started when he saw the look of horror overtaking Kate, burlesquing surprise. "No need to look like that," he soothed. "I applaud acquisitiveness and good acting — they constitute my own special vocation! Had things turned out differently, I might even had rewarded you, though perhaps not quite to the limit of your expectations!" He shrugged the sagging roof-beam shoulders in a parody of regret. "But things turned out like *this*, didn't they, with the result that *I* have been forced to use *you*. Not so unfair really." He frowned at the watch on his thick wrist. "But look at me making speeches!"

The black spindle-legs pranced ahead of him until he was directly in front of Hal, a cane's length away. Crawford was no longer playful — now the eyes were cold and bleak as tundra. "You will drive the Jeep," he told Hal, then indicated Julie. "She will sit beside you, monitored by Greg in the back seat. Your wife will drive my Jaguar. I will say this to you all once, clearly and simply: both vehicles are equipped with cellular phones. If Greg or I should learn of trouble in either vehicle, there will be tragic repercussions." He looked at Hal. "I really only need *you* to answer my questions. Do you see? Good. Shall we go?"

"No!" Julie bared small, white teeth. "You intend to kill us anyway. I'm not going six inches with a disease like you!"

To Hal's sudden horror, she spat, a fine spray that barely touched him. Crawford saw Greg react, swung a cane sideways to block his gunman's advance. He leered down at Julie, the skin around the bird-head shrinking, producing a smile on a skull.

"Tell me...what are your people? Hakka? Undoubtedly. The Hakka are as coarse as they are stunted." The death's head smile grew. "Can't you do any better than that? You discredit a race that makes a *career* of gobbing phlegm! Try again, Hakka, *provoke* me! Let us brawl here all evening, and in the meantime, perhaps the little girl — perhaps Rain will arrive home and then we can make this a family affair."

A thin, unearthly wail rose from Kate's throat. Crawford gave Hal an indifferent shrug. "What can I say? I heard you from your doorstep. You were shouting."

Hal's courage rose on a wellspring of anger and loathing. Suddenly the dryness was gone from his mouth; he felt recklessly, desperately articulate. "I should have remembered: dead babies are your specialty." A shadow of uncertainty passed over Crawford's features. "Oh yes," Hal continued, "we know all about you: murder, kidnapping, extortion, trafficking in narcotics..." Hal raised a defiant smile, like a flag. "How's business, Fairbairn? Or do you prefer Carpet King? Sounds a bit...I dunno...a bit *retail*, don't you think, Jules?"

"Definitely."

The revelation had a paralyzing effect on both Crawford and Greg. Hal saw it and pressed his advantage. "Naturally we had to make a number of inquiries to learn your little secrets, Fairbairn. We talked, people talked to us. Whatever you do to us, no matter how you rig it, an awful lot of people are going to put two and two together. You know something? You're fucked. And if you think you can sweep *this* under one of your precious carpets, you're..."

Hal never finished. Suddenly everyone was looking towards the vestibule.

It came again, louder: a knocking at the front door.

Julie tried to shout, but only got as far as drawing breath. The blow came so suddenly she barely flinched. Driven by Crawford's powerful arm, the ebony cane whispered to her head, the hard wood striking her above the left ear with a thick *crack*. Julie collapsed as neatly into Hal's arms as if they had rehearsed it for a play.

Instantly Greg was behind Kate with his brown hand over her mouth and the silenced muzzle jammed against her temple.

Crawford's voice came as an urgent hissing: "Who? Rain? Who is it? *Tell* me!"

The front door opened. A deep male voice boomed in the vestibule: "Hal? Hellooo? Left ya lights on the Jeep, buddy!"

A familiar voice. Local. Not Doc Woolley. *Who?*

Heavy steps, clumping boots against the slate. Even as Hal made the connection and felt the instinct to cry out to OPP Sergeant Gates, he looked at Greg and saw him tense behind the gun, saw the certain promise in his lifeless eyes: I *will kill her first.*

They were still on the west side of the living room, behind the end wall of the kitchen. Gates only had a tunnel view north to the woodstove. He couldn't see them. There was still time for him to balk at coming all the way in, uninvited, on a trifling matter.

And save himself.

But Gates was a country cop. The Jeep's lights were a good excuse for a social call. And maybe by now the trained cop, country or not, could sense a certain quality to the silence in the church.

If there was a scent of danger, it wasn't strong enough to make him careful. Gates actually smiled for an instant as he came into the living room, larger than life, a big blue angel. A smile for Hal, fading as he grasped key elements of the scene — the gun at Kate's head, Julie's limp form in Hal's arms.

Gates reached instinctively for his sidearm and Greg shot him twice in the torso — two undramatic smacks from the silenced weapon. For no apparent reason, the sergeant's peaked hat hopped off his head as if jerked on a wire. He didn't utter a sound as he began to walk doggedly — absurdly — backwards out of the room, exactly reversing his entrance. Greg released Kate and went to the middle of the living room and aimed carefully into the vestibule. For a moment Hal thought Greg had fired a third shot, but the sound was Gates's bare head smacking the tiles.

CHAPTER
34

A quarter mile beyond the tracks was a T-junction where the gravel road met a narrow paved one. A small green and white sign told her Wesleyville was one kilometre east. The OPP hadn't left her in the lurch, must have known she couldn't go wrong after the tracks.

It was almost full dark as Tyah entered Wesleyville. Without the faded welcome sign in her headlights, she might have driven right through without seeing a village: there were no streetlights, no sidewalks, nobody about. Sunday in the country. No doubt everyone was in church. Then Tyah remembered what the cop had said and realized that she was looking for a church.

She had begun to wonder whether she'd missed it when her lights picked up the police car parked on the north shoulder. As she drove nearer she could see a pretty yellow building illuminated by its porch light, set back beneath the swaying shapes of trees.

The police car was the only vehicle outside the church — no white Jeep. Drawing in behind it, she saw that it was empty. Well...the cop knew Hal Sebastian, was probably in there yukking it up about women drivers.

She killed her engine and got out. The wind caught her hair, plastering it to her face as she climbed stone steps to the white front door.

She knocked and waited, then knocked a little louder, then looked for a bell. She put her ear to the door and for a moment thought she heard a small scraping sound inside, from floor level, and wondered if Hal Sebastian had a dog. Then the wind gusted again, quarrelling in the eaves, erasing the sound. Beside the steps, some kind of tall shrub tapped against a window, an insistent, unnerving morse code.

So where was the cop? Around the back, maybe, doing his neighbourhood cop thing, checking doors and windows in Hal Sebastian's absence? Tyah stepped back from the door and peered as far as she could around the side of the church. There was just enough light left to make out jutting gravestones, tilted and broken like neglected teeth. "Hello? Anyone there?" But only the wind answered, sighing through the trees.

Tyah shivered, longing suddenly for the insulated comfort of the LTD, to be back on the highway with the heater going and the radio playing, on her way to Montreal.

One more try and then she would go. She made a fist and thumped hard on the door, which had been off the latch and now swung partly open.

Surprised and embarrassed, Tyah called through the opening: "Anybody home?" and this time she heard a deep, answering groan, almost at her feet. Terrified, she pushed away from the door and in doing so thrust it fully open.

For the second time that day, Tyah found herself looking down at a bleeding man.

"Oh Jesus Christ..."

The OPP sergeant groaned again. Trembling, Tyah crossed the threshold into the vestibule and stood over him, still unable to believe her eyes. He was lying on his back, the front of his dark uniform sheeny with blood. As she knelt beside him she could see two neat, oozing holes in his tunic. When he tried to raise his head, Tyah slipped her hand behind it, felt wetness there too. At her touch, his eyelids fluttered open, the eyes rolling, trying desperately to fix on her.

"Took...took..."

Tyah cradled his head. "It's okay, okay...I'm going to call an ambulance now. You're going to be okay, you're going to be just fine."

"Jeep...the Jeep!"

"What?"

"Jeep...lights on...*Jeep*!"

Something was happening to him now, a tremor that started in his feet, rattling his boot heels horribly against the slate tiles, growing more violent as the charge passed up through his body, bucking him off the floor. He reached up, clawing the air like a drowning man until Tyah caught his hand. For a few seconds he held her in a crushing grip, then his cold hand went limp. The eyes were still wide open but they were no longer seeing her. He had stopped breathing.

He was dead.

Tyah's first instinct was to find a phone. She ran to the nearest doorway, fumbled for the lights, saw a kitchen, then a wall-phone. She snatched the receiver off the cradle then hesitated for a moment as another, possibly better, certainly crazier idea took irresistible hold.

The Chinese at Dowde and now this...it was surely no coincidence. They had come for Hal Sebastian just as they had come for Tyah. Had come and gone...*minutes ago*!

"Shit!"

Tyah slammed the phone back on the wall and ran into the vestibule.

He was still staring at nothing. Still dead. Beyond her help now.

She turned and flew out of the door and down the steps, trusting herself, hoping that when she stopped long enough to examine this decision, it would seem a little less crazy than it did now.

Tyah threw herself into the LTD, started up, raked the selector into DRIVE. The big car surged into the road, its screaming tires raising a blue shroud over the dead sergeant's car.

The lakeshore road was paved but it was tortuous. She took the first hard bend too fast for the heavy, soft-sprung car, felt the back end drift, wagging crazily as she fought her way out of the curve, within a hair of losing control. She messed up the second corner, too, but on the third she began to get the feel of things. Some drift, some shimmy, but the tail wasn't wagging the dog any more.

Gas.

Brake.

Gas.

Brake...harder, as lights swung around the bend towards her. Tyah snapped her head sideways as the vehicle passed, caught a flash of a red pickup.

Okay.

Gas. Brake. Gas.

She almost had the rhythm now, had the LTD waltzing. After a couple of miles she had gained enough confidence to free up enough concentration to look beyond the next corner — maybe even figure out what she thought she was up to here.

"Look for a white Jeep Cherokee," Hal had said. Well, that's what she was doing: looking for a Jeep. The cop had said a Jeep, too. Someone had taken Hal in a Jeep.

Someone?

Midland?

Someone was taking Hal east in a Jeep. Had to be east, or she would have passed them on her way into Wesleyville, and there hadn't been a single vehicle. She had timed the train at seven minutes. The cop had probably waited at least a couple, which meant that he'd gotten to the church at the very most five minutes ahead of her. Say three minutes to go in and get shot, which left two. Whoever had shot him and made off with Hal Sebastian had left about two minutes before she arrived. Add the time she spent at the church and you were back to five.

Five minutes. A Jeep going east with a five-minute start.

Gas. Brake. Gas.

She checked the fuel gauge: full in Toronto, it now stood at slightly better than three quarters. Okay. At least if she *did* spot a Jeep, she could probably stay with it until it reached its destination or stopped for gas, and *that* was when Tyah would call the police.

Not too crazy, was it? Crazy would have been hanging around

with a dead cop, waiting for a bunch of live cops to make her start from the very beginning (imagine *that*!) while someone

Midland?

got further and further away with Hal Sebastian.

Okay...maybe she *wouldn't* see a Jeep on this road. Maybe they'd already turned north to the highway. Maybe she would follow a Jeep all the way to Grandma's house and bring a SWAT team down on a perfectly nice family eating Sunday dinner.

Maybe she was just a crazy junkie after all.

Tyah reckoned she was overdosing on adrenalin by now. She was getting lightheaded, fairy-light — a feeling that was magically transferring itself to her whale of a car. The LTD's tires barely seemed to touch the pavement as she steered through the next corner with one hand, reaching into the back for her Stetson, which had been too bulky to pack in Vanessa's donated suitcase in the trunk. It was the hat she used to dance in, the genuine article, made in Texas with a bunch of wild turkey feathers in the band. Tyah loved this hat. She had seen herself hanging onto it when she rode through detox, never dreaming she would have to wear it so soon, that the craziness would start here, coming down in buckets in a no-place called Wesleyville.

Tyah's wild and crazy hat!

Fuckin' ay!

Her exhilaration began to evaporate as soon as she passed the first highway sign. A mile later, passing the second one, reason returned: what if they had followed it, turned north to join the 401? If she called the police right now, they could get the Jeep's licence number, put out an all points bulletin, might still have a chance to pick them up. Looking for a Jeep on this road, she might be wasting precious minutes. Life-saving minutes.

By the time she saw the third highway shield with its north-pointing arrow, Tyah was cursing, furious with herself: she had been criminally stupid and selfish to try and take matters into her own hands.

She pumped viciously on the brake pedal, almost losing control as the LTD floundered through the junction, coming to rest a hundred yards past the turnoff. Tyah jammed the console shift into reverse, was half-turned in her seat when she stopped and faced forward again, peering up the road through narrow eyes.

It was the first real straight for the last mile and a half, which was why she hadn't seen them before: tail-lights, set higher and wider apart than the lights on a regular car — the way they might appear on a van or a pickup truck.

Or a Jeep.

CHAPTER
35

"Eighty!"

The cordite-smelling muzzle jabbed the back of Hal's neck.

"All right. *Keep* it there!"

Hal could see Greg's tanned, mannequin head in the rearview mirror, swivelling every few moments to check the empty blackness uncoiling behind them; he could feel the tension coming off Greg in waves, like fever-heat.

Eighty kilometres per hour was the speed limit on the lakeshore road. They were not to break it, Crawford had instructed Greg. By sticking to the quiet country road and driving inconspicuously, they would minimize the risk of getting stopped. The Jaguar would go on ahead, taking advantage of the presence of a cellular phone in both vehicles: at the first sign of outside trouble, Crawford could give Greg advance warning, and vice versa. Crawford had planned for Kate to drive, but after the shooting, she was clearly in no fit state.

Something had happened to Kate, something that frightened Hal as much as the shattering violence that had precipitated it. Kate had needed no encouragement or assistance in leaving the church. She had smiled at Hal, she had smiled at Crawford and Greg, her eyes wide with innocent excitement, like a child anticipating a vacation trip. She had seemed puzzled by the body, the way a young child would be puzzled to see a police officer lying on the hall floor.

Hal was also afraid — terrified — for Julie, unconscious in the Jeep's rear compartment. There was no longer any reason to try and hide it from himself: he was deeply in love with Julie Lee. He wanted Julie, as he believed she wanted him. Carrying her out of the church in his arms, he had leaned close to check her breathing; finding it strong and regular, he had kissed her lips, gently and quickly. A first kiss, and a fervent promise: there would be time to claim each other. He would make the time. Hal swore it.

He couldn't pray for deliverance; he didn't know how to pray, or where to send his prayers. But he could think. He was good at thinking. A lot better than glamour boy sitting behind him.

Hal had been thinking very fast and very hard since Wesleyville. He had decided that braking was the answer to Greg. A sudden, violent application of the brakes, for which Hal would be prepared and Greg would not. Greg was stronger and professionally violent, but the element of surprise would be Hal's. As long as he could recover first, there would be a chance of getting the gun.

He would have to get it cleanly — shooting Greg (even if he could do it) would ruin phase two, and phase two was as vital as disarming him. Vital because Crawford had been thinking, too, when he divided them and threatened reprisals. Merely eliminating Greg would have unthinkable consequences for Kate. Even seriously wounding him was out of the question; for phase two to work, Hal would need Greg's cooperation.

So much for theory, Hal thought, as he felt cold, hard reality jabbing the back of his neck. Greg's voice took on a new urgency: "Keep it very steady. Try anything at all and I'm going to shoot the Chinese. Okay?" *Jab.* "You understand?"

Hal nodded, although he didn't understand, not until Greg's head momentarily cleared the mirror and he saw headlights, perhaps a quarter mile back along the road. Apart from the red pickup a few minutes ago, heading in the opposite direction, this was the only vehicle they had encountered.

The headlights did nothing to raise his hopes. Quite the opposite. Apart from being highly unlikely, pursuit would probably spell disaster; having just killed a cop, Greg had less than ever to lose — he could, and would, shoot anyone he pleased.

The following car was travelling a lot faster than the Jeep. The headlights in Hal's mirror bloomed, and now he was watching taillights, already disappearing around the next bend. A big North American car. No flashing red beacon, no Untouchables shooting out the tires, no James Bond, no Batman. No angel of mercy.

Suddenly Hal felt more alone than ever before in his life. There was no one else. It was up to him. The rest of their lives depended on how he handled a few crucial seconds. Julie, Kate, Rain...

Rain.

His Monkey.

Little clown.

With the thought of never seeing his daughter again came a feeling of despair so complete and so unexpected, it was like being taken by a riptide. Hal felt himself going under, unmanned by the darkness closing over him, pulling him down.

CHAPTER
36

Tyah maintained her speed after passing the Jeep, until she was far enough ahead not to arouse suspicion, but could still see the headlights behind her.

The fact that it *was* a white Jeep was all she had been able to confirm. Their conservative speed had made it easy to pass, but night and tinted windows had dashed her hopes of seeing inside.

Doubt began to gnaw at her again. Would cop-killers and kidnappers be travelling at such a sedate pace? Falling behind them again would be bound to alert them; on the other hand, by driving half a mile ahead as Tyah was now doing, she risked losing them if they turned off.

She was in an agony of indecision when her lights picked up a triangular yellow sign warning of construction ahead. Around the next corner she saw the road works themselves and braked hard for a set of temporary lights in the process of changing to red.

The road's oncoming lane had been newly poured here. It was fenced off for a hundred yards, leaving only the south lane open, the reason for the traffic lights. The closed lane was blocked at Tyah's end by a giant backhoe, startling yellow against the night. She could see another yellow monster, a compactor, parked beside the opposing set of traffic lights at the far end of the site. Along each side of the road, the grass shoulders had been gouged into eight-foot drainage ditches waiting to be filled in with gravel and dirt, protected by fencing strung between steel oil drums. A cursory inspection told Tyah that she was, by her presence in the single open lane, effectively blocking the whole thoroughfare.

The light changed to green but Tyah didn't move.

For a few moments she sat, thrilled and appalled by the idea that was forming in her mind.

She had Hyacinth's gun. They wouldn't be expecting trouble from a woman in a big old Ford...

Forget it! It was a lunatic idea. A dangerous idea.

But was it a bad idea? As bad as losing them altogether or going on a wild goose chase?

Tyah knew that if she didn't act quickly she would decide against it or lose her nerve.

She acted. She turned off her engine but left the lights on. She reached under the seat for the smooth, compact shape of the revolver and slipped it into her pocket. She felt under the dash for the hood release lever and pulled it. Then she opened her door and climbed out into the cold night. She walked to the front of the car, pressed the catch under the wide hood, which sighed up on hydraulic lifts, releasing a blast of oily-smelling heat from the hard-worked engine.

Would she recognize Hal Sebastian? She had seen him only twice, nearly two years ago, in a dark club. She could remember nothing but long hair and gold-rimmed glasses and an incorporeal smile, hung up in her memory like the Cheshire Cat's smile.

Would *they* recognize *her*? Probably yes, if it was the same people who sent the Chinese to Dowde Street a few hours ago. With that in mind, Tyah caught her hair and stuffed it under her cowboy hat and pulled the brim low over her face. As long as she could get to the Jeep, open the door, get her gun up before they took a good look at her face.

Lights flickered back along the road. Tyah experienced a nauseating wave of terror, worsening as the play of headlights grew nearer, rounding the last bend. When the traffic lights turned green, she could barely suppress the urge to jump back into her car, restart the engine and drive away.

She could hear the Jeep now. The backhoe beside her was ablaze, dazzling yellow in its lights. She came out from behind the LTD's hood and walked into the blinding glare of headlights, a woman in a cowboy hat with engine trouble, raising her arms in a helpless-lady-driver-shrug. She reached the Jeep, grasped the door handle on the driver's side with her left hand. Her right hand, concealed below the window-line, slipped the revolver from her right pocket as she opened the door.

But there was nothing to aim at.

For the first crucial seconds Tyah gaped blindly into the dark interior, her contracted pupils still adjusted for the Jeep's bright lights, seeing nothing but their afterimage, twin suns against the shadows.

Disoriented, desperate, she played for time.

"Anybody know anything about cars? I stalled at the lights and she won't start." Her bravado was pathetically unconvincing, but it didn't matter now. By the time her pupils dilated enough to see Hal Sebastian

short hair

horn-rims

no smile

she could also see the Jeep's second occupant, sitting in the back of the passenger side, pointing a long-barrelled handgun at her head.

"Hello, Tyah Whiteside," said a gloating voice.

Tyah saw living-dead eyes in a tanned, comic-book handsome face. She froze in terror, the revolver hanging uselessly at her side.

"Ho missed you, did he?" said the voice. "I won't. Bye bye."

The last thing she saw, in protracted detail, was his finger tightening around the trigger. It was too late now to do anything but shut her eyes and gain a millisecond of grace. No fear. No pain when it came — only surprise that she actually *heard* the shot, the choked *smack* of the silenced weapon.

Tyah opened her eyes again and stared in wonder at the sight that greeted her: an angel rearing up behind her murderer, hauling back on his arm, struggling for possession of the gun. A second commotion erupted beside her as Hal Sebastian turned and flung himself onto the tanned man. Tyah watched, mesmerized as the gun swung wildly, thrust between the front seats, aimed straight at her abdomen. It jerked slightly and went off, the muzzle-blast scorching her left hand as the heavy bullet passed through the steering wheel to shatter the instrument cluster, waking her at last with a stinging spray of plastic fragments.

In an instant she came to her senses and was kneeling on the driver's seat with the short muzzle of Hyacinth's little .22 jammed into the killer's throat just below his chin.

With a sob of rage and effort, Hal Sebastian wrenched the gun from the tanned man's hand and pointed it, trembling, at his ear.

"Hands on your head!" he screamed, beside himself. "*NOW!*" The man obeyed. "Julie! Are you okay?"

"Sort of."

He glanced wildly at Tyah. "Jesus Christ!" he panted. "I don't...I don't believe this! You're Tyah Whiteside!"

Julie was more composed. "There's rope here!" She held up a loose tangle of yellow nylon rope.

Hal pulled himself together. "Put your hands in the air!" he told the man. "Palms together! DO IT!" The tanned man hesitated, his eyes flicking from Tyah to Hal, measuring his chances. But there were two guns at his head, and he could hear the ragged edge to Hal's voice. Tyah jabbed the .22 into his throat for good measure. He made a small choking sound, then raised steepled hands above his head.

Julie wound the yellow rope around his wrists, made a knot, jerked it tight, wound some more. Tyah recognized her now — the Chinese girl, that day at the Doyle.

"Now we've got to get Kate back," muttered Hal. He was furiously chewing his bottom lip.

Julie said: "Crawford's got her, right?"

"Who's Kate?" Tyah said.

Hal snapped a look at her. "There's another car. A man called Crawford has my wife. Did you come on your own, no police?"

"No. I found a dead one, though."

Julie said: "We'd better call them. Tyah, there's a cellular phone…"

"No!" cried Hal. "The moment Crawford smells police he'll kill her!" A desperate light burned in his grey eyes but the gun was steady in his hand now, his voice suddenly calm. "No, we're going to call Crawford. Greg's going to call him. We're stalled at the lights, right? Crawford is going to drive back and pick us up. When he's close enough, we're going to take Kate back!" He glanced at Tyah. "Nothing wrong with your car, is there? You can drive it off the road?"

She nodded uncertainly. "Did this guy shoot the cop?"

"Yes."

Tyah had a full view of Greg's face. He was staring at her with icy contempt. She said simply: "I don't think Greg wants to help."

Hal tried to sound menacing: "If he doesn't, he knows…"

Tyah laid a restraining hand on his shoulder. "Wait." She glanced at Julie behind him. "Are you done?" Julie was, with a vengeance; Greg's hands puffed out, fat purple above his bonds. "Pull his arms back. Hook his hands behind his head. Good — hold him there."

If Greg was in pain he gave little indication of it. He merely licked his lips, the dead eyes remaining inexorably cold. Tyah had seen them before. Shane had those eyes.

Tyah transferred the .22 to her left hand. When Greg saw where her free right hand was going he instinctively tried to double up, pulling Julie off balance.

"Hold him!" snapped Tyah. Her practised right hand unzipped the expensive, silky trousers and snaked through the open fly then into his boxer shorts. It took her expert fingers two seconds to explore the nest of warm flesh, to form her thumb and forefinger into a snug noose around the neck of Greg's shrinking scrotum.

She spoke to him through clenched teeth: "These are good people you've got in this car."

Greg's mouth hung slightly open.

"Not me, though," Tyah continued. "I'm not good. I'm bad. I guess you know all about that, don't you, Shane?" Tyah was too angry to be aware of her slip. "I'm a whore, right? I'm a whore and a fuckin' junkie and you know what else? I don't *give* a fuck!"

Tyah tightened the noose. Beads of perspiration sprang from Greg's forehead. The anger was growing, suffocating her, like lead weights piled on her chest. "So listen very, very good, you suntanned bag of shit. You're going to do *exactly* what Hal tells you, or I am going to pull these off. I mean, I am really...honest to God...going to rip off your balls. Get it?"

She pinched the noose tighter and tugged. From Greg's open mouth came a deep, involuntary groan.

Hal Sebastian was shocked. "Tyah...Jesus..."

"Shut up!" She fought for breath, for enough restraint not to do it right now, not to tear them right now by their crackling roots — for the presence of mind to remember where she was, why she was doing this.

She reached behind her for the phone. "Are you ready?"

Unbelievably, Greg whispered: "I don't know the number."

He screamed.

"Ready, Greg?"

CHAPTER
37

The car always smelled so good after Kate had been away at school. Grandy never sent Pearce the chauffeur to collect her for the holidays; he always came himself. It was a tradition.

It was so exciting to be going home. She thought about her room. Nan would have all her holiday clothes ready in the cupboards and drawers, smelling of mothballs! There would be a mug of Ovaltine on her night table and a hot-water bottle in her bed. They didn't allow hot-water bottles at school although it was always cold in the dormitory.

Mmmmmm...bed! She had been feeling sleepy for miles, although it was hard to get comfortable, curled up in the seat. The seat seemed smaller than she remembered. She wriggled sideways and drew her knees up to her chin and played the game she always played in the car at night. If you closed your eyes so they were just little slits, you could pretend that the dashboard lights were an airport far below, or a lost city under the sea, or an Aladdin's cave full of glittering jewels.

Kate closed her eyes completely and just listened to the silky purr of the engine and let the butter-soft leather caress her cheek and thought about home. She couldn't remember ever having missed it so much. It must have been an extra-long term — it felt as though she'd been away for years. Years since she had smelled Grandy's cigars or the polish-smell in the boot room after Pearce had finished the shoes; years since she had heard Nan ring the gong for meals, or the sleepy tick-tock of the grandfather clock in the dining room, or the fountain chuckling into the goldfish pond in the centre of the rose garden.

Funny, though, how clearly she could see Grandy's Persian carpets, as though she had looked at them all yesterday. In her mind, she could walk up the big staircase and see each one in perfect detail, just like a slide show or pictures in a book. She could remember the lovely names, too: Qum, Tabriz, Isfahan, Shiraz — Sinbad names! Aladdin names! In a little while she would *really* see them!

Kate's sleepy reverie was interrupted by a peculiar warbling sound behind her, between the seats. She wriggled around, surprised to see Grandy answering a telephone. Kate didn't think you could have telephones in cars, except police cars and ambulances and things; she'd certainly never seen a phone in the Bentley before.

She was surprised, and rather frightened too, by Grandy's face, which had gone nasty and tight, a bit like a skull. He sounded so *cross*, and when he slammed the phone down he said a dirty, ugly word. The car was slowing down now. Stopping.

They were turning round!

"Grandy?"

He didn't say anything. Kate felt herself pressed against the back of the seat as the car accelerated at top speed, back the way they had come.

"Grandy?"

"Be quiet."

"We're not going back, are we? You're not taking me back... you're not..." His touch at the back of Kate's neck quieted her. The halter of his huge warm hand soothed and reassured her for a brief moment before it tightened like a vice and the walnut dashboard hurtled towards her face.

CHAPTER
38

"What did you have in mind, Greg? Just for the record. Some kind of accident? Is that why you needed the Jeep? Over the cliff was it, burned beyond recognition?"

Julie's questions were rhetorical. Greg's ordeal with Tyah Whiteside had drained him; he sat hunched forward in the back seat, silently brooding over his bound hands, now resting protectively in his lap; his suntan had turned a sickly khaki colour.

Julie didn't look much better. Unconsciousness had been only the first symptom of her concussion; she was blinking too often, Hal noticed, as though she had trouble focusing, and she had grown alarmingly pale. Of course she wouldn't admit any of it and had stubbornly refused to trade places with Tyah Whiteside, on the sidelines with the LTD. Tyah had found a farm track just beyond the far end of the construction zone; they had watched her reverse down it, then douse her lights.

At 6:18 by the dash clock, Hal saw headlights behind them, coming from the west.

"Could it be him?" Julie asked anxiously. "Would he circle round, come from behind?" If it *were* Crawford, the rest of phase two would be seriously jeopardized.

"I don't think so," Hal said guardedly. "It doesn't look like a Jaguar. It's too soon, anyway — Greg called him less than five minutes ago."

"But we're only guessing how far ahead he was. Why don't I get in position?"

"It's too late now, he'd see you."

As the headlights grew, Hal saw with relief that it was a pickup — the red pickup they had passed earlier; Hal recognized the plastic stone-deflector mounted above the radiator. He could read the wording on it this time — "Gene's Machine" — in someone's idea of Gothic script. The traffic light was green; Hal lowered his window and waved the truck on, but it drew alongside in spite of him.

On its way west the pickup had been empty, but it now carried a load, a green and yellow John Deere lawn tractor fitted with a snowblower attachment. Like the crew at the Bond Head marina, Gene Ferris had heard the weather forecast. He leaned across the bench seat and rolled down the passenger window.

"Stuck?"

"We're okay, we're fine, thanks," Hal reassured him. He glanced nervously into the back seat where Julie was covering Greg with Tyah's revolver.

"What's the matter? Got four-wheel-drive on that thing don't yous?" Gene Ferris knew all about yuppies — they drove Jeeps and wore horn-rimmed glasses like this asshole. Gene was feeling crabby because the snowblower had defeated him all morning while his father claimed to have hooked it up and changed the Deere's oil and filter and cleaned the plug in thirty-five minutes flat, which in Gene's opinion was a goddamn lie.

"We're just fine, thank you," Hal reiterated, inwardly cursing. If Crawford came now...

"Then what yous doin' in the middle of the damn road, holding up traffic?" The signal turned red but Ferris chose to drive through anyway, muttering about yuppies buying four-wheel-drives to run two blocks to the goddamn dry cleaners. Suspicious, too, three of them sitting in a darkened vehicle like that. If he didn't think any better of it by the time he got home, he might just call the goddamn OPP out of Port Hope.

Hal watched the pickup out of sight, then turned to Julie. "I guess we'd better get ready. Are you going to be all right? I could do it, you know. Just because Crawford doesn't see me up here with Greg, it doesn't necessarily mean…"

"Stop it." She opened her door and climbed out, swaying unsteadily for a moment, holding onto the door frame.

"Julie…"

"I'm fine. You want this guy in the front, right?"

Hal covered him too, with the silenced pistol, while Greg got stiffly out of the back and onto the front seat next to Hal, where Crawford would expect to see him. Greg's docility was to be expected, but even so, Hal found it slightly unnerving: neither he nor Julie had ever touched a handgun before in their lives, and the professional must surely know it.

Julie shut the rear door and walked away from the Jeep towards her station behind one of the backhoe's giant wheels. Hal called through his open window: "Julie?"

She stopped, turned slowly. Hal knew what he wanted to say, but now he found that he couldn't quite say it. Not yet. Not while Kate was still out there, still in grave danger. Not until this was finished.

Then he realized he didn't need to say anything; he could see the same unspoken words — the same promise — reflected in Julie's eyes. Once again he felt the powerful current pass between them and this time he didn't switch it off. Now he wanted it to flow forever.

"Be very careful, Julie."

"You too, Sebastian-san."

Hal drove the Jeep into position, beside the lights and slightly west of the backhoe. He was plugging the open lane now, fervently hoping that no more vehicles would come, forcing him to move.

At 6:25 he did see lights at the far end of the construction zone. His hand strayed to the ignition key, then stopped as he realized it was Crawford.

The Jaguar slid cautiously through a green signal — *sniffing*, thought Hal and shivered, precipitating a runnel of cold sweat down his ribs. He turned his headlights on low beam and flashed them, tightening his sweaty grip on the big pistol aimed at Greg's side.

"Don't move a single muscle."

Hal flashed his lights again, encouragingly, and the Jaguar kept on coming. It had reached the fifty-yard mark now, the mid-point of the construction run.

Come on, come on! Almost home.

But was Julie all right? Was she ready?

What was Kate's condition?

How suspicious would Crawford be that no one was getting out of the Jeep?

Hal fought desperately to stay calm. The Jaguar was twenty yards away now and still coming. He considered flashing his lights a third time, then thought better of it. He could see them now, behind the Jag's headlights — Crawford's bulk, the huddled shape of his wife.

Hal watched, pouring sweat, as the Jaguar came to a stop fifteen feet away, in line with the backhoe, its engine a silky whisper.

They were here.

Hal watched Crawford lower his window and put his head out, heard him shout angrily at Greg: "What the hell are you waiting for? Get them in here!"

Now, Julie. NOW!

And there she was, a little quicksilver shape darting out of the closed lane, low under the fence and around behind the Jaguar, the revolver in her hand. Julie reached the driver's side and thrust the gun through Crawford's open window. Hal heard a guttural cry of surprise and rage, then Julie shouting:

"Kate, get out! Get out of the car!"

The Kate-shape didn't move.

"Get out!" yelled Julie, but still Kate remained hunched in her seat.

Forget Greg. Hal snatched the keys from the ignition and catapulted out of the Jeep. He reached the Jaguar and tore at the door handle.

It was locked.

"Unlock it!" screamed Julie, her voice cracking, and Crawford obeyed.

For an instant Hal froze, horrified by the blood around Kate's swollen nose and mouth, by her utterly vacant expression. Then he reached down and lifted her from the seat.

With his attention on Kate, Hal failed to see Julie swooning dizzily, gagging, the revolver wilting in her hand. But Crawford saw it.

One second the Jaguar was there, the next second it was gone, the open passenger door flapping like a broken wing, its engine note rising from a whisper to a tortured scream as Crawford lashed it back along the run in reverse gear.

"He's getting away!" shouted Hal, and then he saw Tyah Whiteside.

No one had noticed the LTD sliding into place beside the compactor at the east end of the open lane. But it was there now, blocking Crawford's escape route with a sudden, glorious blaze of headlights and a blaring fanfare from the horn.

Crawford saw it and braked too late. The Jaguar slammed into Tyah's big car with a bang Hal could feel in his stomach.

The LTD was blind now, but Hal could still see the Jag's headlights. There was a sound of rending metal, and now, incredibly, those lights were moving, growing, sweeping side to side as Crawford hurled his crippled car back down the run, searching desperately for a way out of the trap.

Hal carried Kate to the relative safety of the yellow backhoe, sat her up behind one of its giant wheels and raced back into the open lane where he could see Julie illuminated by the Jeep's headlights, on her knees, throwing up over the new tarmac.

"Okay, Jules, come on...let's get out of the road now. Come on, Julie, he's coming back!" Hal lifted her to her feet and half-led, half-carried her towards the sanctuary of the backhoe.

Kate was no longer there.

"Kate!" he shouted. He screamed her name: KATY!"

Then he saw her, beyond the sphere of the Jeep's lights, silhouetted for a moment by Crawford's sweeping beams. She was about twenty-five yards down the open lane on the construction side, a dream figure dissolving into the night, trailing her hand along the fence.

God in Heaven stay on the side.

Even as Hal began to run, the Jaguar's lights swept again and he saw that she had wandered, disoriented, away from the fence towards the middle of the lane.

Hal's legs became pistons, his voice a desperate roar:

"KATEEEEE...NOOOOOOO..."

Had the Jaguar maintained its moderate speed and questing course, Hal might have reached her. But Crawford must now have realized how completely the trap was sprung. He set the car on a straight, accelerating course, frustration giving way to insane rage as he bore down on this nearest destructible human object. The car screamed his vengeance for him as it snatched Kate up and hurled her into the darkness and rushed on, a twelve-cylinder battering ram, towards the Jeep. At the last moment, Crawford must have opted for the drainage ditch because he swerved, striking the Jeep obliquely, the Jaguar spinning like a green bottle as it thrashed into the trench.

For several seconds there was silence as the night grew fragrant with the rich, dangerous smell of premium gasoline. The Jaguar's tail-to-head collision with the LTD had ruptured its tank, the contents of which were now gushing into the trench.

None of the twelve cylinders was still firing; it was a short on a severed main feed wire that sparked the gas.

Greg was closest to the Jaguar, hobbling in darkness up the road behind the Jeep, trying to put maximum distance between himself and this fiasco before he broke across country. He had ripped out the Jeep's cellular and the Jag was a write-off — he figured at least fifteen minutes before cops.

Smart to do the phone in. He was thinking like a professional again, which meant he was thinking several moves ahead. Getting his hands free was the first priority, then transportation to a warm, safe place (he knew of several possibilities) where he could figure out how to pay back the Whiteside whore before he took his long trip south.

Greg had been trying very hard to keep his mind away from the dreary agony between his legs, but walking, even bowlegged, was making that impossible; his testicles felt like two smashed, runny eggs. Not a career move, not a professional decision to make a personal hit when the heat was on, but this was a matter of pride. He had already decided that he wasn't going to kill her; he was going to do something much worse than that. It would be a lot of fun deciding just what.

The sound of the Jag blowing — *WHOOOMPH* — came from behind him to his left. Greg stopped and turned, first alarmed at how near the inferno seemed, then gratified by the fierce bloom of heat against his face (like a sunlamp) until he remembered that he was watching his nest egg go up in smoke. Shit! He'd been counting on an early retirement when the old man kicked off; no chance of that now.

Greg was on his way again when the rolling, heat-driven fumes enveloped him; the stink of burning rubber and paint and plastic and another smell, too, underneath all that, strangely sweet and appetizing. Like roasting pork, he thought, just before he realized what it was and fainted to the choiring of a police siren, Greg's all-time least favourite music.

EPILOGUE

It had been Rain's idea to pack a picnic lunch for her father's birthday: ham and Swiss cheese sandwiches, good coffee in a thermos, ripe bananas — nothing fancy, which was how he liked it. She put his cards in the basket, the ones he had already opened and the one that had come this morning after he left for work. Rain knew by the writing on the envelope that it was from Tyah. There was a BC postmark because she was doing the wardrobe for a big budget film out of Vancouver. Wherever she happened to be on location, she never forgot birthdays.

Her mother drove too fast as usual, even up the long private drive, alarming the Krishna people taking their lunchtime promenade. She parked by the rear side entrance, next to Hal's pickup. She had ten minutes of business to attend to with the bursar, she told the girls, and disappeared into the big house. Michele said she was going to stay in the car and listen to the radio until their mother came back.

"But it's such a beautiful day!"

Typical sixteen, Rain thought as she got out into the warm sunshine. She walked around the house to the south front to look for a good picnic spot on the wide lawn. It was a gift of a day for late October, warm and clear. The devotees of Lord Krishna were taking advantage of it, strolling meditatively in twos and threes, the gentle breeze stirring their saffron robes.

Rain smiled, thinking how much it amused her father that the International Society for Krishna Consciousness had made such a comeback after forty years. He confessed to having flirted with the idea himself once, way back when, of cutting off his long hair and banging a tambourine. But that wasn't the reason he had taken this commission, much larger than he would normally accept. It was simply the right thing to do, he said, to make his peace with this house; a kind of reconciliation.

Apart from the name — it was called Vrndavana North now — all the changes to Mead End were inside. From out here it still looked like a gracious English country house — easier to imagine black tie and elegant dinner parties than robes and mantras. Before the Krishnas bought it, the property had belonged to the government, some top secret nonsense, and before that...

Her parents had never tried to make a secret of the family history. Rain had been given a junior version as soon as she began to ask why Michele had black hair like Mummy while she didn't, why only Michele had Mummy's eyes. In fact, Rain was extraordinarily like Hal — tall and dark-blond, with his clear grey eyes.

Rain saw her father come out of the grand south entrance, talking to one of his workers. He caught sight of her and waved that he was almost done. He was fifty-six today, but the years had been generous, had chiselled his face and left him plenty of thick grey hair to wear in a bushy pony-tail.

He finished his business and trotted down the wide front steps, his wooden toolbox rattling; he was never without it, even on a simple site inspection; the box was as much a statement as the long hair or his famous "I leave all the brainwork to your mother," which was far from the truth. He liked to see himself as a craftsman, and he was.

Father and daughter were alike in more than looks. He caught her reflective mood before a word passed between them, turned and stood beside her, looking at the house.

Rain said at last: "This was her dream house, wasn't it?" It was not meant or taken as a question. After a moment she felt his arm around her waist, felt a little acknowledging squeeze. Rain put her own arm around him and drew him close.

"Happy birthday, Daddy."

Behind the round glasses, his grey eyes were soft with tears, and happiness too. Then he smiled and squeezed again.

"Hare Krishna, Monkey."

THE END

GREGORY WARD

After working in advertising and related fields for 11 years, Gregory Ward became a freelance scriptwriter. Widely acclaimed, THE CARPET KING was his first thriller, and he is presently at work on a second, WATER DAMAGE. He lives with his wife, the designer Sally Thurlow, and their two children in Newcastle, Ontario.